THE HOUSE OF LONG SHADOWS

HOUSE OF SOULS: BOOK 1

AMBROSE IBSEN

Subscribe to Ambrose Ibsen's newsletter here:

http://eepurl.com/bovafj

❀ Created with Vellum

ONE

Have you ever, as they say, slept the sleep of the dead?

I have.

It's the most peaceful thing in the world—the closest thing to non-existence I've ever felt.

By its definition, it's a dreamless sleep. It's a sleep without borders, where existence is a very tenuous thing. My life had been reduced to a burning candle left out in the rain, the flame bobbing and dodging and only narrowly avoiding the drop that might snuff it out for good. And if it had been snuffed out then, I would have passed on without even knowing it. Pain and suffering and fear don't exist, don't register, in a mind so buried in sleep as I've described.

I awoke with a jerk. Possibly *several* jerks, but my body was too numb to count them.

Next came a wave of confusion. Consciousness was alien to me.

Movement gradually returned to my limbs and the first thing I felt, aside from the pulsing in my joints, was cold steel pressing into my forearms.

My sense of smell came back to me and I inhaled the stale, recycled air. It was tinged with the sterile scent of bleach-based disinfectant. Crunchy linens had been bunched up around my legs. A loose-fitting gown had been left matted to my chest with cold sweat.

It's a hospital, I thought.

Reinvigorated by terror, I opened my eyes.

By that time, an orderly and a woman in a white lab coat had stationed themselves beside my hospital bed, and were discussing my miraculous awakening in hushed tones. This woman in the coat, I puzzled out, was probably my doctor.

"Mr. Taylor?" The doctor's voice was calm, measured. Her hands moved to the stethoscope around her neck, but she didn't do anything with it, merely fidgeted with one of the pearly eartips. "Mr. Taylor, can you hear me?"

The doctor had a strong aroma about her—on first whiff it seemed to me a common brand of spearmint and eucalyptus hand cream that I'd smelled somewhere before. Maybe it was simply a lagging of my senses, or else there was a note in it that roused some olfactory memory, but the smell made me gag. Hot bile rose into my throat and I barely held it in check as I nodded in reply.

I knew what it was.

Her hand lotion smelled like the noxious flowers of a Callery pear tree.

And with that realization, the terror came rushing back into me.

The house.

The accident.

All of it.

I began to scream, I think. And I cried, too, grabbing hold of her white coat like a blubbering child might grasp his mother's apron.

The orderly—a young Lou Ferrigno lookalike—held me down at the shoulders while the doctor sought to comfort me. "Mr. Taylor, please try to relax. You're OK. You're safe here!"

That was a lie, and I knew it.

The Incredible Hulk pressed me down gently into the bed until I shut up.

When she thought she could get a word in, the doctor leaned over me and smiled, combing a lock of long, brown hair behind her ear. It looked oily and unwashed, like she was in the middle of a stretch of 16-hour shifts and hadn't had the time for self-care. The bags under her eyes only drove home this impression further. Her breath smelled liked coffee—the cheap kind they offer for free in hospital waiting rooms. Tired though she looked, she put up with me and tried to comfort me. The cloying smell of lotion was coming in extra strong now. My mouth watered as my stomach threatened a mutiny. "Mr. Taylor, you're safe. You're in good hands. I'm your doctor. Do you remember what happened? Why you're here in the hospital?"

I screamed in her face like a madman, but not because I'd lost my mind. In fact, I was completely sane, and that was the problem.

I screamed because I remembered it all.

I remembered that house on Morgan Road.

I remembered the Callery pear tree out front.

The voices.

The long shadows.

And most of all, I remembered...

"Mr. Taylor! Please, try to calm down. It's OK. Everything will be fine. You were in a terrible accident, but now you're safe and sound."

I wasn't sure if there was anyone else in the room with us. I tried to turn my head, but a sharp pain in my neck dissuaded me. I found my lips were parched as stone, and I dragged my sandpaper tongue across them before replying, "Is there... is there anyone else here with us?"

"No," she assured me. "The aide left. It's just you and I."

I strained to glance to my right, and in the chair against the opposite wall I spied a hazy white-haired silhouette.

It's... it's her... She's in here with me...

When I began to scream, there was nothing the doctor could say to calm me. Only a sedative saw me quieten.

TWO

"Hey, thanks for tuning in! This is your main man, Kevin Taylor. I'm here to—"

The tripod shifted a few degrees and the camera dipped towards the ground. I'd done a poor job of tightening one of the hinges and now my shot was compromised.

"Oh, wonderful."

I re-centered the shot, made certain that the front of the house was completely in frame. Smoothing back my hair and composing myself, I stepped over to the spot I'd marked on the lawn with a large stone, put on a winning smile and attempted my opening monologue again.

"Hey, VideoTube! This is FlipperKevin, your favorite fixer-upper. I've got a real treat today. I'm standing here in a Detroit neighborhood, in front of—"

Overhead, a plane roared by. I knew how that was going to sound in post. My voice would be almost completely blocked out.

"*Seriously?*"

It seemed like the plane would never pass, like it was going to circle back around and keep ruining my shots. I watched it disappear into the East and then spent a moment collecting my thoughts.

It felt unseasonably warm for spring. Wearing my full work clothing so that I might look like a bonafide renovator didn't help. The heavy tool belt stuffed with junk I had no intention of using just then was beginning to slip down to my hips, along with the waist of my paint-stained jeans. My canvas work shirt, similarly stained with splotches of white paint, felt like a hair shirt even with the sleeves rolled up. For a few months I'd been trying to pull off a James Dean sort of thing with my hair, slicking it back into a neat pompadour, but in the direct sunlight my sweat had a way of dissolving the pomade I'd combed in and when it traveled down my brow it made my eyes sting.

When all was silent, I cleared my throat and attempted—for the *third* time—to record the introduction to my video.

"Hey, VideoTube! This is your main man, FlipperKevin, coming at you with an exciting new video series!" I paused, waiting for something to go wrong—for a car to backfire, for a random gust of wind to knock the camera over. When nothing happened, I continued cautiously. "I'm here in front of this gorgeous old house in Detroit. What's that? It doesn't look all that gorgeous to you? Well, I'll have you know she's got great bones, and when I'm through with her she'll look like new. Any guesses as to how much this house ran me?" I smirked. "You aren't going to believe this, but I picked up this fixer-upper for a mere thousand bucks!" Here, I inserted a dramatic pause and incredulous eyebrow waggle. "I announced in my last video that my next challenge was going to be the renovation of a derelict house —a complete head-to-toe, one-man fix—within a single month's time. Well, guys, this is it! I'm going to make this house livable in just thirty days. And I'm going to put out daily videos detailing the entire process."

I looked back at the house, pointing out some of its features for the viewers. "As you can see, this place is in sorry shape. It hasn't been lived in for years—probably decades." Stepping towards the tripod, I swiveled the camera in a gentle arc to capture a bit of the surrounding neighborhood. "*All* of the houses on this street—the few that are still standing, anyhow—are abandoned. This house was the only one with any hope of being refurbished, and I jumped on it. It'll be *perfect* for this renovation project, and since basically everything needs replaced, I'll be able to show you guys all kinds of useful skills, such as how to hang drywall, how to install new cabinetry, and more. Looking at this sorry old house, I know it seems like a tall order to get it squared away in just one month's time, but with a little love and some elbow grease, we'll get her back on her feet!"

I glanced back at the tottering old house and couldn't help adding, "*At least, I hope so,*" under my breath.

Truth was, this house was in terrible shape.

Days prior, I'd purchased 889 Morgan Road for a cool thousand from the City of Detroit. The old house, built in the American Craftsman style sometime in the 70's, had been owned by the city, and they'd been shocked when I'd expressed interest in purchasing it. After inspecting the other standing houses on Morgan Road I'd been impressed enough by this one to snatch up the deed that very afternoon.

This ramshackle two-story house was going to be the star of my newest VideoTube project—a project, I hoped, that would bring me loads of new subscribers, ad revenue and, *possibly*, a network TV deal.

For a few weeks I'd been driving around the Midwest looking for a house in need of some love. Ohio and Indiana had boasted no few candidates, but it wasn't until I'd started looking in Michigan that I'd stumbled upon the *real* bargains. Houses in and around Detroit, especially in the rougher areas, were listed for less than a thousand dollars. I almost hadn't believed it at first. I mean, an entire house for the price of a laptop? For the price of a root canal? It seemed too good to be true.

But it wasn't. A trip through the city brought up a number of houses in flippable condition for less money than a high-end flatscreen TV. Of course, the materials necessary to overhaul such houses wouldn't come cheap, but after doing some digging and familiarizing myself with local vendors, I realized I could totally renovate such a house for less than fifteen grand, provided that I wasn't too picky about the countertops or other cosmetic flourishes.

Really, this part of the city, so filled with rundown houses, was a renovator's dream. There were even government programs that gave houses in empty neighborhoods away *gratis* to cops or medical professionals who intended to move to the area and refurbish them. As a professional VideoTuber, I didn't qualify for any kind of government help, but the thousand bucks for this little gem in the rough hadn't exactly set me back too far, and I'd jumped on it, hopeful that the ad revenue on my upcoming videos alone would recoup my initial investment.

I turned back to the camera, lifting it off the tripod and zooming in on the exterior. "Gonna need new siding. Probably a new roof, too, as you can see. The inside is a mess. I'll show you more of that in a moment. The windows are in surprisingly good shape, which is awesome! And look at all of this open space! There are two vacant lots next to this place where houses used to stand. No one to complain about all the noise when I get to work. What more could you ask for?" I panned across the length of the property, took in the upper story, the front entrance, the porch.

And the tree.

The awful tree.

The property boasted a single ornamental, a squat little Callery pear covered in white flowers that reeked something like old urine or dead fish. It was pretty enough from a distance, but to get up close to it—or downwind, in this case—was to hate it. The stench was strongest in the front yard, though sometimes the breeze would carry the funk inside the house where it would mingle with the aroma of general decrepitude and become something truly nauseating. I made a mental note, not for the first time, to chop the thing down with extreme prejudice.

As best I could tell the house had only been used by squatters or partying kids over the past fifteen to twenty years. There was no shortage of graffiti on its walls, and evidences of old house parties—discarded beer cans, sun-bleached articles of clothing—were easy to find. Even so, beneath the wear and tear, the house appeared to have a stable skeleton.

I started inside, bringing the camera with me. Shoving open the front door, I took a slow pan of the living room and adjacent dining room. "We've got original hardwood floors, mostly intact," I said, focusing on the floor and tapping the creaky boards with my boot. "Lots of room for entertaining." I passed through the dining room and wandered through the kitchen, taking my time in recording its various warts.

The kitchen was done up with peeling white linoleum marked with little orange stars that must have been tacky even by the standards of 1975. The cabinets were made of good wood but were so badly cracked—some having fallen to the floor—that they hardly seemed worth saving. The dented-up sink was still in place but wobbled at the slightest provocation owing to the deterioration of its bracing. An ancient stove and a refrigerator missing its door sat in their respective nooks opposite the sink, and to the left of the cabinets was the kitchen's sole window, offering a view of the front yard and of that tree I hated so much.

I rounded the corner and returned to the living room, approaching the dust-caked stairs, with their thick, hand-carved bannister. The bannister wasn't really to my liking and had the initials of countless partiers of yore etched into its length, but it looked like it weighed two hundred pounds and was probably easier to restore than it was to replace. A quick sanding and staining and it would look fine.

Despite having been vacant for years, the house's most important features struck me as impressively solid. The stairs were no exception, and I climbed them to the second level, where I took some shots of the three bedrooms and bathroom and tugged repeatedly at the waist of my sagging jeans. It was cooler indoors, if only because I had some cover from the sun, and as I went I made sure to pry open the windows to get some fresh air circulating.

Each of the rooms looked out upon the front lawn, and only the window in the master bedroom had any visible damage—a hairline crack straight across the center. The closet in that room was almost big enough to serve as a fourth bedroom, and a handful of twisted wire hangers remained on the slumping dowel mounted to the wall within. There was something else, too. The locks on two of the bedrooms seemed unnecessarily complicated. The master bedroom had a lock mounted on the outside of the door. Another room, this one nearest the top of the stairs, had a meaty hasp on the inside of the door where a padlock might have been used to keep it shut. Strange, but these unattractive fixtures could be pried away without much trouble.

The bathroom was in hideous shape and would require more work than most anything else in the joint. To start with, in contrast to the rest of the house, the shower had been very poorly constructed and was on the verge of falling to pieces. A single, well-aimed nudge of the bulging shower tiles would have been enough to bring it crumbling down. The toilet was cracked and unusable; the sink, though functional, was stained and ugly. The floors were made of the same dirty tiles as lined the shower and would need—you guessed it —replaced.

Walking through the rooms again and taking stock of all the work ahead of me, my head began to spin. The house had been a bargain, it was true, but in exchange for the ludicrous savings I'd be making a considerable investment in hard labor. I began to feel a bit over-whelmed.

My VideoTube channel had really taken off in the past year, with more than two million subscribers and counting. That put me near the top of the stack in the home improvement category, and the ad revenue from each of my videos was more than enough to keep me running. More importantly, the success of my videos had gotten the attention of certain higher ups at the Home Improvement Network, who'd expressed vague interest in giving me my own home improvement program on cable TV. They thought I was likable enough, skilled enough for such a gig, and provided that my subscriber count and popularity continued on the digital platform, there was a good chance I could be a TV star in the future—and that I'd be able to enjoy all of the wealth and other perks that came with such celebrity. *That* was why I was doing this.

So, come what may, I was going to fix this house in a month. There could be no waffling. Taking this house from turd to treasure was a great gimmick and would likely net me more attention than any of my previous video projects. If anything was going to get TV execs knocking on my door, an audacious stunt like this was it.

Peering occasionally into the camera, I gave little quips about the state of the house, the rooms. Cracking jokes and always appearing "on" and motivated is essential to finding success in this business. People don't merely watch my videos to learn about home improvement—they want to be *entertained*. Sometimes, you get to feeling like a dancing monkey, constantly churning out content for more views, more subscribers, more ad revenue. When your biggest concern is the marketability of your content, the videos themselves sometimes take a dive in quality and it becomes too easy to put out a glut of soulless fluff. Some of my sloppiest videos rank among my highest in terms of views and ad revenue.

For instance, I'd done a video once about how to unclog toilets. You may be thinking to yourself that it's a stupid idea for a video, and you'd be half-right, but my clear and cheery delivery, coupled with my sharp video editing, resulted in its garnering more than ten million views. Don't believe me? Search VideoTube for "Flipper-Kevin Top Ten Toilet Hacks" and see for yourself. Go on, I'll wait. The comments on that one were so over-the-top thankful that you'd have thought I'd cured Cancer. The ad monies for that single video have since paid off my cargo van.

Having recorded enough footage to start with, I hurriedly

wrapped things up. "There you have it, folks. I've got my work cut out for me, haven't I? Stay tuned! I start work on this place tomorrow and you can expect daily videos from me all next month. I can't wait to get this house into fighting shape!"

I shut off the camera and took a deep breath.

The smile faded, the tool belt hit the floor.

I wished the fridge in the kitchen worked, and that it was stocked with cold beer.

Alas.

It was time to haul my stuff inside. The rear compartment of my van was packed nearly to bursting with tools and materials. I'd brought along a few things to make my stay more comfortable, too. I figured that, so long as the house wasn't a complete nightmare on the inside, I'd save time and money by simply crashing on an air mattress in the living room, and so I'd packed some of the comforts of home, such as a folding table for my laptop, a portable camping shower and a hotplate. If it turned out the house was too unpleasant to sleep in, there was no shortage of cheap motels a stone's throw away.

I dragged a number of saws into the kitchen, stacked boxes of nails and screws on the sorry-looking linoleum, and gave the living room and dining room a pretty thorough pass with my Shop-Vac. I then prepared for the herculean task of lifting my portable work bench out of the van, and was in the process of picking out a good place to set it in the kitchen when my eyes drifted to the window and I startled.

The Callery pear tree, its noxious stink seeping into my nostrils on the draft, was squared in my sights—except, for an instant, I thought I'd seen something moving amidst its bouffant of white flowers.

A person.

Nearing the window and staring thoughtfully at the tree, I saw that I'd been mistaken. Though, for that brief moment, I'd have sworn that I'd seen a pale arm near its nutty trunk, and a slim body half-masked by its width besides.

I rubbed my eyes and looked again. There wasn't anyone there.

Of course there wasn't. Mine was the only inhabited house on the entire block.

I appraised the tree in my periphery for a time, mostly as an excuse to catch my breath and put off the unenviable task of hauling in my heaviest pieces of kit, and wondered what trick of the light had been responsible for the illusion.

I leaned towards the glass, my long nose nearly touching the pane, and glared at the tree. "I have a feeling you and I aren't going to get along, are we?"

The smelly white flowers swayed in the breeze.

THREE

By the time I got everything moved in the afternoon was spent.

It took some serious mop-pushing to get the dust—deep-set and practically baked onto the boards—off the living room floors, and almost an hour of chasing cobwebs and their attendant eight-legged occupants with the hose of my Shop-Vac, before the living room was even close to habitable. All the while I kept the window open, letting the space air out.

I'd contacted the local electric company ahead of time and had electricity in the place. Well, sort of. Only a handful of the outlets actually worked. Probably I'd have to poke around in the walls and toy with the wires to get things running properly. I was concerned that, when the time came, I wouldn't be able to draw enough electricity from the functioning outlets to get my power tools going. If push came to shove, I'd purchase a gasoline-powered portable generator—something I'd been meaning to pick up for some time anyhow—and the problem would be solved. Seeing as how the costs of renovation were piling up however, I wanted to avoid the expense if at all possible and hoped the aged wiring in the house would fit my needs.

The water was on, too, but I'd set that up more out of curiosity than necessity. The pipes were old, and when water did finally come through the taps in a sputtering rush, it was discolored, foul-smelling. There'd be no drinking it, lest I gulp up a nice dose of lead. Still, the fact that water was coming through them at all was a good sign. The only issue—and an easy one to fix, at that—was that the pipes rattled fiercely when they first got going. I let the water run in the kitchen sink and watched it sluggishly spiral down the drain, going from rust-colored to almost clear. Thankfully, there were no leaks or major backups.

A white folding table roughly five feet across went up against one of the living room walls where, years ago, people had scribbled their names in permanent marker or burnt them in with cigarettes. On it, I set my laptop, printer and the sacks of camera gear I'd brought with me. This would serve as a command center of sorts, a place where I could edit videos and get all of my work done on the digital front. A metal folding chair completed the ensemble. I inflated the air mattress against the wall opposite the table. I then set about replacing the locks on the front and back doors of the house with sturdy hard-ware before heeding the roar of my stomach and prepping a quick meal.

Before eating, I set up my camera between the living room and dining room to capture my mealtime ritual. I struck a match theatri-cally, lit the single burner of my camping stove and poured a can of beef stew into a pot to simmer, monologuing about the virtues of "roughing it".

People love that kind of thing—the nitty-gritty details, the stuff that happens in between renovations. It makes you look more human, more relatable. *Authentic*.

While waiting for the stew to bubble I took a stroll upstairs, taking measurements of the doorways and closets, and it was then that I first noticed a peculiar quirk. It had eluded me on my first few passes, but now that the light was fading and shadows were gather-ing, it stood out to me like a sore thumb. I couldn't put my finger on why this was, however some aspect of the upstairs hall made for exceptionally long shadows. Standing near the top of the stairs with just a hint of light to my back, my shadow stretched inordinately far. It was a curious effect.

Returning to my stew and taking care to watch my shadow throughout the house, I noticed that the effect persisted elsewhere— in the dining room, the living room, the kitchen. Shadows, even those of inanimate things, seemed unnaturally long. The sun was getting low in the sky and I tried attributing the phenomenon to that, but even so I was baffled by the length of them.

In my head, I tried working this into some kind of perk—a cool anomaly, rather than a strange flaw. *Well,* I told myself, *the shadows travel far in this joint, so if someone breaks in and tries to sneak up on you, you'll see them long before they get close!*

Somehow, that didn't really put me at ease, and my mind was subsequently filled with visions of violent home invasions.

I sat down to eat, feeling for the first time—*but certainly not the last*—appreciably vulnerable in the quiet old house.

Truth was that I had little to fear. This was an empty neighborhood, and hardly anyone drove down the street outside. Moreover, I wasn't exactly *helpless.* To hear my viewers tell it—especially the *female* ones—I was pretty lean and mean. Standing at an even six feet, with the calloused hands of a workman and a fair bit of hardearned muscle, I looked older than my twenty-five years. I had a house full of tools, most of 'em sharp, and in the event of hostilities I'd think nothing of defending myself with a claw hammer like a psycho in a horror flick. The windows were secure, with old-fashioned but sturdy locks, and the hardware I'd installed on the front and back doors that very afternoon was solid enough to withstand a lot of abuse.

I was safe, and I knew it.

Even so, staring down at my shadow, which stretched nearly into the next room, incited doubt.

There shouldn't have been anything unsettling about it. I mean, it was *my own shadow,* for crying out loud! I moved, it moved. I shook my head, it shook its head. I nearly dropped my pot of stew like an idiot because I was too busy staring at the floor, and it did the same.

But it was eerie. There was no way around it.

I burnt my mouth on a spoonful of stew and all thoughts of shadows slipped away from me.

When the meal was finished, I gave the pot a quick wipe-down. My hunger had been satisfied, but as I paced aimlessly through the downstairs, digesting, my mind held onto a vague anxiety, and I decided that the best thing for it was to leave the house. Just for a little while. The fresh air—sans the reek of that tree out front—would fix me right up. Sure, there was a ton of work to be done, and I still had a video to put together, but maybe I could run an errand in town before dark...

I searched for a compelling excuse to put off my work and escape the house.

It occurred to me that if I was paranoid about the possibility of break-ins I could mount a motion-activated light outside. It would alert me to the presence of an intruder before they got to the door, and might even serve as a deterrent. The very idea brought me some relief, and I prepared to head into town at once in pursuit of this sensible—nay, *imperative* acquisition.

Having given myself permission to bolt, I left my unease at the door and hopped into my van, heading to the nearest hardware store. I made sure to snag my camera before rushing out into the mounting dusk.

FOUR

I zoomed in on the sign from the driver's side window.

It read ROOKER AND BROS. HARDWARE in big, black letters, and a poorly-drawn character—a pinkish stick figure, really, in a hardhat—leaned against the 'E' in HARDWARE in an awkward pose.

"Ain't that quaint," I said, peeking into the camera with a grin.

The place was very obviously a local operation, and compared to the Home Depots I was used to haunting in other cities, it looked depressing on the inside. The big glass windows near its entrance made it look like a greenhouse. Said windows were cloudy with condensation as an undoubtedly rundown air conditioner in the store struggled against the spring heatwave. There were two other cars in the parking lot, one of them double-parked, and I figured that they belonged to employees because from where I sat I couldn't pick out so much as a single customer walking about the aisles. The lights inside were an off-putting mustard yellow, and handwritten signs made of sun-faded card stock in neon colors clung for dear life from the windows nearest the door. The ink on some of them was beginning to run as the condensation wreaked havoc.

I shut off the camera but left it hanging around my neck as I exited the car. Hopefully one of the employees would be open to a little interview, or at least to my recording inside the store. Footage of me picking out supplies, or of talking shop with knowledgable employees, was excellent filler for my videos, and I'd argue that it was good advertising for the shops involved, too.

As I neared the door, I was blindsided by a little handwritten sticker beneath the NO SMOKING sign, which read NO PHOTOGRAPHY.

Ugh.

Feeling more than a little self-conscious about the big ol' camera dangling from my neck, I slipped into the store and approached the registers up front, where a middle-aged guy with a green apron rubbed at the counter with a bleach wipe. Another guy, this one barely college-aged, was busy stacking cans of spray paint for a nearby display. They both looked up at me the moment I entered, and they both spared me the same dispassionate nod. But it was the older guy, the cashier, who kept his eyes on me as I got closer and who said something about the camera.

"No photography," said the man, dropping the spent wipe into a trash bin and brushing his hands off on his apron. He was lanky, with thinning reddish-blonde hair and a dense, manicured mustache grown to compensate for his lack up top. He looked straight into my eyes, then down at the camera around my neck with so much annoyance it may as well have been a suicide bomb vest.

I didn't reply at once—and when I did, I actually started to stammer like an idiot. Something about this guy had caught me off guard. "Y-Yeah, sorry. I, uh... I'm not gonna use it. Just forgot to take it off."

The guy, whose name tag read "Chip", looked just like my dad.

Chip scratched at his ear and quirked his lip in something close to a smile. "If you do, I'll throw you out. It's there on the door," he said, pointing to the sticker I'd only just discovered.

For a minute there I was in a trance, marveling at the resemblance between this guy and my father.

My *dead* father.

Chip's hair was a different color. My dad's had been dark brown, like mine. And dad's mustache had been more of a handlebar. But other than that, this cashier could have been my father's twin. Even his mannerisms, his tone of voice, were eerily similar.

He glared at me like I was stupid, and I know that I certainly looked it. After my awkward pause, I forced a laugh and glanced dazedly around the store. "I'm just looking for, uh... lights."

He arched a brow, waited for me to go on with his lips pursed. Just like my dad would have done to someone he felt was wasting his time.

"Motion-activated lights. Like, for outside," I clarified.

He nodded and stepped out from behind the counter, leading me away from the checkout area, through the aisles dedicated to paints and power tools, before finally pausing in a section crammed with light fixtures and bulbs. "Got a few of 'em here," he said, pointing to a couple of boxes on the lower shelf.

"Thanks." My voice was distant, though; my attention was on *him*, rather than the merchandise. I couldn't stop staring at the guy. He probably thought I was coming onto him or something, with how intently I looked him over. The resemblance had me a little spooked.

He looked to the camera again, donning a smile that revealed small, crooked teeth.

Just like that, the illusion was broken. His teeth looked nothing like my dad's, and I almost breathed a sigh of relief. I found I could focus on my surroundings again as he asked, "What's the camera for, anyhow?"

"Oh." I tugged on the strap. "I'm actually shooting videos for my VideoTube channel. See, I renovate houses and make videos detailing the process. I bought a house in town and have been trying to gather footage. I was hoping I'd be able to interview someone at the store, or document my shopping trip."

"No recording," said Chip, like a doll with a pull string. Then, looking me up and down afresh, he grinned incredulously. "Now... what channel you on? I ain't ever seen you on TV."

I laughed. "No, I'm not on TV. Not yet, anyhow. These videos are online. On VideoTube. I've got lots of subscribers, though. I'm not super famous or anything, but I've been recognized on the street by viewers a couple times..."

Chip wasn't impressed. A single "Hm," and he was on his way back to the register.

Left to my own devices, I sighed and looked back at the goods on the shelves, trying to recall what I'd come for.

The motion-activated light, dummy.

Beneath a stack of boxes containing floor lamps, I found Rooker and Bros' stock of outdoor, motion-activated lights, and to say that I was unimpressed would be an understatement. There was one box, its edges frayed, that seemed to contain a pair of solar-powered lawn spotlights. *Spruce up your lawn with our premium LED landscape lighting!* read the sales copy on the side.

I gave the box a little shake and heard bits of loose glass rattling around.

I was going to have to give those a *hard pass*.

More in line with my needs was a second product. This one sat beside it in a cube-shaped box caked in dust. I had to get down on one knee just to free it from the shelf. Inside was a motion-activated LED floodlight. A bulleted list of benefits, all of them pertaining to home security, were printed on the lid of the box. This one fit the bill, though as I gave it a careful shake I discovered the handwritten price sticker on it and very nearly put it back in protest. It was easily thirty or forty bucks more expensive than a similar unit at a big box store, and it looked like it'd been sitting on the shelf since the Great Depression, to boot.

I did some mental math, wondered where the nearest Lowe's was, and even considered haggling with ol' Chip on the price. In the end, because I hate going to more than one store, I sucked it up and decided to buy it.

Truthfully, I also wanted to talk to my dad's lookalike some more.

Returning to the front of the store with the dusty box held at arm's length, I was struck for a second time by his resemblance to my late father. Standing there in front of the guy was surreal. I felt like I'd gone back in time about two years. Even the setting—a dingy hardware store—worked perfectly. It was exactly the sort of place my father would have shopped, and the two of us had spent a lot of time haunting such stores in the years before his death.

"That'll be ninety-five twenty-two," said Chip, looking into my glazed eyes expectantly.

I handed over a few twenties—one too few, as it turned out. I surrendered another and waited for my change.

He dropped the cash into the drawer and tore the receipt from the feed. Then, nudging the box towards me, he gave a little grunt, as if to say, "Out you go." I went to leave, but as I did so he suddenly donned that same grin from earlier and asked, "You say you bought a house around these parts. Where at?"

"It's a house on Morgan Road. You know it?"

The grin faded, like he thought I was pulling his leg. "Sure, I know it. Why'd you buy a house out there?"

Even though I knew this guy was a perfect stranger, I still *felt* like I was being scolded by my dad, and I explained myself to Chip accordingly, seeking to justify my actions. "W-Well, you know, it was dirt cheap. And it's got good bones—very solid. I like a fixer-upper, and this house hit all the marks. Hoping to have the work finished in a month's time."

Chip glanced at the other employee—the kid had moved on to sorting different varieties of air fresheners on the counter—then shrugged. "Well, best of luck to ya."

I took the box under my arm, but didn't leave right away. "Most of the houses down that way are abandoned," I said. "On Morgan Road, I mean. Why's that? When did they all empty out? Do you know the area well?" I was genuinely interested in his answer, but at the same time I wanted to prolong my conversation with this fatherly stand-in.

He scratched at his mustache. "Oh, yeah. Bunch of crack houses and meth labs down there. At least, once upon a time. I ain't been by that part of town in awhile, but I thought every house along that stretch had fallen to pieces by now. I remember those houses being lived in when I was a boy. Was a decent neighborhood back then, but I'm getting old." He chuckled. "Surprised you found one worth fixing. And even then, stranger, I've got to level with you—I don't understand why you'd bother. I mean, a house in a bad neighborhood like that... Someone's just gonna mess it up again. Why spend time fixing up a lemon, anyhow?"

I could have spent time trying to explain the dynamics of my profession to him—that I was renovating the house as a stunt to grab eyeballs, ad money and a potential nod from television executives—but instead I gave a weak shrug. "Maybe you're right," I said. The honest truth was that I didn't care one iota for the house. So long as the renovations went smoothly and netted me the kind of success and attention I was looking for, I didn't much care what became of it once I was done. Perhaps I'd put it up for sale, or rent it out. Whatever I did with the finished product, I'd do my best to make sure it wasn't my problem anymore.

Chip nodded. "Thanks for shopping local," he offered.

I returned his nod in kind, but had to stop myself from uttering, "See you, dad," as I left the store.

FIVE

The chance meeting with my father's doppelganger at the hardware store had my thoughts going all over the place. I was so distracted by that little encounter, in fact, that when I got home—

No, come to think of it, "home" isn't the right word. Looking back on it now, I don't think I ever once considered the house on Morgan Road to be "home", exactly. The name on the deed was mine, and I was going to be sleeping at the place, fixing it, but even on that first night I wished for my association with it to end there. From the very start, I'd made some sort of subconscious pledge to hold it at arm's length, not to get too comfortable.

Anyhow, I was so hung up on thoughts of my dad that the house's remoteness and its penchant for casting extra-lengthy shadows didn't even register in my mind as I pulled into the battered drive. I trudged inside with my new purchase in hand and immediately went rummaging for the tools I'd need to install it.

The motion-activated light would go in where the old porch light was now situated. The existing fixture was cracked and dirty, and it took the easing out of three rusted screws before I could access the wires underneath. I held a small flashlight between my teeth so that I could see what I was doing. Joining the wires of my new LED to the wires in the light box was easy enough, and when I'd fastened the new fixture so that it was flush against the exterior, I stood back and waved my arms.

The light flickered on and rendered me blind for a few seconds straight.

Which, I guess, was exactly what I wanted it to do.

There'd been a number of switches on the back corresponding to different functions—namely, the brightness and duration of the light every time it was set off. I'd opted for maximum brightness and had selected the one minute option. This way, if anything triggered it, I'd have a full minute to scan the area before the light powered down. The box claimed that the light picked up movement to a distance of thirty feet, which would cover as far as the edge of the street. Blinking away the stars it left in my vision, I felt I'd made a good buy.

I went into the house, locked the door, and prepared to edit some video. Tired as I was, I much preferred the thought of going to bed, but if I was going to start this challenge the right way I needed to upload some content and get the hype train rolling.

I dropped down into my chair and leaned over my laptop, getting to it at once. When I'd transferred the day's footage from my SD card into iMovie, I began sifting through it all, cringing at the corniness of my monologues. I trimmed away the false starts, the stutters, and in time I'd managed to whip up a semi-passable video. It began with my peppy introduction on the lawn and various shots of the exterior set to catchy royalty-free music. Then came my tour of the inside, detailing just how much work lay ahead. To the very front end I added the same animated intro that I used on all of my videos, and then I waited for iMovie to export the finished product.

All told, it took nearly an hour for me to dig through the day's footage, select the usable bits, and assemble a five minute video. Back when I'd first started and hadn't known the software, it had some-times taken me two, even three hours to make something halfway decent. Now, so long as the sound and picture quality in my recordings was solid, it was a relatively quick and painless process. The one thing I never got used to was watching myself on the screen, though.

I rather disliked the sound of my voice, and I couldn't help but flinch at my own jokes and hijinks on camera. The viewers lapped it up without fail, but watching my own cheery put-ons was kind of grating, and I was always relieved when the job was done. I never watched my videos after they hit VideoTube—couldn't stand it.

While waiting for iMovie to spit out my finalized video, I decided to check my email. As expected, my inbox was bursting. There was the usual garbage—spam, messages from various online retailers informing me of "incredible" new sales—along with a few dozen messages from viewers. Now and then viewers would email me to let me know they enjoyed my videos—that they'd managed to fix some longstanding problem in their homes thanks to my guidance. I always appreciated comments like those, though I seldom replied to them. There was a second variety of fan mail—more common that I liked, and which I *never* replied to as a rule—which contained requests for help. *Dear FlipperKevin, how do I replace my sliding door?* or, *Dear FlipperKevin, I'm a big fan. I was wondering if you could tell me which brand of nail gun you like best. I'm at Home Depot and would really appreciate it if you could answer quickly!* or sometimes, *FlipperKevin, I want to be a successful VideoTuber like you. I just bought thousands of dollars in camera gear, and I was wondering if maybe you wanted to collaborate on some videos. Hit me up if you're ever in...*

It should have been flattering to get so many messages from perfect strangers, and at the start of my success, it had been. Lately, though, it had gotten old. I hated having people email me out of the blue, acting like I was their personal resource. It reminded me of how my dad, a carpenter with decades of experience, had always gotten questions from people all around town...

Thoughts of my father rushed in like a wave for the second time that evening. Bitterness crept into me. Anger and melancholy, too.

"Delete. Delete. Delete," I muttered as I cleared out all the junk in my inbox. There was something cathartic about deleting so many emails, in watching the inbox gradually empty out. I focused on that, rather than on memories of my dad and his lookalike at the store.

It was getting late. Tomorrow the real work was going to start. I needed rest if I was going to make a dent in my mile-long to-do list. There was so much on my plate, and trying to decide where to begin, or what time to start working, was a little overwhelming. While trying to come up with an action plan for the coming day, I caught myself thinking, *Dad always suggested getting up just before dawn. He liked to start early in the day. He'd always drag me out of bed at five...*

I stopped short, kneading angrily at my temples. The old man was being persistent tonight; try as I might I couldn't get him out of my head.

I carried the laptop over to the bed and eased myself down, trying to steer my mind towards more pleasant things. Finally, I got a notification from iMovie that my video was done baking, and I immediately pulled up my VideoTube account and uploaded it for mass consumption. On the mediocre signal I was getting from my cellphone tether, the video took its sweet time uploading to the site. Once uploaded, I was informed that it would take roughly ten minutes to process and go live.

I don't remember what I did while waiting for the video to premiere. I know I finished clearing out my inbox, and I recall tucking a pillow under my chin. Before I realized it, though, I'd drifted off in front of the computer.

And when I finally awoke about an hour later, I noticed something was wrong.

SIX

The dining room window was open.

It'd been the cold reaching through that window that had awoken me—a cold that somehow didn't mesh with the warm spring night I'd known only an hour previous.

Though the breeze had been a rude shock to my body, my mind was very much concerned with other things as I eyed the open window groggily.

And then *not so* groggily.

I was sure—reasonably sure—that I hadn't left it open. Earlier in the day, before setting off to the hardware store, I'd shut and locked them all. It was possible that I'd forgotten this one, the one in the dining room just a few feet from the front door, but I couldn't see how. I set my computer aside, pushed off of the air mattress, and craned my neck towards the next room. The motion-activated light on the porch wasn't on, and for a moment I was comforted by that fact.

The light only stays on for a minute, remember? That's more than enough time for someone to sneak in...

My mind was on a roll that night, clinging chiefly to bad memories and worst-case scenarios.

Taking stock of my immediate surroundings, I peered into the kitchen. Empty. I then crossed the room on the balls of my feet and approached the open window. Trying to sneak through the house was futile; the groaning floorboards announced me before I even passed by the front door.

Peering around stacks of boxes, I found there was nothing out of place in the dining room. Just that window and a brisk wind kicking dust into the air. I pushed the window shut and fastened the lock until the mechanism creaked, but the chill persisted. So much so that I considered digging one of my sweatshirts out of the boxes.

Looking outside, I was stunned at the darkness. Except for a dull suggestion of moonlight that got lost somewhere in the clouds, there was no light to see by. The scenery all bled together into a single ribbon of black.

I'd been ready to let it all go, to limp back to bed and go into hibernation, but something kept my eye riveted to the window. I stared through the glass expectantly, but the night was dark and still as the inside of an inkwell. *The glass.* On the outside of the window-pane, barely visible in the weak light coming from the dining room, I could make out something.

A handprint.

My first thought—a hopeful one—was that I'd left it there myself; that I'd touched the window earlier without realizing it.

A quick comparison of the print against my own hand convinced me otherwise. It was smaller than mine.

Maybe it had been there awhile, I told myself. The house had sat abandoned for years, after all. But then, had it been there earlier in the day? Had I noticed it before, when opening and closing the windows? I couldn't say that I had. So small a detail as that would probably have escaped my notice. I'd been busy then, a little frazzled. The only reason I was fixating on it now was because the window had been left open and I had no recollection of opening it.

I brought a hand to my tightening chest and kneaded at my heart like a lump of brioche dough. Was there someone in the house? I doubted I'd been asleep so soundly that someone could have slipped in without my noticing it, and yet the possibility remained. For a long while I stood and listened.

The shifting of *my own* weight prompted a lengthy creak, but the house was otherwise silent.

I wanted to call out, to ask if anyone was there, but couldn't find the words. And anyway, the very idea of asking such a question struck me as idiotic. If someone *had* entered the house, they weren't likely to just come on out with a toss of their shoulders, hands on top of their heads.

I focused on the silence, tried to parse something from it. The downstairs was clear. If there *was* an intruder, he was in the upstairs. And he was quiet as a mouse. I pictured the empty bedrooms in the upper level—pictured, with a shudder, a figure standing in one of those shadowed rooms, stock-still. *Waiting.* The house settled against the breeze with a light groan as if to say it was so.

It's probably nothing, I told myself, looking back to the air mattress. And I wanted to believe it. But all desire for sleep was gone now and had been replaced by a trenchant unease that somewhere, just outside of my view, an intruder was lurking.

I saw no alternative but to check each room. Only when I'd managed to verify my solitude would I be able to relax.

Stopping in the dining room, I pulled a hefty adjustable wrench from my toolbox and wielded it like a club before turning the corner and starting towards the stairs. Shuffling from room to room with the wrench in my fist, I must have looked like a Neanderthal trying to sneak up on a saber-toothed cat.

What could someone possibly want in the upstairs? I wondered, mostly in a futile attempt to convince myself that the matter required no further investigation. The three bedrooms and bathroom located on the second story offered nothing. I hadn't even brought any of my supplies up there. The bathroom was hardly functional and the rooms were filthy as the day I'd bought the place. Approaching the stairs, I couldn't shake the image from my head of someone standing silently in one of those bedrooms, though. Someone in the middle of a dark room, the door closed, simply waiting to be discovered.

I hadn't so much as touched the bannister when I halted at the foot of the stairs. A jolt of terror left me limp, and the wrench suddenly became too heavy for my noodle arm to bear. From what should have been that quiet and unoccupied second level, I heard a noise—a slow and even creak as of a man-sized load shifting on the tired floors. But what I heard did not frighten me half as much as what I *saw*.

I'd noticed in the dusk the house's strange tendency to warp—to lengthen—shadows to a curious degree. From the bottom of the stairs, perfectly timed so as to correspond to the aforementioned creaking, I watched a long, vaguely man-shaped shadow shift upon the wall opposite the bannister. It remained there only for an instant, receding soundlessly, almost as though its caster had grown aware of my surveillance.

If the intruder made a sound then, I didn't hear it for the bass beat of my heart in my ears.

"Who's there?" My voice lacked the steadiness to make demands, but I did my best to mask my fear. I clutched hard at the wrench, gave it a shake like I meant to bean someone at the slightest incentive.

There was no reply.

Taking the first few steps hurriedly, loudly, in the hopes of spooking the trespasser into revealing himself, I shouted the question again. "Who's there? I'm calling the police."

Recalling that my phone was back in the living room, I lamented at what was in truth an idle threat. Calling the cops would have been a smart thing to do under the circumstances, but doing so now would require me to turn my back on whoever was lurking upstairs. Having made it nearly half-way up, I couldn't afford to risk it. I pressed on.

The shadow did not return, and the intruder made no sound. It was possible he'd taken refuge in one of the rooms, or had his back pressed to a wall. When I had only four steps to go, I mounted them in a single jump, bursting into the upstairs hall and waving around the wrench with an animalistic cry. Somewhere in this chaotic surprise attack, I found the wherewithal to switch on the hall light, too.

The hallway was empty. I looked to the dim-glowing window at the end of the hall, which was likely responsible for the shadow-play, and then to the four doorways. All of them were ajar, as I'd left them.

I calmed down enough to inspect the upper level without further shouts or theatrics, and when I was done I found no one lurking in any of the rooms. I wasn't sure what I'd seen, where the shadow had come from, but that it didn't correspond to any late-night intruder was now apparent. Without the daylight to spruce them up with brightness, the rooms in the upstairs struck me with their ugliness. It was in shadow, rather than daylight, that their defects and filthiness became clearest to me. Peering into the ruined bathroom with only the light of the hall to see by, I wondered if such a place could ever be set right—if any amount of renovation could ever make a house like this worth living in.

So, no one had broken in. I'd left a window open and freaked myself out for no good reason. I supposed that made sense, even if I couldn't remember leaving said window open. I'd done stupider things in my life. Putting out the hallway light, I marched back downstairs.

On the way to the living room, I stopped at the window to take another look at the handprint, but for some reason I couldn't find it. I must have looked like a real idiot, leaning this way and that, inspecting every inch of the pane, but no matter how long I searched, it didn't turn up. The handprint that'd been there only minutes ago had vanished without a trace.

Like the shadow I'd seen coming from the upstairs, it was possible that the handprint, too, had been nothing. I'd been sleepy when I'd first glimpsed it, not at all in a steady state of mind.

I returned to the air mattress. Keeping the wrench within reach

*—just in case—*I pulled the blanket up to my chin to beat back the chill that still plodded around the room. There was time enough to salvage the night's sleep, to wake up rested, even, and I rolled onto my side with a yawn.

I would have gotten to sleep a whole lot faster if not for the scratching.

From the wall directly behind my head, I heard a light scrabbling noise, as of rodents scurrying. A furtive SCRITCH SCRITCH SCRITCH came in even intervals, traveling up and down the wall. I could hear them working their teeth against the baseboards, too. The sound left me feeling disgusted, and I made a mental note to purchase some mouse traps—or *rat* traps, depending on what I was dealing with. Though not a fan of rodents or other pests, my work often saw me coming face-to-face with them. I knew the scratching would eventually cease, or that I'd finally get tired enough to ignore it and drift off regardless.

What I hadn't anticipated was just how long those things would go at it, how energetically.

I slipped in and out of sleep for a time, the most furious scratch-ings always seeming to occur when I was on the verge of drifting off. It was like the pests wanted to get my attention, like they wanted me to stay up and chat. Eventually, in my tired stupor, I reached behind me and pounded at the wall to shut them up. That did the job, and they retreated to some other spot in the house to keep up their infernal racket.

I don't know what time it was when I finally fell asleep. It wasn't long after I'd knocked on the wall and dispersed the rodents, I was sure. My dreams for the night were vague, comprised of real-life settings mixed with illusory ones, as I straddled the borders of sleep and wakefulness.

And in one of those dreams—or what I told myself *must have been* a dream—I'd heard something just after pounding on the wall with my open palm. Upon remembering it, I assured myself it'd been nothing but my imagination, that it was impossible. But not long after the last rodent had gone running, I thought I'd heard something else coming from behind the wall.

A low, rumbling laugh.

SEVEN

I lingered in bed past my alarm, and when I eventually rose it wasn't because I was looking forward to the mountain of work that awaited me. No, it was the realization that my newest video had gone live the night prior that ultimately drew me out of bed. I hunkered down at the table with my laptop to see how many views and comments I'd racked up overnight.

As expected, the feedback was piling up nicely. In the hours since it had been posted, I'd already managed nearly forty-thousand views. Cracking open a bottle of lukewarm water to chase the dust out of my throat, I started scrolling through the comments, curious what my viewers thought about this upcoming challenge.

Most were enthusiastic, supportive, but as usual there were some doubters in the mix, too.

User YungPoo44 wrote: *This whole thing is fake. Seriously, I'll bet FlipperKevin has a whole team of professionals doing the real work. You guys are so stupid, giving him all of these views. He probably doesn't even know how to use a drill. #fake*

Comments like these were nothing new. A lot of people thought that my channel was fake. A certain subset of viewers believed that I had a huge team of professional contractors at my disposal—along with an endless stream of cash to pay them with—and that they did all of the work while I took the credit. Honestly, sitting in the dusty living room with burning eyes and a crick in my neck, that sounded like a fine arrangement.

One of the most "liked" comments came from user ErikaBB. They wrote: *Ooh, what's this? Does Flipper Kevin have a special friend over?* They included a timestamp which pointed to the 1:47 mark in my video. I wasn't sure what this user was talking about, but the stream of replies to it piqued my curiosity.

YungPoo44 made a reappearance in the replies to this comment, writing, *See? It's fake. I TOLD YOU.*

Other users opined. *I dunno,* added one, *does anyone really believe that one dude could fix a rundown house in a single month? Of course he brought help.*

Still another: *I wonder if that's his gf???*

I wasn't sure what they were talking about, but apparently, at a minute and forty-seven seconds into my video, there was something these viewers were willing to accept as proof of my having others in the house to do the heavy lifting. I queued up the video to that mark and watched closely, wondering what the fuss was all about.

I had to pause and study the clip for almost a minute before I noticed it.

The scene in question showcased the outside of the house. Specifically, the front of the place, as seen from the front lawn. At 1:47, after briefly focusing on the porch, I'd stepped back and taken a quick shot of the upper story.

And that was when I saw what looked to be someone standing in one of the upstairs windows.

It was the window corresponding to the master bedroom, the one with the crack in it. Standing a foot or two from the glass was what looked like a sickly woman in a lightly-colored garb. A thin, summery dress, a nightgown—something like that. Despite my footage having been shot in high definition, the image of the woman was rather grainy.

"*What in the world?*" I asked aloud, rubbing at the screen with my fingertip. I wondered, rather optimistically, if it wasn't just a woman-shaped smudge on the display.

It wasn't.

Baffled and not a little unsettled, I decided to dig into the raw footage. How had I not noticed this before? Had I captured this figure elsewhere in my shoot? Was there anyone there at all, or was I just seeing things? Pulling up the original, unedited files, I zoomed in as far as I could on this particular scene, and was dismayed to find that the figure was still there in the window. Despite the zoom, the image didn't become any clearer than it was on VideoTube—if anything, it got more distorted.

I couldn't see her eyes no matter how long I stared. I could make out what looked like a mouth, though—yawning, black, toothless. It reminded me of an anaconda's; jaw unhinged to swallow up an entire deer. One thin arm was pressed to a bent torso, and the overall impression was of a sickly woman nearly doubled over in uncontrollable laughter.

A laughing woman?

I pored over the footage—dug into the files that'd come straight from my camera—and could find no other trace of this figure in any other shot. During a subsequent pan to that very window, shortly before I'd carried the camera into the house, she'd vanished altogether, and examinations of the other windows yielded no sign of her.

Immediately, I tried to think up an explanation.

First of all, I was sure that I'd been alone in the house since arriving the day before. The fright of the previous night—a thing for which, in the daylight, I was now rather ashamed—had proven that beyond a shadow of a doubt. There couldn't have been anyone in that window at that time—and if there had been, there would have been no way for them to escape my view. I supposed it was possible that they'd fled through the back door, but the fact was that we would have almost certainly run into each other upon my entrance to the house mere moments after having taken that shot of the upper level. At the very least, I would have heard someone running down the stairs, across the creaky lower story, or slamming the back door.

More likely than not, this was a weird effect of the light. A reflection of something in the lawn, like the Callery pear tree, I guessed. Really, the outline of the figure was so vague and powdery that one could have read almost anything into it. And anyhow, it didn't resemble anything like a real person. No human being I'd ever met had a mouth like *that*. This alone was sufficient to disqualify it as proof of an intruder in my house.

Still, it was unsettling.

Pushing away from the computer and rifling through my backpack for some breakfast, I replayed my memories of the previous day. Could there have been someone in the house the day before? A squatter? *No, that isn't possible,* I thought for the hundredth time. I'd been in and out of the house all day, had replaced the locks and ensured their sturdiness. Except for that issue I'd had with the window after dark, those had all stayed locked, too. No one could have gotten in without my knowing it, and anyone already in the house would have been found out almost immediately.

I was half-way into unwrapping a granola bar when my hands got a little weak. I remembered the handprint I'd seen on the dining room window the night before and shot up from my chair. What if that handprint belonged to the person I'd captured in my footage? What if they'd found some way to open the window from the outside?

Returning to the window, I knelt down and took a long look at the glass. The warm morning sun came through it, leaving the dusty wooden sill fragrant. There were no handprints to be found. A smudge here and there, but nothing else.

Without a good explanation, I turned to the next best thing: Putting it out of my mind completely.

It was nothing. *Obviously nothing.* And even if there *had* been someone in the house, they wouldn't be getting in again. This house wasn't abandoned anymore. It was mine, and I'd taken some care to secure it. The light I'd installed on the porch would ward off any nighttime visitors and I'd make sure the doors and windows stayed closed and locked when I wasn't around.

There's nothing to worry about.

When I'd polished off a second granola bar and washed my face with a damp cloth, I began plotting out my day. The hardest thing, for me, has always been picking a starting point for my projects. In my experience, it's best to single out one room and work on it exclusively until it's finished. Seeing as how I was spending most of my time in the living room, I settled upon fixing that room up first. Incidentally, it also seemed the easiest choice.

The living room was about fifteen by twenty. I'd given the space a pretty solid clean the day before so that I was well-acquainted with its defects already. The biggest thing it needed, aside from a bit of electrical work to get its outlets working again, was some new drywall. The wall behind my air mattress had begun sagging over the years and looked on the verge of cracking. I wasn't sure if it was due to water damage or mold, but ripping out the bad drywall and hanging some new would be simple enough, and I liked the idea of easing into this project with such an easy task. Hanging drywall was one of my specialties.

I made a quick list of things to buy, took some measurements, and then set off for the nearest Home Depot.

But before I hopped into the van, I paused on the porch. I locked the door and tested it. It didn't budge. I walked around the house, through the dewy lawn, and did the same with the back door. Both doors were perfectly secure. Despite knowing they were shut, the paranoiac in me insisted that I check all of the lower story windows. When I saw that they were all closed, I finally set off.

I backed out of the driveway, and as I did so I couldn't help but look up at the window to the master bedroom. There was no one standing in it, but I wondered whether someone would enter into view if I waited long enough.

I thought better of testing that hypothesis, and drove away faster than was wise on the crumbling road.

EIGHT

I can still remember the first time I put up drywall. It can seem like a daunting task if you've never done it before, and I recall that I was doubly nervous because at that time I still hadn't gotten used to working alongside my dad. He'd made it look so easy, but then he'd been building and renovating houses since before I'd been born. It could be that I've prettied up the memory in retrospect, but I sincerely think he could have done drywall—and most any other job —blindfolded.

It'd been a cold autumn day, rainy, and we'd been hired to hang some new drywall in an apartment building. There'd been a leak in the roof and the existing drywall had bubbled and cracked in several places. We'd patched the roof the day before on what had been my first time on top of a three-story building. To this day, I don't do very well with heights, and roof work ranks among my least favorite jobs.

On the day we'd first done drywall together—after he'd enjoyed his pre-work Camel on the apartment's balcony, of course—he'd pulled up the waistband of his dungarees and gotten straight to work. We took turns breaking up the existing drywall, and in just under an hour we'd gotten the new stuff up. I've been working in houses for a little while now and have put up my fair share of drywall solo, but even now I'm in awe of how smoothly things went that first time, when I was under his wing. It was truly textbook.

My father had never been a talkative man. As a kid, he'd been more likely to get annoyed by my childish questions about life than to answer them. In that apartment I discovered a side of my father I'd never seen before, though. He'd answered *all* of my questions with uncharacteristic patience, as if the subject matter required the utmost care—as if he were passing on some treasured oral tradition. I'd never known my father to be an especially passionate person, but in his attention to detail and calm guidance I'd glimpsed something like real enthusiasm behind the silent, tough-guy veneer. In a small way, I'd felt like I'd really gotten to know the man that rainy afternoon.

We'd gone back home when the job was done, showered, and eaten in near silence as was our habit. But that evening, my dad did something that left me completely blindsided. He came out of the kitchen with two beers while I was sitting in front of the TV. He handed me one and told me I'd done a "good job" that day.

I hadn't known what to say. I ended up doing the smart thing and opted not to say anything, lest I ruin the moment. Instead, I sipped the beer and basked in the sun of my father's approval. Pabst Blue Ribbon had never tasted so good.

That's what I was thinking about as I loaded everything into the back of the van.

I'd picked up sheets of drywall, shims, drywall screws and compound. I had everything else I needed back at the house. After hitting up a drive-thru and treating myself to an early lunch, I made a slow return to the job site, taking in the scenery as I went.

This part of Detroit didn't have anything I could call a "scenic route", to be honest. Every building I passed—both commercial and residential—looked punished by neglect. Those that *had* been reasonably kept up—a pawnshop, a delicatessen—had thick bars on the windows to dissuade prowlers from patronizing them after hours, and only added to the grotty, unfriendly atmosphere. And then I started down side streets, through neighborhoods.

Along these roads, where there were boards thrown over potholes, the houses looked lived-in. That is, at first. Here and there you'd see someone sitting on a porch, or cutting the grass. A mailman trudged down the sidewalk delivering letters. Signs of life. But the longer I drove—and the closer I got to my own property on Morgan Road—the less activity I saw. I began to encounter the odd empty house here and there, the occasional abandoned lot.

Activity waned the further one went into the tangled network of streets, giving the impression that entire neighborhoods had been cut off by some unseen vise, until finally one was surrounded only by dereliction. Morgan Road and everything adjacent to it was practically a gangrenous limb. It had been excised from the whole, left to rot in the open. Eventually, it would all crumble away, but for now it was a sprawling monument to decay.

Driving through these streets and doing a bit of exploring to delay the work ahead of me, I discovered an interesting feature that was little more than five minutes from the house.

A graveyard.

It seemed rather small. Seeing as how I didn't spend a lot of time in such places, I had only the graveyard in the Florida panhandle where my old man was buried for reference. This patch, perhaps the size of a football field and crowded with faded, lopsided headstones, struck me as tiny.

With some french fries to finish and a desire to stretch my legs, I parked along the curb and decided to take a closer look. There was no gate, no sign posted to warn off visitors. In fact, the signage that had once provided the graveyard's name was nowhere to be found. Only rust marks on the concrete pillars at the entrance indicated where it had once been.

The grass was tall, and there weren't any flowers at the graves. Most of the inscriptions near the front were hard to read, worn down by the rain and wind, but as best I could tell the bulk of the headstones belonged to people who had died prior to World War II.

I walked between the graves, munched on cold french fries and inspected the sorry-looking ornamental angels whose wings had been weathered to nubs. Like the broken down houses that surrounded this place, the unkempt state of the grounds invoked a certain disgust. And unease. When the people who'd lived in this area had scattered to the four winds, they'd abandoned more than their homes. This graveyard, whose many stones had been intentioned to act as memorials, was forgotten. Save for a few, it was impossible to make out the names on the monuments. Anyone could have been buried in the plots. That the legacy of any human could be reduced to a blurry headstone was distressing enough, but as I walked back to the van and spied the tottering houses across the street, so indicative of the area's profound deterioration, I wondered what else had been forgotten. What memories had been abandoned in those houses? What histories, what sins, had been swept under the rug in their desertion?

Who had lived in the house I was fixing up, and what had they been like?

Having gotten my fill of the scenery, and of moody introspection, I drove back to the house. As I left the graveyard, the day's work seemed a good deal more appealing than only moments before. Everywhere I looked, there was ruin. This place had forgotten beauty, traded it for rot and disorder. By renovating the house, I realized I had the opportunity to set something right, to reintroduce species such as beauty and stability to an ecosystem where, for too long now, they'd been considered extinct. I fancied myself a prospector panning for gold, wondering if I'd unearth something interesting in this restoration that had, like the names on those headstones, long been hidden.

I GRINNED into the camera and held out a handful of drywall

screws like a drug dealer offering a fix. "So," I said, "these are the supplies we'll be using for the job today. Working with drywall can be a bit intimidating when you're first getting started, but I promise it's actually pretty simple. It helps to have a friend present, but as I'm about to show you, this is entirely doable as a one-man job."

After unpacking the van and putting away my air mattress, I'd piled the new drywall and my other supplies around the living room in an aesthetic formation and set up the camera about ten feet from the wall I was set to replace. I'd also moved my laptop and other belongings into the dining room to keep them from getting showered in dust. Finally, before starting, I'd shut off all power from the room and removed the covers from all of the wall boxes.

"As you can see here," I said, pointing to the bubbles and fissures in the drywall, "this poor wall has had it. I'm hoping there won't be any water damage back here, but you never can tell. I could probably cut away the damaged portions and just patch it up with new drywall, but I want to get a good look at what we're dealing with. I also want to have good access to the wiring. So, you get to watch me replace the whole wall. How's that sound?"

Having introduced the tools for the job and covered the problem areas, I was now set to do a bit of demolition. I walked over to the camera and adjusted the tripod to better capture my movements in frame. The light coming in from the window in the dining room was good, but I had a studio light positioned off-camera that I could use in case the day became overcast.

"This is my favorite part," I said, picking up a hammer. "The tear-down is actually a lot of fun, and I've found it's a great way to relieve stress. You just want to make sure that you only break the drywall and don't damage the studs behind it. Go hard, but not *too* hard." I feigned deep thought, arching a brow and pursing my lips, while considering where to land the first blow. Lifting the hammer to just above eye level, I took a step back and made a slow practice strike, like I was sizing up my golf swing. "How about right here?"

On went a dust mask and a pair of safety glasses.

Then came the wind up.

And the release.

With a measured swing, I sent the hammer through the drywall. It sank in without much effort and left a small divot. I then focused on increasing the size of that first opening length-wise, until I'd knocked a straight line of material out. I turned to the camera and got a little closer so that my voice would still be audible despite the mask. "So, what I've done here is create a little line of holes in the wall. These are handholds—I'll be able to grip the drywall from here and tear it down. See?" Returning to the wall, I made more holes, more handholds, and when I'd managed to leave the wall pockmarked from one end to the other, I tossed away the hammer. "All right! Here comes my favorite part. Time to get my hands dirty."

I put on a pair of cowhide work gloves and playfully flexed my bicep for the camera.

It felt lame, but I knew it would come together in the edit. At least, I told myself as much. Joking around in front of the camera —*talking to myself*—was awkward no matter how I sliced it.

I reached up and slipped my gloved fingers into the handholds. With a grunt, I began pulling the drywall apart. A large piece cracked off in my grip, and I waved it around for the camera. "It's easy as that!" I reached up and took another chunk down, making a pile of the broken stuff at my feet. Peering at the studs behind, the inside of the wall appeared in decent order. Ancient dust circulated, clinging to my forearms, as I yanked another piece free, and another.

Not wanting to spend all day in front of the camera, I started hurrying through the teardown process. Just a few minutes into my wrenching away the drywall, the pile on the floor began to grow rather tall. I'd intended to rent a dumpster for all of the refuse involved in this renovation, but had forgotten to, and would have to store it on the lawn, or in garbage bags, for the time being.

I was half-way through breaking down the extant drywall and hadn't found anything serious behind it. No leaks, no mold. I was chuffed. "I'm not done just yet," I told the camera, "but it's looking like there are no major issues behind this wall—just some damaged drywall. Thank goodness."

I moved to my right, began prying at a new length of material.

I was rambling on, half to myself and half to the camera.

But as I let that next piece drop, I suddenly shut up. There was something tangled and white on one of the newly-exposed studs. It looked like a dense tangle of cobwebs, and I grimaced beneath my mask. "Uh-oh," I said, "might have some creepy crawlies to deal with."

Ready to stomp on any monster spider that might emerge from the gap, I ripped away another chunk of drywall, revealing the gap between the web-encrusted stud and the next.

And then I got a really good look at the bunch of silk.

Except, it didn't really look like silk anymore. It seemed too coarse, wiry, to be cobwebs.

I glanced back at the camera as though I expected the thing to comment.

"Not sure what this is," I mumbled.

With trepidation, I reached into the wall and teased the white strands, tugged them a bit. *A frayed wire?* I wondered. *A tangle of fur?* The strands seemed fastened to something lower down, and the rasping sound they made as they passed tautly over the fingers of my leather gloves reminded me of hair.

I gripped the exposed edge of the drywall and decided to work my way downward.

Teeth grit, I pulled away another segment. It cracked off loudly and a shower of whitish dust hit my jeans.

I then dropped the chunk of drywall—not because I was ready to tear away another, but because I'd suddenly been robbed of my ability to hold it.

Someone looked out at me from the new gap in the drywall.

A shock of thick, white hair was wrapped around the stud. I'd first seen the very edge of this tangle only moments ago, but I now saw the leathery, eyeless head it was attached to, and I spied also the beginnings of a thin, mummified body occupying the space beneath the yet-unbroken drywall.

A corpse.

A corpse had been propped up in the narrow space between the two studs.

Though I hadn't yet revealed the entirety of the body, I could fill in the blanks well enough. The edge of a soiled, off-white garment was teased. There wasn't a lot of space back there; I envisioned the limbs tucked up towards the trunk, stiff and brittle, like those of a dead insect left to bake on a hot dash.

In my haste to back away from the horror in the wall, I tripped over my pile of refuse and hit the floor. Dust stuck to my palms, to my hair, like powdered sugar as I landed on my face. I didn't feel any pain, nor any shame, however. I scrambled to my feet, hit the front door and crashed out onto the lawn.

Next thing I knew I was yanking off the dust mask and dialing 9-1-1.

NINE

Detective Sherman straddled a chair as the video started, his belly pressing into the backrest. His partner, Bateman, remained standing to my left, arms crossed.

They were both trying their hardest not to laugh.

"How can you stand talking to yourself like that?" asked Sherman, shaking his head, as I appeared on screen and explained the drywall teardown process. "It's embarrassing."

I didn't respond, merely shrugged. It was embarrassing. This was unedited footage. I'd never intended anyone to see *everything*—not my mistakes, my stutters. With proper editing—that is, visual effects and music—my videos were entertaining! These cops didn't get it, though. To them, I seemed like a loon, monologuing in an empty house while ripping apart a wall. It made for a bizarre cinematic experience, and it was only because they'd expressed interest in seeing the footage that I was still in the interrogation room at all.

I'd been at the police station for a few hours now. Exhausted by the back and forth with cops, the hours of sitting—both in the back of a cruiser, and in the grey, stuffy interrogation room—my terror had largely been dulled and I no longer felt rocked by the horrific find in the house. That is, until the detectives handling the case had asked me to hook up my camera to one of their televisions. I'd cooperated, hesitantly, not wanting to revisit that moment when I'd discovered the corpse.

We ended up watching it three times.

The cops absolutely lost it when, some minutes into it, I flexed my bicep for the camera. They'd glance at each other, howling, as if to say, "Get a load of this!" I'll be honest, it left my ego a little bruised. But there was one part they thought even funnier than that.

Each time I unearthed the body and scrambled out of the house like a frightened Scooby-Do character, they gasped with laughter.

I don't think they were *trying* to be jerks. Initially, when they'd brought me in, they'd just had a few questions. They didn't suspect me of anything, as it was clear the body had been in the house a long time—maybe since before I'd even been born. But when they'd learned that I'd captured the find on tape, they'd asked to see the video and had sent someone back to the house to grab my camera.

After this third viewing, Sherman got up and shut off the TV, tugging on his belt. The gut beneath his blue dress shirt shifted like a giant boil full of cottage cheese. He reeked of sweat. "Well, we've removed the body. Don't know much, yet. Female, not sure on the age. Waiting on more details. At this point, she's a Jane Doe. And it's possible she'll stay that way."

"Why's that?" I asked.

"It's complicated. See, there's no telling how long the old girl has been hidden away like that. We'll need the medical examiner to tell us how she died and how long ago. We did a little digging and found that no one's lived in that house since the late 80's, early 90's. In the almost thirty years since that house was last occupied, it's been used by all kinds of people, and some of 'em might have used it as a convenient place to hide a body. Unless we find some forensic evidence that helps us get an ID, or we can link it to a previous missing person's case, it's a safe bet she'll remain a mystery. What a way to go."

Bateman, the slenderer of the two, stroked his beard and grew deadly serious for a moment, brow furrowed. "I say, was there a cask of Amontillado back there?"

The two roared with laughter.

I'd set the cops up with a copy of my video and knew full well that they'd be showing all of their buddies. FlipperKevin's freakout was going to entertain the entire department for some time to come, I was sure of it.

I was too tired to care and hoped they'd hurry up and release me.

Sherman pushed in his chair and rested an arm atop the TV. "Our guys had a look back there, behind the wall, and didn't find anything else. Seems this is just a spot of bad luck for you, Mr. Taylor. I take it the realtor didn't mention that particular amenity, eh?" He smirked. "If you notice anything else, give us a call. Otherwise, unless you have some questions, you're free to go."

"I can go back to the house?" I asked. The phrasing sounded hopeful, like I was ready to return to my work, but in the back of my mind I hoped the detectives would bar me from re-entering the premises until a lengthy investigation was complete.

"You may," replied Bateman. "The body has been removed, photographs were taken and forensics wrapped things up on their end. Collecting evidence in an indoor location—behind a single wall—isn't too complicated. If this had been a grislier case, you might have had to find a hotel for a week, but the nature of this find doesn't require that kind of cordoning. At the present time, we have no need for further access to the house. You can get back to whatever it was you were doing." He looked to my camera and fought back a smirk. "Any other questions?"

Let me tell you, I had questions. Oodles of 'em. I wasn't sure that these sweaty pricks would be able to answer them, but I decided to try my luck anyhow. "How does something like this happen? I mean... who could have done this? And why?"

Sherman straightened his glasses. "Dunno. In the time that it was occupied, the house had no criminal history to speak of. Whatever happened, I'd wager it occurred in the house's lengthy vacancy. All sorts will take advantage of a house like that; the homeless, lowlives looking for a place to sell dope or guns... Maybe a drug dealer stuck her back there, or else she got on someone's bad side during a house party. Point is, if you poke around in abandoned old houses like those long enough, you're bound to find something a little unsavory. Which leads me to wonder why an enterprising young man like yourself would bother fixing one up. That neighborhood wouldn't be *my* first choice, that's for sure."

Bateman started towards the door, adding, "Don't take this the wrong way, Mr. Taylor, but this isn't really that huge a deal. Old, unidentified remains are rather common, in fact. People find bones in their attics, in their gardens... I've seen a lot of bodies in my day, and though I'm not a betting man, I'd guesstimate this individual to have died maybe twenty or thirty years ago. After so much time, it's highly unlikely anyone's looking for her, waiting for her, so this case just isn't going to be a huge priority. Our department has got a lot of *current* cases going. I reckon that, while we've been in this room talking, at least one person in this city's gotten shot or raped. I wouldn't be surprised if we never got straight answers about this woman hiding behind your wall, so don't hold your breath. Cases like these have a way of going unsolved unless other evidence turns up. The 'hows' and 'whys' may never come to light."

Finally, they let me gather my things and go. One of them offered me a ride back to the house, which I politely refused. I couldn't stomach the idea of spending more time with them. My place wasn't so far from the station, anyway. I could walk, and would welcome the solitude.

They saw me to the exit, and I thanked the two of them, though I wasn't sure why. Except for removing the body and laughing heartily at my footage, the cops hadn't really done anything. I left the building and ambled onto the sidewalk, disoriented by the darkness. It was an hour or two past sunset and the night was both too dim and too warm for my liking.

"So... what now?" I sighed.

I was a skiff left unmoored; the pier was fading from view and the choppy waters ahead didn't bode well. I'd spent so much time hoping the cops would let me go that I hadn't put much thought into what I'd do with the remainder of my day once they did. Would I go back to the house? Crash in a hotel? Hop into my van and drive until I no longer recognized my surroundings?

Walking silently, I replayed the day's events in my head: The drive through town; the discovery of the body; the long wait in the police station; the relentless barrage of questions; the mocking laughter of those two detectives as they reviewed my recording. Even as I held the camera, recalled the dreadful footage on it, the ordeal didn't feel real to me. A dead body? On *my* property? That kind of stuff was only supposed to happen on true crime TV shows.

I quickened my pace, fell deeper into thought. The orange street-lights flickered as I strode away from the station and passed a long, abandoned lot where a pair of stray cats chased one another in the tall grass. I was making my way to the house, but wondered what I was going to do when I got there.

Like it or not, there was still the 30-day renovation challenge to think about. It was a very public affair, not the kind of thing I could easily abandon. My newfound unwillingness to work in the house was about to become my biggest problem, it seemed. I mean, how could I ditch this audacious project and leave my brand unscathed? What was I going to tell my viewers? *Sorry, guys. Found a dead body in this house so I'm going to throw in the towel. Be sure to like and subscribe!* I couldn't talk to my fans about what I'd found in the wall. To do so would detract from the point of my challenge and taint my whole channel with a kind of morbid sensationalism. Moreover, ethics aside, I couldn't post footage of the body as proof for my viewers, since VideoTube's guidelines understandably restricted content that displayed real human corpses. If I showed the corpse to the world in an effort to convince my subscribers, it was possible that VideoTube would terminate my account permanently.

The idea of working in that house, of sleeping anywhere near that open wall where a body had been stashed, made me ill. I'd slept right up against it the night before, with only an inch of material between me and the then-undiscovered dead woman. Just the memory of that, of the scratching I'd heard from behind that very wall, called to mind all kinds of twisted and unwelcome images. *Maybe it wasn't mice you heard last night, but the sound of the body shifting; of skeletal fingers picking at the inside of the wall...*

I wasn't going to be able to sell it off—no one in their right mind would buy such a house, especially if the local news lit up with reports of a dead body being found inside. Financially, that didn't bother me too much. I could eat the cost. What *did* bother me about giving up the challenge was the hit to my credibility. I had a reputation to consider, and I feared that a very public failure like this one would torpedo my career. I'd done smaller challenges in the past, and despite tight deadlines or other bumps in the road I'd never backed out of them. If I bailed on this house, though, my hopes of securing a TV deal in the near-future were toast.

What would dad think? A ghost of a smile teased my lips as the question popped into my head. Then, just as quickly, I frowned, because I knew how my father would react at the prospect of quitting a job. *He'd laugh at you.* My father wouldn't have quit for anything. In all his years he'd never backed out of a job. Not a single one. He'd valued his reputation too much to be a quitter, sometimes to the point of danger. Once, he'd worked on a house infested with brown recluse spiders. Houses packed full of black mold. He'd been the kind of guy to show up to work with a fever—hard-working and determined to a fault. He hadn't been much of a father, but he'd been a model workman.

My father wouldn't have cared a jot about finding a corpse at a worksite. *So, what? Ain't no body in the house now. Keep working on it,* he would've said while taking a puff from his Camel. *You're gonna have to toughen up if you wanna get paid, kiddo. Worse things to find in a house than a dried-up ol' stiff. Lemme tell you... once, I worked on this mess of a house where...*

I could practically hear his voice in my ear.

I crossed a busy intersection and then jogged a little while, starting into the network of semi-abandoned streets that would lead me back to Morgan Road. The occasional headlight painted my surroundings in streaks of yellow as I went, reading the street signs and pushing into familiar territory.

If I wanted to, I could pack up my most valuable things and stay at a hotel for the night, coming back for the other stuff later. Maybe by morning I'd be able to decide what to do with the house. A good night's sleep in a proper bed, some hard drinks and room service sounded incredible. I considered another course of action, that of simply hauling all of my equipment back into the van and leaving Michigan for good. It would take awhile to get everything packed, but even so this plan had a lot of appeal. I wanted to put as much distance between myself and that crumbling nightmare of a house as I could.

I took my time meandering along the lonely stretch of Morgan Road and arrived at the house to find all of the lights on in the downstairs. The front lawn looked pretty well trampled, and the overgrown grass had been mashed down by the tires of police cruisers. As I walked up the drive, the motion-activated light I'd installed the evening before went off, blinding me. I cursed all the way to the front door.

Stepping inside, I was dismayed to find the downstairs a complete mess. Muddy bootprints marred the already dusty floors. Bits of drywall had been scattered across the room. My things had been rearranged, jostled, by foreign hands. Violated. The house had never been cozy or inviting to me, but in its current state of disarray I found myself unable to turn up a single redeeming characteristic.

And that didn't even begin to cover the apprehension I felt as I looked to the open wall in the living room.

I stepped towards it slowly, cautiously. I didn't even get within ten feet of the wall, opting instead to stand on tip-toe. I had to be sure that the body was, in fact, gone.

Of course it was. Not a trace of it remained. Even the tangle of white hair I'd seen on one of the studs had been removed by the authorities. They'd been very thorough, had probably probed behind the other walls and taken no shortage of pictures. I'd only been allowed to return to the house because the cops had found no other evidence of note in their hours-long search.

The lack of a body should have been a comfort, but it wasn't. Body or no body, I still *felt* it there, mucking up the place. And so I called out, irritated, in a voice that echoed off of the bare walls. "Why'd you have to go and die in *this* house, huh? Of all the houses to die in, it just had to be *this* one? The house I'd staked my future on? I had plans for this house. And now they're ruined. Thanks, lady. *Thanks a lot.*"

I paused, suddenly sickened with guilt. I'd spent a lot of time that day worrying about how this terrible inconvenience was going to alter *my* day-to-day without once sparing the least bit of sympathy for the victim. Finding a dead body in your house is a pretty terrible thing, but it isn't half as bad as being walled up yourself. The woman hadn't ended up back there by accident; no, there'd been some foul-play involved. It was possible she'd been dead before being immured, and had only been stashed in the wall by some evil-doer to keep her corpse—and his misdeeds—hidden. Or maybe, like some unfortunate victim in a Poe story, she'd been put back there by someone to die a slow and horrible death, while still alive and kickin'.

I didn't want to think about the specifics. I had enough on my mind without imagining what it might be like to slowly die in a cramped space like that.

"On that note, it's time to go," I said. I didn't want to be there anymore.

The atmosphere had changed, maybe permanently. In that moment, deciding that I needed to pack my things and go, it wasn't even fear that compelled me, but disgust. What a wretched little house this was. The cops had been right; I'd been a real idiot to buy it in the first place. A headache nipped at my brainstem as I turned and had a look around the room, trying to decide where to begin.

The laptop went into my backpack. I loaded up another bag with camera gear, then set about identifying other essentials. When I'd gotten the most important items sorted, I realized I still didn't have a destination in mind. I was leaving the house, but where would I go?

I sat on the folding chair and massaged my temples. The first thing I wanted was a hot shower. I pulled out my phone and started looking into luxury hotels in the area. I didn't care if I had to drive twenty, forty miles. I wanted someplace swank after the day I'd had.

Before diving into the search results for quality lodgings, I decided to peek at my email, and again lamented the fact that I was about to disappoint all of my subscribers. I could already imagine the deluge of comments I was going to get. The haters would be vindicated. *See?* they would write, *FlipperKevin is a sham. He can't fix anything to save his life. This was just a stupid gimmick to earn him more views. He's only in it for the money. I'm unsubscribing.*

It was possible that my finding the body would make the local news. No journalist had been by yet, and seeing as how this part of town was completely derelict, perhaps there was no media interest in the case. Still, it was possible someone would drop by for an interview, or that the police would give a statement. I considered this fact, wondered if I couldn't point my viewers to any number of articles that might pop up in the next twenty-four hours. I wondered, too, whether they'd be understanding of my decision to end the challenge prematurely if they had all the facts.

Maybe I'd record a hasty statement, briefly explaining my intention to end the 30-day challenge. While pondering what I'd say in such a recording, something in my email distracted me.

I had a message waiting for me from Mona Neeb—a woman I'd had some correspondence with before.

Mona Neeb, from the Home Improvement Network.

Dazedly, I opened the email. *Hello, Kevin!* she wrote. *This is*

Mona from HIN. Not sure if you remember me. We talked a few months back? Anyhow, I wanted to drop you a line to let you know that this new series of yours, the thirty-day renovation, is exciting, and it's piqued the interest of some of the producers here. We look forward to following this new project. It looks like you've already gotten quite the reception! Your views and viewer-engagement are incredible. Many of us are following your daily updates with great interest, and there's talk that a show in this format could do huge ratings on our network. When you're finished with this project, provided it all goes well, I'd like to set up a meeting with you at our main office so that we can discuss the particulars. You'd expressed interest in your own show during our last chat, and I believe you'd be the perfect host for such a project.

She left her contact info in the email so that we might arrange a meeting at the Home Improvement Network offices. What really stuck with me, though—the line I read again and again like a meditative mantra—was the last bit of her message.

Best of luck to you in completing this challenge, Kevin! All of us here at HIN will be watching!

Translation: *Don't mess this up and you might get to be a television star!*

I groaned, and it took everything I had not to throw my phone across the room.

I was stuck fixing this house now, and I knew it.

It would have broken my heart to disappoint subscribers, to eat the costs I'd hitherto racked up in this renovation, but after what I'd been through the past day, I'd been prepared to cancel the challenge.

This email changed everything, though. I couldn't pack up and flee after what I'd just read. As I'd hoped, this VideoTube series was set to become my golden ticket. I could have a real shot at the big-time, so long as I completed this renovation. Mona Neeb wanted me to fix this house up in thirty days; to do less, or to walk away from the house, was to walk away from fame.

The roller coaster of emotions I'd ridden that day left me feeling ragged. I re-read Mona's email and laughed. I think I cried a little, too. And then I stood up, unpacked my laptop and camera gear, and got to work.

It didn't matter if there were ten, a hundred, corpses in this joint.

I was going to get the work done. I didn't have any choice now.

TEN

When I wasn't hard at work editing my video, I was glancing back at the open wall, expecting a shriveled corpse to materialize.

While picking and choosing which bits of my footage to use for the day's video, I was forced, briefly, to revisit the moment I'd made the horrific discovery. Watching it in private now, mere feet from where the body had been found, the hair on the back of my neck stood at attention. Despite this, I was arrested by morbid curiosity. I had a desire to know—to *really know*—who it was I'd found in this house, and hoped that a measured look at their remains might help me to quell my nerves.

I paused on a frame where the corpse could be seen clearly, studying it for a time. "See?" I told myself aloud, gripping my knees with shaky hands. "It's just an old body. Like a mummy."

Yes, it was rather like a mummy. The shriveled, papery skin and empty eye sockets reminded me of mummies I'd seen in museums on school field trips. The long, white hair testified to advanced age and seeming femininity, and though only her head and neck had been unearthed at that point, the fact she'd been small—shrunken— was not much in doubt. I hadn't gotten a look at the entire body; the cops hadn't shown me, and I'd had no interest in pursuing the matter. The leathern face staring at me from the screen was enough.

I puzzled over the circumstances that'd seen her confined back there, but promptly stopped myself. It wasn't any of my business, and the less time spent musing on such things the better.

Something caught my attention as I let the video play. On screen, I'd just gone running from the house after unearthing the body, and the woman's cadaverous face was in perfect view. If I hadn't known any better—if the corpse had actually had eyes to see with—I would have sworn that it was staring intently at the camera. As it was, I thought it a rather peculiar thing that the body had been discovered in that very place where its eyes would meet the camera straight on. I laughed it off, but in the back of my mind I couldn't help imagining that it was no accident; that, as if anticipating my recording, the corpse had positioned itself ahead of time, so that it might be captured in just such a way.

I started cleaning up the video, adding the usual flourishes, and then watched the rough cut. The cops had had a point; my material in this video was pretty lame. I threw in a couple of lens flares and hoped that they would distract from my bad jokes. Adding a bit of music and adjusting the brightness in a few shots, I then picked up my camera and prepared to shoot a quick addition. I had to show the viewers what the finished product looked like.

Before sitting down to edit the video, I'd hurriedly torn away the remaining drywall, leaving all of the studs exposed. When I'd set up my studio light to give the impression of daylight and therefore perfect continuity, I summoned my cheeriest voice and tried to hide my fatigue. Panning over the exposed wall, I began narrating. "And that's all for today. Got all of the drywall down, but unfortunately I encountered some technical difficulties. I'll get the new stuff hung tomorrow and will detail the entire process. There's no real damage behind this wall, so it'll be easy-peasy. Thank you for watching! Don't forget to 'like' this video if you found it helpful. And if you want to follow me on this journey for the next thirty days, be sure to subscribe to my channel!"

With that out of the way, I spliced in the new footage and threw in some extra razzmatazz on the editing front—more sound effects, the usual intro animation. When iMovie had processed the file I threw it onto VideoTube, which immediately began processing it. It would go live in fifteen to twenty minutes.

I spent those fifteen minutes straightening out the living room. I stuffed the broken drywall into garbage bags, ran the vacuum awhile to suck up all of the dust before I had a chance to breathe it in, and even pulled out a mop to clear up the muddy prints the cops had left behind. It was more care than this house deserved, but at some point that evening I'd decided I was going to stay there for the night, and I wanted to make it as comfortable as I could.

It wasn't that the fear had altogether left me. I was still thoroughly creeped out by the idea that a body had been hidden behind these very walls. The email from the Home Improvement Network had been quite a shot in the arm however, and my mounting fatigue had me wanting to crash hard and soon. Sleeping on the air mattress as I'd done the night before was the easiest thing. When this thirty-day job was finished, I'd stay in a five-star hotel and live it up. Steak dinners, booze, cigars—the whole nine yards. I didn't have time for any of that at present, though. Staying in the house would help keep me on task.

Reflecting on my father had also taken its toll. Knowing how he'd react if I, his prissy son, chose to cancel this challenge, or spend the nights in a hotel out of fear, I decided to man up. I'd slept in this house the night before, after all. I hadn't known it then, but there'd been a dead body inches away. Now it was gone, so there was literally nothing to fear. I decided to power through my lingering unease and just sleep at the worksite, if only to remain manly in the eyes of my dead father.

The day's video was taken care of. The 30-day challenge continued. "Crisis averted," I said, pushing away from the table and pacing around in the living room. I stretched, catching a whiff of my serious BO, and wished the place had a working shower. I could have theoretically used the shower in the upstairs bathroom; the faucet and shower head still worked. The water wasn't the freshest here, though, and the idea of cozying up to the grimy, crumbling tiles up there didn't sit too well, so I dug out my camp shower and hauled it outside, along with a liter or two of bottled water.

The night remained warm, and except for my porch light, and a flickering streetlight at the very end of the road towards the graveyard, there were no other artificial lights around. Just me and Mr. Moon. Approaching the Callery pear tree, nose wrinkled for its stench, I fixed the clip of the camp shower to a sturdy branch, stripped down to my underwear and started rinsing off.

I stood beneath the lazy spray, scrubbing, until the water was spent. When I was finished, I found that the ritual left me reasonably refreshed. And tired. I hadn't eaten since lunch, and my stomach burned with a ravenous hunger. The wind dried me off within a few minutes and I returned inside, smashing half a box worth of protein bars and an entire bag of beef jerky. I promised to treat myself to a big, hearty breakfast before getting to work the next morning, but for now the pre-packaged stuff would have to do. Wiping at my eyes, I set up the air mattress—this time in the middle of the living room, away from the exposed wall—and made sure all of the doors and windows downstairs were locked.

The day had left me stressed, no doubt, and thinking about all the work still ahead of me left me doubly so. Nonetheless, my work here had taken a very happy turn since receiving Mona's email. There was a light at the end of the tunnel—a real possibility of stardom. I flopped onto the air mattress with a sigh, stretching out, and draped a blanket over myself. I shut off the light in the living room and rolled onto my side. I was so tired I could have fallen asleep within minutes.

And I would have, if only I hadn't noticed something.

As I closed my eyes and courted sleep, something bright knocked on the outside of my eyelids and drew my attention. I blinked against it, sitting up slightly. It was coming from the dining room—from the window.

I tensed as I realized what it was.

The motion-activated porch light had come on. It had detected movement.

ELEVEN

I almost didn't get up to look.

A raccoon or stray dog might have been the culprit. It was possible, too, that the police had stopped by with more questions, though I hadn't heard any cars pull up and there were no footsteps coming up to the porch. I hesitated, taking in the ponderous silence, but at remembering that I had only a minute before the light went off, I finally crept into the next room to investigate.

On the way over, I paused to peer through the peephole in the front door. The porch was clear, and I crossed into the dining room to have a look through the window. The scene outside, set aglow by the harsh LED light, was an unfamiliar mess of black and green. Every tall blade of grass threw up an angular shadow that swayed in the breeze like the spines of some dangerous animal. The tree's white flowers caught the light, glowing eerily, while the trunk, dark and coarse, blended in with the surrounding night.

I held my breath, looked for the person or animal who'd triggered the light.

I searched as far and long as I could, but came no closer to discerning what'd set it off. The potholed street sat empty, and what I could make out of the vacant lot across the way appeared perfectly desolate. In some places where the grass was especially tall, I wondered if something didn't lurk; if something hadn't dipped down into the overgrowth for cover at sensing my gaze. I stared at the pockets of shadow where the light didn't quite reach, and though I fancied I could feel a thousand eyes staring back at me from those shadowed spaces, nothing emerged to give that feeling any weight. The yard was empty, and whatever had set off my porch light was now out of view. Perhaps it had been an animal, and it had run off, spooked, when the light came on. If it had been a person, then it was possible they'd lost their nerve in a similar way and bolted.

The light went off and the yard exploded in darkness. Shadows that had been held at bay by the light only moments ago crashed over the property like a tsunami now, leaving only a sea of shifting pitch. The white flowers continued to glow eerily, as though they'd absorbed the light, but most every other feature—the swaying fronds, the cracks in the road—had been masked in a blackness more brilliant than the flash of 1600 lumens that had reigned only seconds prior.

It was nothing. You should have stayed in bed.

I turned away from the window, only to pause mid-turn with a jerk.

The light came on again. I heard the device click, as if it had a tongue and were saying, *Now, don't go anywhere!*

It was malfunctioning. That had to be it. It hadn't gone off the night before as far as I could remember. Now, it was flashing on for seemingly no reason. I glanced through the window, looking for an owl or squirrel I could blame this on, but came up empty-handed.

I grabbed up a box cutter and shuffled towards the door. Another look through the peephole revealed nothing. Sucking in a deep breath, I placed my hand on the deadbolt and prepared to step into the night.

If someone had come to visit me this late at night, unannounced, then they sure weren't up to any good. Thus the box cutter. I wanted to step out onto the porch to take a closer look—and to scare off anyone who might be lurking. If I found someone on my property, I'd warn them off and call the cops. Or, if it turned out to be an animal of some kind, I could have a good laugh about it and go to bed. Either way, I wasn't able to see the whole property through the dining room window and needed to get outside to make sure there was no one hanging around.

With a quick movement, I unlocked the deadbolt and threw open the door. The light rushed into my eyes as I did so, and I saw stars as I stepped out onto the porch. "All right," I demanded. "Who's there?"

I canvassed the whole front of the property and waited for an answer.

I saw no one, and if they were hiding out of sight, they weren't feeling too talkative, because they didn't reply. No stray cats I could use as scapegoats emerged, either. In the space between breaths, the outdoors became terribly still, and the silence convinced me that I was, in fact, alone.

Without warning, the light to my right went off, and I found myself suddenly buried in that dense inkiness I'd marveled at through the window. I flinched as the world around me went black, and it took me only a few seconds of standing there, startled, to realize I didn't much like it on that porch. I felt vulnerable and fled into the house like a coward, slamming the door shut and throwing the deadbolt.

"The light's not working," I said, massaging my jaw. I threw the box cutter into an open toolbox and paced between the dining room and living room. In the corner of my eye, I kept watch on the window, waiting to see if the light would go off again.

It didn't. The rest of the night, in fact, it remained off.

I put on a lamp in the living room and sat down on the air mattress, easing my nerves back into shape. After the exhausting day I'd had, some stress and edginess were to be expected. The house—the entire neighborhood—wasn't remotely inviting. This was only my second night roughing it in the house, too; it was far too soon to feel comfortable in the place. Even then I knew I'd never feel especially secure there, but over time I hoped I'd get used to its quirks. Maybe by the end of this challenge I'd even get to the point where I didn't jump at every shadow, or startle at every creak.

I opted to leave the light on, at least until I was tired enough to sleep. Minutes ago I'd been on the verge of drifting off; now I felt a bit wired.

Hanging drywall. Tearing up linoleum. Replacing cabinets. Inspecting the pipes... Without realizing it, I began going through a mental check-list of all the jobs I was soon to tackle. I would have kept along that track if not for the intermittent scratching behind the walls. It started quietly enough; the tentative nibbles of an unseen rodent, the sound of bristly fur brushing against the inside of the baseboards. I flopped onto my side, irritated, and wished I'd set traps.

But then the noises of the mice got me thinking about other things.

My mind was filled with dread visions of a bony hand scratching at the inside of the wall; of that coarse, white hair rasping against the studs; of staring, empty sockets. What if there were others in the house, other bodies, just waiting to be found? The fact that I'd started my work on that very wall was enough to stir up new unease. Why *that* wall? Had I been drawn to it in some way, subconsciously? Had the scratching of the night before been a plea on the part of the corpse—a wish to be discovered?

Eventually, I fell asleep. All night, my dreams were occupied with themes of home invasion, of things reaching out to me from the walls, or from around dark corners.

In one such dream, I found myself wandering through a dark house. Alerted to an ominous glow outside a nearby window, I leaned towards what looked to be a peephole in a cartoonishly large door. Staring hard into that peephole, I could see nothing. There was only darkness; darkness and a stale, warm breeze, as if the seal around it wasn't very good.

The dream ended when I suddenly realized I wasn't staring into a peephole at all, but rather, into an open mouth. A long, hot tongue lashed against my staring eye, and I awoke with my heart trying to break out of my chest.

When I finally got up for the day, the lamp on the table was still on. I hadn't been able to find the courage to shut it off.

TWELVE

After ignoring the bleating of my alarm, I finally crawled out of bed around nine in the morning. When I say I "crawled", I mean it literally. I felt drained.

I changed into my work clothes—a pair of tattered overalls—and opted for a baseball cap, rather than taking the time to wrestle my unruly hair into shape. Only then did I allow myself to sit down at the computer and check the reception to my newest video.

Thankfully, the views were huge and the comments were almost unanimously positive. The only sour notes in the chorus dealt with my supposed helper from the last video—that is, the figure that had appeared in the upstairs window. There were still murmurs of my being a hack, of the entire challenge being staged, but if I ignored them long enough I knew the haters would eventually get bored and mosey on. I felt a pang of discomfort at remembering that strange figure in the window, but shook it off and focused on the positive feedback that had rolled in overnight.

Though I hadn't gotten much rest, the interest in my recent uploads buoyed my mood so that I could—*almost*—ignore the creakiness in my joints and the ache behind my eyes. Before logging off, I did something else at the computer. Hooking up my printer, I printed off the email I'd gotten from Mona Neeb at HIN the day before and taped it up to the wall. As the going got tough, revisiting that email would keep my spirits up; remind me of why I was doing this all to begin with.

I was set to begin my day.

Though I'd promised myself a hefty breakfast, I decided to forego it for something simpler. Having slept poorly, my stomach felt at odds with the thought of a big meal and I nibbled half-heartedly on a granola bar while pacing around the front lawn. It was a nice day out, sunny and mild, though the clouds in the distance were tinged with grey and I wondered if there wouldn't be rain before too long. The grass was weighed down with dew, and as I trudged through it, some of the blades reaching nearly to my knees, I tried thinking of places in town where I could rent a lawnmower.

I recalled, with a guilty laugh, how spooked I'd been the night before when I'd thought I'd seen someone in the yard. If anyone did come around at night, trimming things up would give such prowlers fewer places to hide. I turned to the Callery pear, tapping the trunk with the heel of my boot and knocking away a patch of bark. Crunching the granola bar wrapper in my fist, I gave the tree another kick, having gotten about as much of its stench as I could stand in one go. "I'm gonna get to you soon," I said.

Having left the living room wall unfinished, the first task of the day was clear enough. I set up my camera, tugged on my suspenders and got the drywall hung in just over an hour, jabbering on about each step of the process. When that job was done, I did a slow, proud pan of the finished wall. "And that is how you hang drywall, folks. I know I make it look easy, but with some patience and practice you'll master this in no time."

Being more awake now and having done some work, my stomach caught up with me and I felt the first rumblings of true hunger. That big breakfast—more of a brunch at this point—was sounding mighty fine. I ventured into the kitchen and tested the rickety tap, rinsing the dust off my hands in the cold spray. The faucet worked, albeit with a terrible rattling every time the water came on. I wasn't sure how easy a fix it would be. Perhaps, if the pipes were good, I'd be able to re-fasten them with a bit of plumber's tape, rather than replace them entirely. Though the water didn't strike me as good for drinking, I liked having a sink I could use for quick rinsing. It was a lot more convenient than loading up the camping shower every time I wanted to wash my hands. The drain still worked, and the basin, though crooked and improperly braced, didn't leak.

I decided to check out the pipes before moving onto the other jobs on my to-do list. I didn't want to risk a leak in the walls, and figured that stabilizing them might save me a lot of trouble, not to mention mopping, later on. Beneath the sink was a small wooden panel in the wall; removing it carefully, I gained access to the pipes, which ran to the left of the cabinets. Switching on the tap and listening closely, I was able to estimate the location of the rattling pipes based on the sound they made, and when I'd set up my camera on the kitchen counter, I took up a drywall saw and carefully cut a twelve-by-twelve square in the kitchen wall.

I picked up the camera and gave the viewers a look into the new opening, narrating, "So, what we're looking at are the pipes that lead directly to the kitchen sink. I've cut away a bit of the wall here to access them. It'll be an easy patch-job when we're through. The reason I did this is because these pipes make a terrible rattling noise when you turn on the faucet. There are a few things that can cause this—improper water pressure, or, in this case, the fixing bracket simply fell off, which makes the pipes kick around a little when water flows through. This, I'm happy to say, is a fix so simple a monkey could do it. Literally, all we need to do is fasten these pipes in place with a length of plumber's tape and patch up the hole in the wall." I chuckled, inserting the camera a bit deeper into the opening and surveying more of the space behind the drywall. "I feel like I've really lucked out with this house, man. I'm telling you, the bones are solid. I haven't run into any major damage, any glaring issues..."

I paused, distracted by something in the viewfinder. The dim light on my camera illuminated something just above the topmost edge of the hole I'd made, and I reached inside to have a look. It took a bit of reach, and in the process my fingers grew tangled in cobwebs. The object of my search was not so different in substance, and I knew what it was the very moment I touched it.

I recoiled like I'd been burnt.

My initial suspicion had been confirmed. Through the viewfinder, it'd looked as though a long lock of white hair had been wrapped around one of the pipes. I'd assured myself silently that I was mistaken in thinking so, but as I brought my hand out of the opening with some of the white strands between my fingers, I realized I'd been on the mark.

Wiping my hand against my overalls and nearly tripping over my own feet, I loosed a string of curses and dropped the camera on the counter. The white hair was familiar.

The corpse.

I tried working things out in my head, but good explanations for the presence of that hair were not forthcoming. *It's not the same hair. It can't be. That lady's body was in a completely different room. It's not like she lived behind the walls. Even if she'd been alive back there, she wouldn't have been able to cross from room to room. There wouldn't have been enough space to get around. It belongs to an animal. Or maybe, at some point, someone did work on these pipes and got their hair caught in 'em. That has to be it. It's nothing but a gross coincidence.*

Unsettled and wanting nothing more than to leave the house, I went rifling through my supplies and hurriedly fastened the pipes in place with a strip of plumber's tape. When next I switched on the tap, the pipes were quiet.

And I was glad for it, because in the next moment I was rushing out of the house, desperate for some fresh air.

THIRTEEN

With a burger and fries in the tank, I felt like a new man. At least, physically.

Mentally, things were more complicated.

I didn't like the house. I don't want to make it sound like I *ever* had love for the place, but at the very start of the project the house had been nothing but another in a long line of boring worksites to me. Now it was shaping up to be anything but boring. The dead body notwithstanding, there were a lot of little things about the house that had me on edge. Meditating on them, I pressed my large Coke to my forehead like I was trying to beat back a fever.

There were the shadows in the house, and the tendency of things to go strange after dark. The porch light, though new and properly-installed, had a mind of its own. White hair had turned up in my most recent dive into the walls—was it just coincidence? Viewers on my previous video had pointed out the presence of a figure in one of the house's windows—a figure which, in retrospect, looked rather like the stiff I'd discovered in the living room.

Coincidence, I told myself. The similarity between the two was just a weird coincidence.

I mean, what was the alternative?

I don't know why, but after driving through town I circled back and parked outside the crumbling graveyard, staring through the passenger window at the rows of tottering headstones. However desolate and depressing, there was something peaceful about that spot. It seemed like a good place to sit and think, I guess.

And so I did. I thought about my future with the house. Would I manage to get everything squared away in thirty days? If not for the unease, for the interruptions, it probably would have been a sure thing. The work would be hard, but I was motivated by my recent correspondence with Mona Neeb. Still, I was hesitant to return. Something about the house was really rubbing me the wrong way. It was a shame that I didn't have a partner, someone to spend time with in the house. An extra set of hands would have made the work lighter, but what I really wanted was the company of another living, breathing person. Working in that abandoned neighborhood, it was easy to feel like I was the last man on Earth.

A second pair of hands... I couldn't help thinking of my dad. Things would have been a lot better with him there. He wouldn't have been fond of my chasing a TV deal, but he would have been able to keep me centered on the job, would have kept me from wigging out about the little things. I missed his calm, his air of confidence while working. It was a shame I hadn't inherited those attributes.

I'd spent the better part of my life living with him, but in the end I felt like I hadn't really known him—like we'd merely been two well-acquainted strangers. My parents had split when I was about eight years old. My mother, a self-styled "free spirit" who never failed to remind me that she'd thrown away her youth in birthing a child, emptied the joint bank account, took the car and disappeared. I haven't spoken to her since then; I'm not even sure she's still alive. From that point on it was just me and my dad, living in my childhood home in the Florida panhandle. He'd work long hours, I'd go to school, and like busy roommates we'd sometimes interact when things got slow. It was always perfunctory, though. I didn't get pats on the head for good grades, no "attaboys" for taking a cute girl to prom. My relationship with my father throughout those adolescent years was pretty sterile.

I held a lot of resentment towards him as a teenager. He made sure I was fed and clothed, but didn't much care what I ate or wore. He expected me to stay in school, to earn decent grades, but couldn't name a single one of my friends. My hobbies were a mystery to him, except when he would find me tinkering with an action figure or model airplane and mock me for playing with "baby stuff". When I realized he'd never take anything but a superficial interest in my life, I vowed to leave him behind in that old house just like my mother had done.

I almost succeeded. I did well enough in high school to earn a good scholarship to a university up north, and I moved into the dorms at eighteen. I hadn't applied to the school because I'd wanted to earn a degree—I hadn't even considered a major before flying the coop—rather, I'd done it to get away from my father.

And it showed. My whole college experience back-fired spectacularly. After just one year, where I'd partied nightly, slept little and bottomed-out my GPA, I got kicked out and found myself with no option but to move back down to Florida. With my head down, I brought all of my things back into my childhood bedroom, all the while fielding my dad's smack talk. "Can't believe they let you graduate after just one year!" he'd mocked. "My boy's a real scholar, huh?"

My moving back home came with strings attached. After a week of sulking, my father read me the riot act, threatening to throw me out unless I picked up a job and earned my keep. Though I sent out a handful of applications to local stores and restaurants, I didn't get any calls back. Tired of seeing me laze around, he insisted I accompany him to various job sites. He'd use me to do heavy lifting, to take care of the simple things. In his mind, it was better to have another pair of hands at the workplace than to have a good-for-nothing taking up space on his sofa.

That was how it started.

The first few jobs were awful; I remember hating every minute. At some point, though—maybe it was a month or so after I'd first started tagging along—I found I had a knack for this kind of work. My dad would give me orders. He'd tell me to load the truck with lumber, would order me to buy bags of cement and drive them to the job site, or to help him paint walls in refurbished rentals. Gradually, the demands grew bigger, and I became comfortable around tools.

More surprising, I became comfortable around my dad.

Time passed. I began doing things without being asked, taking on more responsibility. I handled simple repairs on my own and picked my father's brain incessantly. In a way that was alien to me, my father actually answered my questions, and he did so with a willingness—a *joy*—that I'd never seen in him before.

Months went by and we started discussing the jobs ahead of time. He'd let me know the day's itinerary and I'd prepare accordingly, buying supplies per his instructions and doing a fair share of the work. We'd be cutting boards or fixing pipes, and he'd sometimes stop what he was doing to watch me, offering the occasional pointer. Enjoying the attention, I made an effort to constantly up my game, to impress him.

One day, while installing a sliding door, he'd called me "partner", as in, "Will you hand me that flathead, partner?" He'd never talked to me that way before. Stupid and starved for my father's attention as I'd been then, I'd teared up and I had to dig around in the toolbox for close to a minute, lest he notice.

Right up till the end, my father hadn't been a talkative guy. A stereotypical "man of few words", he'd talk at length about his work, but would offer mostly clipped replies when it came to casual conversation. I'm not sure if he knew he was dying—he must have felt something was wrong in the months before he passed—but if he did, he didn't breathe a word of it to me. That was why I was so surprised when, almost two years ago, prior to work one morning, he'd collapsed and coughed up blood.

After an ambulance ride and a hospital stay of some days, where he was in and out of consciousness, a nervous doctor gave us the news. It was stage four stomach cancer. Terminal. There was talk of getting him into hospice, but the doctor confided in me that my dad wasn't likely to make the trip without dying en route, so frail was his condition.

Rather than process this news like a normal person, rather than coming to terms with his mortality and sharing some tenderness with his only son in the days before his passing, you know what my father did? When I came to visit him each day, he'd ask me how the job was going. He wanted to make sure that I was still working each day, and that I hadn't allowed his illness to get in the way of the work he'd previously scheduled with clients.

Barely lucid, his final words to me had had to do with the proper method for patching a crack in a house's foundation. Not long after that conversation, he slipped into a coma he never managed to come out of. He died three days later. There hadn't been any apologies for how he'd treated me growing up, no last-minute "I love you, son". No, he'd used his last moments of coherence to let me know which brand of concrete patcher he liked best.

I inherited the family home, along with a fair bit of money from an old insurance policy he'd taken out after my mother had left. I hated that house, so full of bad memories, and got rid of it as quickly as I could, selling it at a big loss. I buried my old man and pocketed the remainder of the money, suddenly directionless. For a while, I lived in a Florida apartment, doing work for some of my dad's old clients. My future was less than certain, and I considered spending a hefty portion of my nest egg in getting a degree of some kind.

While I was trying to decide what to do with my life, a relative of mine in Wisconsin asked me if I could explain how to replace his shower faucet. Insisting that it was an easy job, I shot a barebones video for him in my bathroom, explaining the process and demonstrating it on my own shower. I uploaded it to VideoTube so that he could easily reference it and almost forgot about it. For whatever reason, random viewers began liking and commenting on my video, claiming that I'd really made it easy to follow along. They requested that I demonstrate other fixes, started contacting me for advice on their own renovations.

Enjoying the attention, I asked my clients around town if I could bring a camera with me to record my daily work. Most didn't have a problem with it. I uploaded videos at irregular intervals, mostly basic stuff—"How to Replace a Chandelier" and "Toilet Installation Basics". The reaction to these videos was more robust than I could have anticipated. My views surged, people subscribed in large numbers to keep up with my content. I didn't know a thing about video editing then, but after chatting with a friend of mine who was good with computers, and who insisted I could make a solid living posting videos on VideoTube, I got serious. I made the videos prettier, more humorous, and I uploaded content more often.

When I began receiving three-figure checks for ad revenue on my videos, I knew I was really onto something. Three figures soon became four. My subscriber count broke the ten-thousand mark. Then the hundred-thousand mark. When I surpassed a million, I was absolutely floored; passing two-million subscribers was even more exciting.

It took me about a year-and-a-half to become one of the best-known home improvement guys on the web. I really didn't have any room to complain. I was on the verge of securing a TV deal, was living very well. Even without that network gig, if I kept doing what I was doing I'd probably be set for life. I felt very proud whenever I reflected on my past successes.

The good vibes ended as soon as I focused on the here and now, however. The house on Morgan Road was standing in the way, casting one of its characteristic long shadows over my mood.

I've never been one to leave a job half-done, but as I stared out across the graveyard I considered ditching the house and re-starting the thirty-day challenge elsewhere. Just the thought of driving back, of working inside it as though nothing had happened, made me queasy. If not for the network email I'd received the day before, which effectively tethered me to the accursed property for the next month, I knew I'd have packed up in the night and left Michigan altogether.

There was no sense in my bellyaching, or in putting off the inevitable. I was going to do the work one way or another. However uncomfortable, I'd be through with the place by June. A month's worth of discomfort and unease in exchange for a lifetime of success; when I thought about the renovation in such terms, it really didn't seem so bad.

I rolled down my window and pulled away from the curb, coasting into town. I made a pit-stop at a dollar store for some cheap mouse traps and then circled back towards Morgan Road. I loosed a sigh as the house entered into view, and from the driveway I decided to forge a kind of peace treaty with it. *Tell you what,* I thought, *I'll fix you up by month's end. Just do me a favor and cut the nonsense. I don't want any more surprises, got it?*

I parked and shuffled up the driveway. The sky was clear but the scent of rain was coming in strong. The humidity in the air seemed to ratchet up the stink of the flowers on the tree out front, so that when I stepped into the house and slammed the door behind me, I was almost thankful to fill my nose with the smell of dust instead. Tossing the packs of mouse traps next to my laptop, I tried to decide on the next order of business.

The drywall in the kitchen needed patched after my earlier work with the pipes. It was as good a place to start as any; a short segment on fixing holes in drywall would be good for a future video. I went looking for my camera, realizing a few moments into my search that I'd left it in the kitchen, on the dusty countertop.

I picked it up, wiping the thin layer of grime from the bottom, and found that I'd accidentally left it recording. *Oops.* The battery was half-dead and would need replaced, lest I accidentally run out of juice while recording a later segment, so I carried it out to the living room to switch it out. I looked at the recorded footage and took a moment to rewind it back to the last bit of my earlier monologue, where I'd been bracing the pipes.

The footage played in reverse on the viewfinder. I watched it in the corner of my eye, waiting for the last bit of my pipe-fastening tutorial to come on screen, while playing with my phone. Just a few minutes into the rewinding however, something appeared in the footage that pulled me away from my social media feed and commanded my full attention. I set down my phone and studied the viewfinder with closeness.

The camera had been left on the counter, pointed towards the wall where I'd made the opening. Furthermore, the kitchen window had also been captured in frame, though only partially. It was in that window that I noticed something—something I hadn't expected to find, and that shouldn't have been there in the first place.

I sat down and began combing through the mistake footage in earnest. I didn't notice it until the plastic housing of the camera began to creak in my grasp, but I was squeezing the device in both hands as though it were a neck I was trying to wring the life out of.

All told, the camera had been left running for about an hour and ten minutes after I'd left the house for my lunch break. I returned to the spot in the footage where I'd finished taping up the pipes. A minute or two later, I could hear the sound of my van firing up outside, of the vehicle backing up and starting down the road.

No sooner had I driven down the street had someone walked up to the house and stood outside the kitchen window. Owing to the camera's placement, only part of the individual's body was actually captured in frame; they'd been recorded from the neck down, their face conveniently cut off from view. Despite that, I had a pretty decent sight of the visitor.

It was a woman, by the looks of it. She seemed to me of average height, with pale skin. Her arms hung limply at her sides, and her body was draped in a dirty, off-white garment that looked almost like a giant pillowcase. From the top of her unseen head came tendrils of silvery white hair that rested on her shoulders and stretched down to her breast. She looked unwell, completely out of place.

And, in terms of dress, hair color and thinness, she bore more that a passing resemblance to the body I'd discovered in the living room wall.

That was chilling enough, but as I continued watching the hour-long recording that had been made in my absence, other details provoked curiosity and, subsequently, alarm.

I watched long segments of the footage—sometimes ten, even twenty minutes in length—and was unsettled by the absolute stillness of the woman.

She didn't move in all that time.

Not at all.

After approaching the window from some unseen point outside, she stood completely motionless, her arms flaccid, as if rooted to the spot. Not even her hair moved, giving the impression that the wind outside, which I'd only minutes ago felt myself, had died off completely in her presence.

There was more. The camera had recorded a number of voices over the course of this hour-long period, some of them masculine, others feminine. One was even child-like. Bafflingly, all of them seemed to issue from the figure in the window; they were muffled as if coming through the glass. This seemed impossible. Unless the woman was some kind of voice-acting genius, I doubted that any single person could possess such a range of voices. Maybe there were others outside the house, out of view of the camera, whose voices had been captured? Reason told me this had to be the case, and yet the longer I watched, the more sure I became that the voices were all issuing from this single woman, as though her unseen face boasted a dozen or more mouths, each with their own unique voices.

I couldn't understand what was being said; without headphones on, it would be impossible to make out the words clearly. I skipped ahead, catching bits and pieces of new voices as I did so, until I reached the end.

It was at the moment that the figure drew away from the window, disappearing from view, that my terror reached a fever pitch, because less than a minute later the sounds of my van pulling into the driveway were captured clearly. Then the sounds of my opening and closing the front door, my pacing through the house, and of my picking up the camera and berating myself for accidentally leaving it on all registered in the recording.

The figure had been standing in the window up until just a few minutes ago.

My blood ran cold. I set the camera down with a bang and rose to my feet, gaze drawn to each of the windows. I expected to find the gibbering woman in one of them, watching me, but found nothing but the mid-day sun.

My departure from the house and her arrival had occurred within moments of each other; so too had my return and her sudden exit.

My heart went off in my chest like a grenade. My brow had grown damp with sweat while watching; my scalp and neck tingled so badly that I nearly scratched them raw. I dove into my toolbox and shoved a utility knife into my pocket. Walking into the kitchen, I looked through the window, searching for signs of the curious visitor and finding none.

She was here only a few minutes ago, I thought, my throat tightening. *And she might still be out there.* Steeling myself, I stomped to the front door, made my way out onto the porch.

It took me a few tries to find my voice. "All right," I shouted. "Who's out here? Show yourself!"

FOURTEEN

For nearly thirty minutes I stalked around the property.

There was no sign of her.

My search for the woman on the recording took me in a circuit around the grounds. I even wandered into the adjacent lots, nearly tripping over the cracked concrete foundations that had once served neighboring houses, and which were now buried by wild grass like Mesoamerican ruins in the Amazon.

For all my efforts, I found only a tension headache and a palpable dread that parked itself in my throat.

There had been someone outside the house. I had the video footage to prove it. Who she'd been, I couldn't say. I had no idea what her reasons were for casing the joint, either. If she'd been a common thief, on the lookout for things to steal, then she must've been the most inept burglar in history, because she'd made no effort to enter the house. I'd gotten more of a creepy, Manson Family vibe from the whole episode; only a lunatic would stand outside a window like that for an hour, unmoving.

What really stuck in my craw was the fact that the woman

looking into the kitchen resembled the woman I'd inadvertently recorded in the upstairs window during my first day at the house. I'd discounted that bit of footage as a weird reflection on the window from the outside—a graphic anomaly. Now, I wasn't so sure.

The woman at the kitchen window also resembled the corpse...

I tried banishing the thought from my mind, but the damage was done.

Any resemblance between this weird visitor and the woman I'd found in the wall was absolutely coincidental. Full stop. Paleness, frailty and white hair were not exactly rare attributes, and I knew that there were probably a hundred women in this county alone who might have fit the description. I hadn't seen her face, but that she'd been a living, breathing person wasn't up for debate.

Still, I couldn't silence thoughts of the corpse altogether. The night before discovering the body I'd heard scratching at the wall. I'd quickly and rightfully credited the local mouse population with that noise, but that hadn't stopped my imagination from doing terrible things upon reflection. *If a corpse could scratch at the inside of a wall, why couldn't it come back to the house, too? You did let her out...*

However annoyed I was with myself for entertaining such stupidities, the dread remained in place. The fear that rippled through me was like an itch I couldn't reach; try as I might to scratch it with any number of implements—or explanations—it persisted.

In an effort to frame the incident more rationally, I approached the house and stationed myself at the kitchen window, in approximately the same spot where the woman had stood. Peering inside, I wondered what had been so fascinating that she'd had to stand there over an hour to fully admire it. From this position I was able to see a few things—the edge of the kitchen counter and the adjacent cabinetry, the boxes of supplies I'd stacked on the floor, the refrigerator with its missing door. None of it was interesting, though. None of it drew me in to the point where I'd have liked to stand and stare for a whole hour.

So, what had she been looking at, then?

Leaning against the outside of the house, arms crossed, an alternative crossed my mind. From that spot outside the window, the visitor would have been able to see the camera I'd absentmindedly left running on the countertop. Maybe she hadn't come looking for anything through that window, but—noticing the camera—had stood there a long while in the hopes of being noticed. Perhaps her little stunt had been intended to unnerve or intimidate—to send a message.

This house had been no stranger to squatters, I reckoned. Having spied the woman in the upstairs window, I'd suspected that she might have been a homeless woman who'd been taking shelter in the building before I'd moved in. If that was the case, then perhaps she'd come around this afternoon, found the doors locked with new hardware, and had been frustrated by her inability to get inside. And so, wanting to intimidate the new owner, she'd stood outside the window, as if saying, "Get out of that house. It's mine."

"Yeah," I admitted aloud, "that makes sense." I was dealing with a disgruntled squatter; it was clear to me now. The woman in the video —in *both* videos—was a homeless woman trying to get back into the once-abandoned house she'd used for shelter. Come to think of it, there was another incident I could throw beneath that same umbrella, too. The porch light had seemingly malfunctioned the night before. At least, I'd thought it had. In fact, it may have been picking up the same woman's movements as she'd walked around the yard. Maybe she'd come back after dark, hoping to find the place empty so that she could spend the night.

I felt a touch of guilt for having been so eager to ward the woman off. This house was the only one on Morgan Road that could have offered shelter to a homeless person. All the others were crumbling, on the verge of turning to dust. If she'd made use of this house in the past, then I couldn't really blame her for being upset at finding it occupied and off-limits. Had the woman approached me, tried to explain her reasons for lingering about the premises, I would have offered to help her in some way.

Still, as bad as I felt knowing I'd nearly threatened an elderly homeless woman with a boxcutter for looking into my window, I wasn't going to tolerate trespassing, and any act of hostility meant to frighten me off was going to be met with action.

Though it may have been a little premature, I allowed myself to relax. It was entirely possible that the woman wouldn't come around again, but if she did, I felt confident I could deal with her. I looked to the Callery pear and considered mounting a trail camera to it for the purpose of gathering evidence. If the woman grew bolder in her visits, I'd have all the proof I'd need to get the authorities involved.

Going back inside, I thought about calling the cops and letting them know the score. Perhaps they'd know the woman, or would be willing to do the occasional drive-by to deter her from coming onto the property. I reconsidered when, with a flush of my cheeks, I recalled my last dealings with the Detroit PD and the way the detectives assigned to my case had laughed at my recordings.

On second thought, I'd keep them out of it for the time being.

Now that I felt reasonably sure that the source of my frustrations was an elderly woman, my courage returned. I'd no longer jump at each noise or every flash of the porch light. I could handle this well enough on my own. She'd given me a solid fright, but surely she didn't represent a true threat.

Making sure the doors were locked, I tried returning to my work.

I *TRIED* RETURNING to my work.

I didn't get far.

Though I patched up the hole in the kitchen drywall and busied myself with a few other small fixes, I was too scatterbrained by recent events to give the work the focus it required. While hammering in a loose piece of molding, I mashed my thumb. Unwrapping the mousetraps, I managed to catch my fingers in them several times while attempting to bait them, then again while leaving them along the baseboards in the kitchen and living room.

I set up a few shots so that I could throw together a quick video. Aside from the drywall patching, I singled out a few of the house's most glaring problem areas and let the viewers know what kind of things they could expect in the days to come. The first area I highlighted was the kitchen, and I tore off a few pieces of the broken cabinetry to show just how degraded it was. In the master bedroom, I recorded some footage of the crack in the window, and promised the viewers I'd show them how to replace the pane.

While in the bedrooms, I was reacquainted once more with those large, imposing locks on two of the doors. There was a sturdy hasp mounted to the inside of the door in the room closest to the top of the stairs. It was the type you could use a padlock with. Why someone felt the need for such a lock on a bedroom door was beyond me. Stranger, though, was the lock on the master bedroom door. It was located on the *outside*. I contemplated its potential uses, but to my mind one would only ever install such a thing to keep something locked *inside* of a room. Engaging that lock would probably have been like locking the door to a jail cell. Had the previous owners had dogs or something—had they used the room to house animals and keep them from the rest of the house?

A tour of the bathroom and a careful bumping of the mold-encrusted tiles was next, and since everything in the room would need replaced—along with a good bit of the walls—I admitted that the bathroom would provide fodder enough for *several* videos. Lastly, I zeroed in on a warped floorboard in the dining room, which I speculated may have been the result of moisture damage from underneath. This would require me to get under the house and into the crawl-space, to search for potential water damage and to inspect the soundness of the foundation.

I filmed myself getting snapped in the fingers by mousetraps for comedic effect and then signed off, having recorded more than I needed for a single day's upload. I transferred all of the raw footage on my camera—including the hour-long bit of the old woman standing outside the kitchen window—onto my computer.

Before sitting down to edit video, I pulled up the number for a local dumpster rental company—JT's Dumpster Rental—and spoke to a man on the phone about having a 15-yard dumpster delivered. The gentleman verified the house's address, filled me in on the price, and then promised to have it delivered by end of business the next day. I had bags of drywall and busted cabinetry piling up in the place, and couldn't wait to get ahold of the dumpster so that I could begin clearing it all out.

When I'd warmed a can of soup over my camping stove and eaten almost an entire sleeve of saltine crackers along with it, I began editing my footage. For close to three hours—until sunset—I putzed around, sorting and clipping the various bits I'd recorded.

I made a folder specifically for the woman who'd been coming by, which I titled INTRUDER, and in it I stuck everything I had on her so far: The hour-long stint outside the kitchen window, the brief appearance in the upstairs. I hoped I wouldn't have anything else to add to that folder, that I'd never see her again. But just in case she did keep coming around, I wanted to make sure I had a visual record of her behavior that I could take to the cops.

By the time I called it quits, I had not one, but two complete videos. I held one back on my computer for future use and uploaded the other, which ran through my bracing of the kitchen pipes and patching of the drywall. I anticipated another wave of encouraging comments from this one and promptly uploaded it to VideoTube.

The day had been long. I'd worked up a sweat over the course of the day, and my overalls were hardly comfortable, but I couldn't find the energy to strip them off or to set up the camping shower outside. Reclining on the air mattress, I found myself at once exhausted and wired; my body was ready to tap out, but my thoughts were still running a mile a minute. I toyed with the idea of running into town for a six pack while waiting for my video to go live, but couldn't summon the will to roll off the bed. It felt so soft and comfortable underneath me that I didn't notice sleep coming up from the rear.

Within twenty minutes, I was out. My thoughts were no less stormy, but my body had had its fill of activity for the day and powered down before I could even reach over and shut off the lights in the living room.

Sleep was sweet while it lasted.

FIFTEEN

I felt weightless as I blinked at the dark, like I was floating along a lazy river. I was only dimly aware of the air mattress beneath me. With no little trouble I wiped my eyes with the back of my hand, trying to wake up fully and gain my bearings. Minutes crept by and I managed to sit up, my body so stiff that it pained me to do so. Reaching blindly for the lamp nearest the bed, I groped for the knob and gave it a turn.

It didn't come on.

I tried looking to my laptop, to the battery packs I'd left charging on the table, but they'd been buried in the darkness, their little glowing lights nowhere to be seen.

I sighed into my hands and rose on unsteady legs. It seemed the power had gone out. Perhaps the house's poor wiring had somehow gone bad. Maybe I'd been drawing too much electricity, or the old power lines had finally given up the ghost. I stood, listening for howling winds, watching for streaks of lightning, but the night was perfectly calm. The weather clearly wasn't the cause, then.

Another possibility crossed my mind.

What if someone cut the power?

Panic struck my heart like a riding crop, prompting its beat to quicken substantially. Nothing seemed familiar in the darkness. I wasn't able to make out the lay of the land and felt, once more, like I was adrift on a black sea. The nearest recognizable landmark, the dining room window, seemed impossibly far from where I stood. Its borders were painted in a thin veneer of moonlight that almost resembled pale frost. Even if I'd gone right up to it and stared out into the yard, it wouldn't have done any good; my previous studies of the window had me well convinced that—without the porch light to pierce the veil of night—I wouldn't be able to tell whether anyone was lurking outside.

Struggling to cast off the last vestiges of sleep, my imagination conjured images of that pale, white-haired woman from earlier in the day. I imagined her shuffling around the property in the perfect darkness, waiting for a chance to sneak inside. The settling of the floors as I shifted my weight almost gave the impression that she was there with me, lurking in some shadow-clotted corner of the room.

The space between my shoulders began to tingle. Though it may have been paranoia—and I told myself that it was—a sensation like the weight of strange eyes fell upon me and I struggled to keep from hyperventilating.

Lights. You need to get the lights working.

I marshaled my wits and tried to remember where the breaker box was located. After a brief pause, I recalled that it was situated on the wall between the kitchen and living room, not at all far from where I presumed I stood. Turning on my heels, I staggered ahead, hands out in front of me, and began running my fingers along the wall.

After a breathless search, I located the cool metal casing and negotiated the latch on the door. Effectively blind, I took a moment to feel out the components within, my nervous fingertips grazing each of the switches. For a time, it was all nonsense to me; I may as well have been standing deep within a shadowed pyramid, trying to puzzle out the meaning of an ancient pictogram etched into a wall. Fearing that I was not alone in the house, the task took on a heart-pounding urgency, and starting from the top I began throwing the breakers—first to the left, and then to the right—without caring what each switch corresponded to.

The lights rushed back on.

My delight, though, was short-lived.

The bulbs in the fixtures flickered as though on the verge of burning out, and when they did come on all the way, they did so with an uncharacteristic glow the color of egg custard. My eyes acclimated to the light almost immediately, and I shut the breaker box, turning to survey the room around me. Everything was as I'd left it—the folding table, the camera gear atop it, the toolbox beside the bed...

Hot bile wormed its way up my throat, and I had to clench my teeth to keep it from spilling out onto the floor. Nothing overt had triggered this response in me. There was no one standing in the living room or kitchen as far as I could see, and nothing was out of place. With nothing physical I could pin my fear on, it soon became apparent that the atmosphere itself was to blame; the mood of the place struck me as gravely disordered.

The air was stuffy, possessed of the tell-tale staleness gained from circulating the contours of another's lungs. It felt like someone was standing close to me, breathing directly into my face; as if all the air I breathed had been held in someone else's mouth in anticipation. The mustard-colored light served to disorient me further. My surroundings were familiar, and yet, they were made unfamiliar by the orange glow.

Then, from the upstairs, came a noise.

A *voice*.

I stiffened, my arms locking up in a jerk. The whooshing of blood in my ears made it hard to listen, but even if the words being spoken didn't fully register, the *character* of the voice was clear as day. The bile rose again like the mercury in a thermometer, and once more, it nearly dribbled over. I threw a hand over my mouth, choking it down, and tried to summon some nerve.

There was someone in the house with me. This time, I was sure of it.

Bumps and creaks and shadows could be explained away.

But a voice?

Arms held tightly at my sides and fists balled, I crept across the room. Pausing at the entrance to the dining room, I craned my neck and looked to the foot of the stairwell, my guts coiling. Placing one hand against the wall to keep myself upright, I forced myself to quiet my breathing and listened. I tried to figure out where, specifically, this voice was coming from.

My legs nearly gave out, and I slumped against the wall.

It wasn't a voice, but *voices*. Plural.

I couldn't say how many.

Shuddering some feet from the stairs, I strained to listen. The dialogue was hard to make out, but that the voices were distinct and diverse was apparent from the very first. However dissimilar the voices may have been from one another, they had one quality in common: They were all utterly discordant.

There was something aberrant about those hushed voices that shook me to my core, something about them that made them terrible, almost painful, to listen to. It was a good thing that the speakers were furtive, quiet. If they'd spoken in anything higher than conspiratorial whispers, I'd have probably punctured my own eardrums as a defense.

In a word, these voices were *inhuman*.

One among them was a grating drone, each syllable pronounced as through the wingbeats of a thousand wasps.

Another, croaking and wheezy, was the sonic equivalent of parched earth. Listening to its repellent notes, one could not but envision a man at the bottom of a dry well, calling up to the listener as he died of thirst, the corners of his mouth cracking apart like clay.

Still a third registered, sounding something like a low, childish whine—a breathy voice, whose highs and lows were reminiscent of an infant's wails and coos, respectively.

There may have been others. It was impossible to glean the full number of speakers by listening to the low rumble of their voices, not the least because I couldn't stand to listen with closeness and pick them all out.

As if hearing this hideous concourse upstairs wasn't bad enough, I felt an extra punch of fear because there was something familiar in the most terrible of these voices. I'd heard them before, on tape. That afternoon, in the recording of the woman outside the kitchen window, some audio had been captured. Low and muffled, the footage had featured numerous voices I hadn't been able to source. I hadn't listened to the recording with much care, but that some of the voices were the same I hadn't the least doubt.

The intruder—*intruders*—piped down as I set foot on the bottom stair.

I'd left a large wrench sitting on the second step, almost as if I'd predicted my need for a weapon, and presently I clutched it in my right hand. The second, third and fourth steps were climbed, and except for a cryptic shuffling—perhaps that of the gregarious trespassers seeking cover—the upstairs was plunged into unbearable silence.

While I fought to announce myself, to issue a threat in a calm tone of voice, a man-shaped shadow passed along the wall of the hallway. It stretched out to an impossible degree, like black taffy, before snapping around the corner and out of view. I almost dropped the wrench, and my free hand shot to the bannister in search of support. With my heart in my throat, I pressed on to the top of the stairs, despite my better judgement.

The shadow remained, cast across the floor of the hallway, though it issued from an unexpected place. There was no one standing there as predicted, no physical body casting the long, unnatural shadow. Somehow, the shadow's fountainhead was the far wall, near the hallway window, just past the last of the bedrooms. There was a long, wide crack in the wall. A crack that hadn't been there before. It looked like a deep fissure in a canyon wall—packed with darkness and ragged on the edges as if hewn by years of weathering.

The shadow receded into the crack.

I followed it, too scared and baffled to know any better. Brandishing the wrench, I uttered a shaky, "W-Who's there?" but I barely heard it myself.

I stood before the gash in the wall, running my fingers along the crumbling edge. *How did this happen?* I wondered. I found all the doors on the upper level were closed. Confident that no one could sneak up on me without exiting one of the rooms and thus announcing themselves, I allowed myself a closer study of the damaged wall.

Leaning towards the crack, I peered inside, curious if the house had been damaged from the outside somehow. I was sure the crack hadn't been there earlier in the day—that it had formed only in the last few hours, while I'd been downstairs, asleep.

As I studied the broken drywall, the edges of the crack spasmed like the borders of a gushing wound. In the space behind the wall I saw something.

Or rather, *someone.*

A thin figure twitched just behind the crack. Brittle limbs like those of a milk-colored mantis brushed against the tattered borders of the opening, and a pale face stared out at me, half-covered by a mop of tangled white hair. There were no eyes in its wide sockets, but that it could see me was beyond doubt. I knew, because it laughed at me.

When the mouth flopped open, as if on broken hinges, it did so to an incredible degree. The jaw clicked, the stub of a chin drooped until it pressed into the figure's throat, and the upper borders of the mouth flared out. It was the vacuous mouth of a marine predator, preparing to suck in an entire school of fish in a single gasp. Boisterous laughter spilled out from this immense, toothless maw;

laughter of every imaginable pitch and character. The noxious voices I'd heard while cowering downstairs now rushed out from deep within the figure's throat, along with others—less recognizable but every bit as horrid.

I staggered back, dizzy. The wrench hit the floor. And so did I. I landed on my backside and pushed myself away, staring up at the horror that now leaned out of the crack in the wall and fixed me in its eyeless sights. Two skeletal hands came to grip the upper and lower lips, and the figure began to open its mouth wider still. The popping of its jaw was drowned out by a cacophony of demoniac laughter—punishingly loud now—and as I stared into the yawning gullet, I thought I saw something stirring in the depths of the fiend's body.

Countless eyeballs—twitching, shifting, staring—looked out at me from within the figure's throat.

MY HEART FELT like it was about to give out on me. I rolled off the air mattress, hitting the floor with a thud, and clutched at my chest. I sucked in air, curled into a ball, but for close to a minute I feared I'd never get my heart under control again.

Wincing through the pain in my breast, I shuddered in a heap until finally the spots in my vision had cleared and I could raise my head.

I was in the living room. The lights were on—exactly the soft white they should have been—and my legs were tangled up in a blanket.

A dream. It'd been a bad, bad dream.

Relieved though I was, it took me several more minutes before I felt sure I was awake and to breathe normally, rather than in gasps. The weight on my chest gradually shifted. The crotch of my overalls was wet with hot urine and I was dripping with sweat from the waist up.

Everyone has nightmares; I've definitely had my fair share over the years. But as I sat on the floor, huffing and shaking, I felt pretty sure that I'd never had one quite so bad as this. Had it lasted much longer it might've killed me, if the runaway patter of my heart was any indicator.

What had caused such an awful dream? Could recent stress alone have provoked those nightmarish visions? I didn't have any other explanation—nothing sane, anyhow.

In time, I stripped off my wet clothes and changed into something fresh. I choked down a bottle of water and paced the entire downstairs a few times, slowly recovering from the shock. It was past three in the morning when I finally felt in control of myself again, and was sure that I wasn't still dreaming—though this latter breakthrough only came after I'd massacred my forearms in a series of pinches.

Even as I calmed down, the scenery of the nightmare continued intruding upon my thoughts—so much so, in fact, that I decided to go into the upstairs. Though I knew it had been a dream, and that there were no cracks in the wall, no monstrous, many-voiced figures lying in wait, I still felt the need to climb the stairs and have a look around. I brought my drywall saw with me, just in case, and headed into the upstairs hallway.

The doors were closed and no long shadows danced along the walls or floors. There wasn't any crack near the window, either, though that didn't keep me from knocking on the wall and, shortly thereafter, carving into it with my saw. Terrified that the dream had been some kind of premonition, or that the walls might hold some horror like the one I'd glimpsed in my sleep, I cut a small hole in the drywall and used my phone's light to peer inside the opening.

There was nothing behind it.

I felt like an idiot for having cut into a perfectly good wall, but at last my paranoia ebbed and I was able to return downstairs, confident that everything had been a dream. A horrifying and hyper-realistic dream, but a dream nonetheless.

I plopped down into the metal folding chair in the living room and tried to relax. Skimming the first few comments on my new video buoyed my mood a little, and glancing over at the printed email from Mona that I'd taped up to the wall soothed me further. Still, the sting of the dream remained. And it was a long time till morning.

SIXTEEN

More comments dribbled in overnight, as did more views. The reception to the newest video was positive, but all the praise in the world
wasn't going to make up for a night of ruined sleep.

Having spent the night nodding off on the air mattress—too
scared of recurring nightmares to fully commit to sleep—I'd chosen to
start my day early. Just before sunrise, with a bag full of dirty clothes
in the passenger seat, I'd gone to a local coin laundry to freshen up
my wardrobe. Afterward, I'd eaten a big meal at the diner across the
street—a place where the coffee was strong and the waffles were as
big as my head.

Driving home with clean clothes and a full stomach shored up
my mood a bit, and by ten I was ready to get some actual work done.

Stepping back into my overalls—scented now with fabric soft-
ener, rather than pee—I prepared to shoot a tour of the house's crawlspace. Of all the remaining jobs, this one seemed like the easiest.
Though crawlspace exploration is hardly ever comfortable, a brief
time spent crawling around on my belly and searching for leaks or
foundational cracks sounded much more appealing than any of the

other heavy-duty renovations that awaited me elsewhere in the house.

More than that, the crawlspace video was sure to be a hit. People loved watching me get my hands dirty, enjoyed seeing me in uncomfortable situations. If I encountered a snake or big spider down there that I could milk for drama, all the better.

I carried my camera and tripod out to the yard and set it up so that I had the side of the house in frame. There was a small access door at ground level that I pointed to as I began recording my monologue. "Hey, folks! FlipperKevin here. Thank you for tuning in. Today, I've got a real treat for you. I'm going to do a full crawlspace inspection. It's cramped down there, and there's no telling what I'll find. Before continuing with my work inside, I really want to get a look at the foundation, though, and ensure that there are no cracks. Some of the floorboards in the downstairs are a little damaged, too, and I want to make sure that it isn't due to water damage from down below."

I did a little sashay and explained the best way to dress for such a task. "I've got overalls on for this job, along with a long-sleeve shirt beneath. Crawlspaces tend to be grimy, and sometimes you find unfriendly critters in 'em. Also," I added, donning a pair of safety glasses, "eye protection is a must."

When I'd pried open the access door, everything was set. I lifted the camera from the tripod, got down on all fours, and switched on the camera light. The entrance to the crawlspace was short and narrow, and the interior wasn't much more accommodating. In order to get around down there, I would have to commando crawl slowly.

Inserting the camera into the opening and then easing myself halfway in, I began narrating. "So, I'm going to focus on a few things. First, I want to make sure the pipes under the house are sound. If there's an issue with moisture down here I need to know about it so that I can install a moisture barrier. I'm also going to look for cracks in the foundation." Setting the camera down gently, I pulled myself further into the crawlspace, leaving only my feet extending into the yard. "When you do this kind of inspection, you have to take your time. Don't try to rush it. Just ease yourself in a little bit at a time. It can be hard to see in these places, and if you go too fast you might bust your head on a bit of pipe or something. Not to mention, there's no telling what's living in your crawlspace. You'll find snakes, spiders, termites, rodents—all kinds of things you don't want to get too cuddly with. Thankfully, they tend to be a lot more scared of you than you are of them."

I was fully inside the crawlspace now. I could get up on my knees and elbows, but sitting any higher was impossible. I did a slow pan of the space, letting the camera light uncover the layout. Cobwebs hung from every feature like discarded party streamers; I brushed them away as I crawled deeper in.

Up ahead, its scaly skin glistening in the light, I discovered a small snake in retreat. I could tell it was a boring old garter snake, but played it up for the camera nonetheless. "Whoa, just found a snake down here," I said, zooming in slightly. "Not sure if you can see it." I paused for dramatic effect. "Gotta be careful down here... don't want to get bit." Later, I'd throw in some heavy music to give this find an extra punch.

Going deeper, I propped myself up on my elbows and surveyed the space to my right, where a mass of pipes sprouted from above. I looked at each one, searched for signs of breaks or leakage. "Pipes look good!" I announced.

The crawlspace to this house was done in the "mud pad" style; that is, a thin layer of concrete was poured over the soil floor. Everywhere I shined my light, the concrete looked in perfect order. There were no major cracks to be found, no puddles or condensation. The concrete pilings that supported the house, too, were in great shape. "I've gotta say, the people who built this house knew what they were doing. It's awesome down here. I might just renovate this whole crawlspace, what do you think? I could put in some plush carpet, throw up a flatscreen over there—"

A noise from overhead brought an end to my joking.

I set down the camera and tensed as the sound of footsteps registered just above my head. *Thud. Thud. Thud.* Three steps, so close that I could feel the vibration they made, and no more.

I froze, remaining silent for a time. When no other steps rang out, I was faced with what seemed like two possibilities. Either I hadn't heard steps at all, but merely something falling over, or someone had gotten into the house and was now standing directly above me, waiting for me to make a move. I found the first explanation much more palatable, and recalling that I'd locked the doors before starting this inspection, I felt reasonably sure that the second scenario was unlikely.

Still, it took me awhile to shake the image of someone standing on the floor directly above my head, unmoving. Visions from my most recent nightmare flashed through my head and my pulse quickened accordingly.

There was a bit more ground to cover, some more pilings to inspect. When I'd checked the last of them, I'd be getting out of here.

I picked up the camera again and sniffed at the earthy air. "Thought I heard something in the house, but it was just the floors settling for a minute there," I said, as if trying to convince myself.

Turning, I inspected the concrete pilings on the left side and found them sound. "It's all good," I said with a hint of relief. "The pilings are all intact. No sign of water damage. Now, how about we get out of here, huh?"

I was ready to head back to the access door, to the yard and the sunlight. As I shifted the camera around, something on the concrete pad beneath me caught my eye. I nearly overlooked it at first, writing it off as some sort of discoloration, but on second glance I realized what it was.

Beside one of the pilings, rendered in a thin layer of white chalk, was a single handprint.

I squinted at it in the murk, and then used the camera light to get a closer look. The handprint wasn't very large; it looked like it belonged to a child or adolescent. Furthermore, a pair of initials, somewhat faded, had been written next to the handprint. "F.W."

I studied the chalk both with the naked eye and through the viewfinder, and tried imagining who had put it there, and when. Probably it had been the work of a previous tenant; a kid, by the looks of it. The thought of a kid coming down to the crawlspace to leave a little message like that one brought a smile to my face, and as I turned and crawled back towards the exit I made sure to keep an eye out for other chalk messages, lest I accidentally wipe them away with my overalls.

I was done in the crawlspace and eager to get out. The air was beginning to feel thin, and though I wasn't claustrophobic, the lack of space was really getting to me. I dragged myself forward, careful not to bang up the camera as I went, and fixed the exit in my sights.

Somehow, the access door seemed incredibly far off, like it had moved since I'd last looked to it. Or like it was slowly shrinking. *That isn't possible,* I thought, picking up the pace. Pushing with my elbows for a bit of extra speed, I knocked the camera against the concrete floor and felt a deep scratch form on the plastic casing. Then, a few feet later, I caught a face-full of cobwebs. When I cleared them away the access door looked no closer than it had only a minute ago.

Suddenly, the crawlspace took on something of hostility. I felt helpless, scared, like the garter snake I'd spooked in entering. I breathed in short gasps, unable to draw in enough oxygen and hating the earthy taste that flooded into my mouth with every inhalation. Like a worm trying desperately to surface from the soil during a downpour, I began wriggling forward as quickly as I could, heedless of bumps and scrapes.

In my haste, I bumped the side of my head on one of the pilings and was momentarily blinded with pain. Feeling like I'd just taken a softball to the head, I rolled onto one side and clutched at my skull, the spot warm and tender. Blinking back tears, I gave the camera a hard shove and sent it sliding closer to the exit.

The camera spun to one side and came to rest just beyond my

reach. Its light now shined directly into my eyes, making it even harder for me to judge the remaining distance. Squinting at the access door and hoping that I was almost there, something entered into my blurry vision that made me halt.

The daylight coming through the access door had momentarily dimmed, as though the clouds had shifted over the sun. Except, clouds were not behind this sudden dimming. The light was being blocked out by the presence of a figure standing just outside the access door. Spotty though my vision was for the brilliance of the camera light, I could make out two pale, aged legs about a foot from the crawlspace entrance. Small, ivory feet crawling with spidery, cerulean veins were planted firmly in the tall grass.

The camera, it would turn out, captured a rather unmanly yelp of surprise on my part. It would not, however, pick up any footage of those pale legs outside the door, because it was pointed at my sorry, cowering face. When I finally found the wherewithal to grab hold of the camera and shout at the person in the yard, I found the legs were no longer in view. Bright sunlight warmed the square entrance to the crawlspace, unhindered by the shadow of any figure.

Moments ago I'd been trying to flee the crawlspace. Now, I emerged carefully, tentatively, like a timid animal leaving its den. I slid the camera out onto the lawn first and then pulled myself through the opening with a grunt. The fresh breeze tasted sweet to me compared to the rarified air down below; I didn't even mind the essence of the Callery pear that rode in on the wind.

"Who's there? I saw you. Come out! Show yourself!"

I made three trips around the house before I allowed myself to relax.

There was no one on the property. The doors were still locked and there was no one to be seen in the yard. Down below, panicking in the dark, my eyes had played tricks on me. That was all. Rubbing at the hot goose egg forming on my head and noticing the scrapes I'd accumulated on my hands and forearms, I cursed myself for being so jumpy. *Congratulations. You've probably got Tetanus now.*

Replacing the access door, I staggered out to my van and dug out the first aid kit I kept in my glove compartment. Leaning against the hood, I dabbed at my fresh cuts with alcohol swabs and dry swallowed a couple of Tylenol.

"Stupid house," I muttered, looking up at the heap from the driveway. I had my reasons for putting up with all of this, for seeing the renovations through, but as I stood there, my head pounding, I had to wonder if it was really worth it.

My father had never walked away from a job, but then he'd always chosen his battles wisely. *Dad would never have picked such an awful house to renovate,* I thought. *He'd have passed on this one without so much as a second glance.* Moreover, he sure wouldn't have bothered fixing such a sorry old house simply for publicity, like I was.

I resolved to ignore thoughts of my father as I balled up the spent alcohol swabs and returned to the house. *It doesn't matter what he would have thought. You and the old man are completely different people, nothing alike. He wouldn't have understood.*

I slammed the door shut and made sure the deadbolt was fast.

Despite my bump in the head, there was more work to be done. There was no time to laze around, nursing wounds. Not if I wanted to wash my hands of this house ASAP.

And I did. I really, really did.

SEVENTEEN

I looked up at the camera with all the enthusiasm of an amateur magician who'd gotten puked on by one too many kids at a birthday party. "Fixing hardwood floors is *that* easy," I said dully.

I ate up a few hours in town, grabbing a salad and haunting a couple of hardware stores for the supplies I'd need to fix the warped floorboard in the dining room. I selected a length of wood and cut it down to size on the portable work bench I'd set up in the kitchen. I stained it in approximately the same color as the other boards and explained the repair process on camera while hammering it into place. There were no jokes in that segment; I wasn't feeling chatty.

When that was through the daylight was almost spent and I reeked like a walking trash can. I carried the camping shower out to the tree, hung it up and stripped off my clothes. There was still enough light to see by, and it was possible that someone would drive down lonely Morgan Road only to find me rinsing in the buff, but I just didn't care.

The water was cold, but after a minute my body got used to it and I stopped shivering. Using a bit of body wash, I lathered myself up and worked some shampoo into my greasy hair. A clumsy carpenter bee bumbled from one of the Callery pear's flowers to the next as the cool spray washed away the suds.

While bathing, my thoughts wandered—first through the day's events, then to more abstract matters. Along the way, my brain hit a snag and I found myself thinking chiefly about the numerous frights I'd had on the property, and of the body I'd found in the wall. Odd noises, queer sightings, hideous dreams and more had plagued me since moving into this house.

What if these scares, these odd coincidences, were related somehow to the body?

Things progressed naturally from the normal to the *paranormal*. Seeking an explanation for recent events that would leave things neat and tidy, I thoughtfully considered the possibility that my house was haunted. It was the first time the notion had occurred to me, despite all I'd been through.

Because I didn't believe in ghosts.

I didn't have a hard and fast reason for my disbelief. I simply didn't believe because I'd never had cause to. I'd never seen a ghost, or experienced anything I couldn't rationally explain. The idea that my recent troubles could be attributed to some supernatural menace felt like a bit of a reach.

But it *was* a convenient, all-encompassing explanation, and that was alluring.

While on the subject of ghosts, I couldn't help but reminisce. I recalled that, as a young child, I *had* believed in something. I'd been afraid of the dark, of the unknown, like most kids, despite never having encountered anything paranormal.

The wind picked up and the cold beads of water on my bare flesh incited me to shudder.

An old memory reared its head.

I'd been seven, maybe eight years old. My parents had still been together, then. It was summertime; I remember because the night was punishingly hot and we didn't have air conditioning. You'd wake up on nights like those with the bedclothes clinging to you like a second skin.

One night, before bed, I'd gone out to the living room to speak to my mother. All these years later, I sometimes have trouble remembering what she looked like. Her hair was dark. So were her eyes. The other details tend to blur. She'd been sitting on the sofa, watching the nightly news and smoking a cigarette.

She gave me a stern look for disturbing her; it was a little past my bedtime. She demanded to know what I was doing up. I confessed to her that I was scared. I'd heard something in my room—in the closet or under the bed, I can't remember—and I didn't want to be alone in there. I pleaded with her to come and check out the room.

With a smirk, my mother mocked me. "A little old for that, aren't you?" she'd said between drags. I remember she had this real debonair way of ashing her cigarettes; she'd flick the back of the thing with her thumb and let the smoke drift up from the corner of her mouth like she was some kind of old movie star.

I was pretty worked up. I didn't want to go back to the room until she'd had a look around. My dad was already asleep. I could hear him snoring away in the next room.

My mother put out her cigarette, and for a time it looked like she was going to humor me. "Let's go," she said, pointing towards my bedroom.

I started back to my room and my mother kept on my heels. She followed me inside and ordered me to sit on my bed. Rather than start looking around for ghouls, she did something that baffled me. She pulled out the chair to my desk and placed it directly beneath the light fixture in the ceiling. Climbing onto it, she began unscrewing the lightbulbs.

The room went dark.

"What are you doing, ma?" I'd asked her.

She'd shushed me as though I were a crying baby, slipping the warm bulbs into the pockets of her sweatpants. And then she'd walked out, closing the door behind her.

I remember fidgeting in that dark room, curling up on my bed. "Ma? Why'd you do that?" I'd asked.

She didn't respond, except to lock the door from the outside with her key.

"Ma! I don't wanna be in here, ma!" A thin band of light came in beneath the door, and in it I could see my mother's feet as she stood in the hall. "I think there's something in the room with me. Please don't leave me here," I'd pleaded.

With a laugh, I heard her lighting another cigarette. Her footsteps receded down the hall, and she replied, "I don't know if there's anything in that room with you, but if there is, you're going to find out real soon."

With that, she planted herself on the sofa, got back to her news program.

I spent that night imprisoned in my room, the lights off, shaking like a leaf. Eventually—I don't know how—I fell asleep. When I awoke in the morning the door was unlocked. Nothing had "gotten" me. No monster had come lumbering out of the murk to gobble me up, and no terrible ghost had appeared at my bedside.

The incident really only served to drive home something I'd already learned by that age: The only thing I had to fear in life was my mother.

I was left shaken, humiliated by it all. From that day on, I'd been too ashamed to put much thought into ghosts—into bogeymen or things that went bump in the night. My fear of the dark never fully left me, but I no longer allowed myself to show it.

Humiliating episodes like that one hastened the split between my parents. Though my father hadn't been an especially warm or protective guy, he'd had no tolerance for the kinds of stunts my mother would pull, and I remember that the two of them would nearly come to blows over her cruelty towards me. My mother packed up and left one morning. She never said goodbye to me, and she expressed no interest in any kind of visitation arrangement. For my father's part, he wasn't exactly enthusiastic about being a single parent, but he made things work in his own impersonal way.

Even now, almost twenty years later, I felt a touch of humiliation coloring my cheeks.

Returning to the house and putting on clean clothes, I tried to get back to business.

There was still a video to put together. The laptop called to me from the table in the living room, but I ignored it, trying to think of more gratifying distractions. I paced around, hands in the pockets of my sweatpants, and finally heeded the laptop's call—but only to turn on a bit of music. Johnny Winter's self-titled. Not having any neighbors to complain about the noise, I cranked the volume up to eleven and air-guitared like a dumb teenager.

Some minutes into my living room jam session—replete with detailed air-fretwork—I was startled by a pounding at the door. My shoulders stiffened and I turned the music down. Evening was in full swing now, and in the dead space between the firm knocks I could hear the nocturnal insects starting up in the lawn. Creeping towards the door, growing vaguely uneasy with every passing moment, I looked through the peephole. The front porch was lit up by the motion-activated light, and in the glow I could make out a figure standing near the door, just barely out of view.

A figure I didn't recognize.

EIGHTEEN

I pried open the door and discovered a short, barrel-chested man with a tattered blue T-shirt on. The T-shirt read, "JT'S DUMPSTER RENTAL EST. 1957—LOCALLY OWNED AND OPERATED." A large truck idled in the street, its hazard lights blinking. It was towing a big ol' dumpster in fire hydrant red.

"Oh," I said, stepping out to meet him with a nervous laugh. "The dumpster rental."

"Yessir," replied the man. I wasn't sure what his name was—didn't care to ask—but in my head I referred to him as the eponymous JT. "Sorry to come around so late," he continued, "you're actually the last delivery of the day. Had a lot of dumpsters to haul. Meant to come around earlier, but it didn't work out. Hope it's no inconvenience."

"Not at all," I said.

He looked into the house from the porch, then glanced around the yard, blinking hard like he was trying to wake from a dream. A smirk teased the corners of his lips, but it suddenly faded and he cleared his throat. "I, uh... I had a bit of trouble finding the house, truth be told. I didn't think anyone still lived out this way."

"I get that a lot," I said with a laugh. "Can't beat the privacy, though."

His smile and accompanying nod seemed guarded, like he was holding something back. Pulling some folded papers from his back pocket—a rental agreement for the dumpster, I soon realized—he explained the terms and lent me a pen so that I could initial and sign in the right places. As I did so, he kept looking up and down the street with what I took to be strong curiosity. Curiosity and, I suspected, veiled disgust. When I handed back the paperwork, he hiked a thumb at the idling truck. "Where you want it?"

"You can drop it on the lawn, next to the tree," I said after a moment.

He walked back to his truck, maneuvered this way and that until —about five minutes later—he'd gotten the dumpster up onto the lawn. Parking the truck, he got out and disconnected it. "That good?" he asked of its placement.

"Yeah," I replied. "That'll be fine. I won't have to carry all the junk in here quite so far that way."

He nodded. Then, stalling, he turned and asked me the question that had probably been bubbling in his mind for several minutes. "Say, you fixing this house, then?"

"Uh-huh."

He looked up and down the street again. "Don't say. Needs a lot of work, I'll bet."

"Sure does."

"I'm glad to see someone doing something with these old houses," continued the dumpster guy, pudgy hands stuffed into the pockets of his oil-stained jeans. "I think it would be great if a millionaire came in and just bought them all. It's a lot of land, and it's just sittin' out here, unused, you know? They'd make good rentals if they were fixed up."

"Wish I could afford to renovate more than just the one," I lied.

"Why you fixing it?" asked the man, arms crossed now. "You gonna sell it off, or...?"

I didn't feel like going through the whole song and dance and simply said, "I just like a good fixer-upper, that's all. House has good bones."

"I see, I see." He laughed, brushing a hand against his ruddy cheek. "When I was young, years back, I remember the houses on this street were all empty. We'd come here to, you know, mess around as kids. Some of 'em were full of punks—drug dealers and whatnot. But we'd use some of the houses for parties. It's been years, but I'm pretty sure I went to a party in this house, once. Good times."

Out of politeness, I listened to this man's *lovely* reminisce.

"Well, you take care," he said, departing. I watched him climb into his truck, spared him a wave, and then slipped back into the house.

Earlier in the day I would have welcomed company; after that bit of back and forth, I was now fully committed to my solitude.

I got back to my computer, turned the music up a bit higher, and began working on my video. Starting through the day's footage, I recalled with no little shame my behavior in the crawlspace—the panic I'd felt, the way I'd sped out of there like a frightened kid. I'd trim all of the unflattering footage away and preserve only the instructive segments. Doing so took me the better part of an hour, at the end of which I found myself with a fully-formed video ready for mass consumption.

The crawlspace video was uploaded and I retired to the air mattress, an arm draped over my eyes.

There was one bit of the footage that stuck out in my mind—a scene I hadn't included in my final video, but which raised some questions in me. I'd found a chalked handprint in the crawlspace, along with a set of initials. *F.W.*

I reckoned that the print had been made a long, long time ago. But whose was it? There was no way to be certain. Still, in the twilight of my day, as the fatigue took hold, I daydreamed about the house's history. I didn't have a lot of facts to fill out its timeline with, and so tried to imagine what the place had seen in its many years.

Before all of the parties, before the decay had set in, what had this house been like and who had lived in it?

Whose ghost is haunting this place?

NINETEEN

It was a touch after 3 AM when the headache pushed me back into the territory of wakefulness.

The pain seemed to issue from the goose egg on the right side of my head, just behind my temple, and though it had gone down substantially since I'd first gotten it in the crawlspace, I could still feel the ping pong ball-sized lump there. It was sore, a bit warm to the touch.

I switched on the lamp nearest the air mattress and went rifling around in my things for some painkillers. As I did so, my back began acting up on me. Leaning over too far, I felt a little spasm in my lumbar region and immediately sat up, lest I topple over in a gnarled heap.

If this was life in my late 20's, I wasn't looking forward to seeing what the next few decades held in store.

I couldn't find the bottle of Tylenol I usually kept in my backpack. There were still a few packets of pain pills out in the van's first aid kit, but as I stood and glimpsed at the incredible darkness that flourished just outside the dining room window, I thought better of going out to retrieve them. I sucked down some water and paced around, a hand pressed to the lump as though I could somehow smooth out the pocket of angry flesh.

Standing with my back to the small bedside lamp, I caught a glimpse of my shadow stretching across the floor. As I walked circles around the room, the shadow followed, growing to the excessive length I'd come to expect. I waved an arm around, cast a little hand puppet up against the wall, but couldn't for the life of me understand why the shadows in this house behaved in such a way. Queerer still was the manner in which my shadow would hook around corners as I turned in my wanderings; the way the edges of my silhouette would hitch for a moment, as if hitting a snag, only to double in length the next instant.

Having tired of all the shadow play, and of the way that the single lamp seemed to render the adjacent rooms in abominable shadow, I set about turning on all of the lights in the downstairs. In doing so, I walked past each of the windows and had a look through them. The night was misty, and thin fingers of fog threaded the air. It looked gloomy, picturesque in a way, but I found myself sorely wishing I'd sprung for some cheap mini blinds for the lower story windows. Thanks to the pervasive fog, I couldn't see much of the outside, and yet I doubted that any nocturnal visitor to the property would have much trouble looking *into* the well-lit house from that same yard. I considered putting out all of the lights and just returning to bed, but the ache in my head kept on and I parked myself in front of the computer instead, looking for something to raise my spirits.

I scrolled through the comments for my newest video, just a few hours old, and was very pleased to read them. Most of the comments dealt with the creepiness of crawlspaces in general. *EEK! A snake! And all of those cobwebs... yuck. I wouldn't be able to go into a crawl-space like that. What if something bit me?* wrote one commenter.

Another, less eloquently, wrote, *Nah. I ain't going down in a place like that. With my luck I'd find a dead body down there!*

I smirked at that one, I'll admit, and fought the urge to reply,

"Actually, in this house, the corpses are kept behind the walls, not in the crawlspace."

I paged through a few more comments, but despite the general tone of interest and encouragement among them I became gradually more unsettled by memories of the cramped space that existed just under my feet. Just remembering what it'd been like, crawling on my stomach, with the access door seeming miles away, chilled my blood and got my heart racing.

I leaned back in my chair and the floorboards groaned under its legs. Staring down at the knotted wooden planks, I wondered if anyone else in the house had heard it—if, by chance, there was someone there now, listening from the crawlspace.

How many times do you have to go through this? I shut my laptop. *There's no one else here.*

I mostly believed it, but even as I stood up and considered returning to bed, a chill surged through me. I felt it in my legs first. Then it came up through my torso, my arms. My teeth chattered. The air in the house was stuffy, uncirculated, but the cold had gotten through to me anyhow. Looking down at my bare feet, at the hardwood boards I was standing on, I fancied it was coming from down below, in that dusty, pitch-black crawlspace. The cold gave way to dread.

I'd felt this apprehension before. The previous night, when I'd been dreaming, I'd felt a subtle, unaccountable change in the air. It was like the feeling before a heavy storm breaks loose; the pressure drops, the air suddenly cools and you can feel the electricity brimming all around you.

I was awake. I certainly *felt* awake. I pinched myself on the forearm once, just to make sure, and the sting of it helped to bring me back to my senses.

A flash of light to my back brought my attention to the dining room window. The porch light had gone off.

"Really? This again?" I said, shuffling quietly to the window. The fog outside did much to bind the light, resulting in a brilliant haze that was almost more difficult to cut through with the naked eye than the preceding darkness had been. I stood there, holding my breath, and looked out across the front of the property.

In the moment before the light shut off, I thought I tracked movement in the yard. The light went out so quickly that I couldn't be sure, and the drifting of the fog only confused things further. When the light cut out and I was left staring into the misty night, I finally allowed myself to exhale and the burst of air from my mouth fogged up the glass.

I'd seen a shadow. Long and fast-moving, it had slipped past the Callery pear outside. It was one with the night now, invisible.

Was I losing my mind? I tell you, it certainly felt like it. I pawed at my eyes and took another look into the yard. But I turned up nothing. Nothing but the smoke-like fog. I made sure the window was locked, then journeyed to the other downstairs windows to make certain they were also properly fastened.

I had my back turned when, from the direction of the living room, I heard a *click*. This noise was followed by a sudden dimming of the overall light in the house. "What the..."

It had sounded like one of my lamps had been turned off—the one near the air mattress, with the twist knob, specifically.

That's not possible, I reminded myself.

Perhaps the bulb had burned out. Or maybe, just maybe, the lamp had malfunctioned.

But then, it had *clicked*. The little black knob on the side made that sound. I knew it well. Someone had turned it off.

That's not possible, I thought again.

Turning back towards the living room, I drew in a deep breath that I could scarcely hold in my lungs. The air mattress came into view, as did the edge of the table where the lamp was situated. Though I'd expected it, the fact that the lamp was indeed off sent a jolt of fright racing through me.

But that find didn't scare me half as much as what awaited me further in.

Standing fully now between the living room and dining room, I had a perfect view of the former, and discovered there was someone sitting in my chair.

A woman.

The woman.

Somehow, I remained standing, but as I stared at the seated figure —with her tangled, winter-colored hair trickling down the backrest of the chair—I lost all feeling in my legs. The figure sat unmoving in the metal chair, directly before my open laptop as if preparing to do some work. Her body, angular for its profound thinness, was cloaked in a stained white gown.

I wasn't sure if time stood still, or if a hundred years leapt by as I stared at the back of her head. And somehow—from the black screen of my open laptop, it appeared—the woman stared back. Though she did not turn to face me, and made no acknowledgement of my presence, that she was watching me intently from that screen, or else by other means, was plain. In the moments that I stood frozen, anchored to the floor, I let my gaze wander towards that screen and I gleaned the broadest strokes of the figure's terrible face reflected therein.

She lacked eyes, but the gaping sockets where eyes had once resided, now partially crusted over with leathery skin, were nearly as expressive. The bulk of her once-elegant nose had largely crumbled away, but asymmetrical nostrils remained. The two holes looked like something left behind by a burrowing parasite. A yawning mouth— too large, too deep, for a human being's—twitched at the corners in silent speech, or perhaps laughter.

I had seen this monster of a woman before, in my dreams.

I'd also captured her on camera, briefly, leering from the window of the master bedroom. The kitchen window, too.

Now, she was seated before me, a mere fifteen feet away. A smell not unlike the stench of the Callery pear tree—though a good deal more rank—met my nostrils as I gawked. It smelled almost like ground beef a few weeks past its sell-by date.

Her mouth continued twitching. She nodded her head in erratic little bobs, like she was either in absolute agreement with some unseen conversation partner, or else dodging psychical punches. Her arms, stick-thin and the color of new notebook paper, were wrapped around her midsection as though she were holding herself together at the waist. Blue, spidery veins traveled up and down her limbs, from the tips of her bare feet to the rigid ends of her skeletal fingers.

Like hers, my mouth moved but no sound came out. My tongue turned to lead and the very concept of language flew out the window.

There was a voice in my head—I *think* it was mine—still repeating that old, hopeful refrain.

It's not possible.

It's not possible.

It's not—

I was still staring at the woman when I felt a cold hand against the back of my arm, along my tricep. Two frigid, unseen fingers pinched my skin, leaving my arm tingling with pain. My heart did a somersault; my heartbeat suddenly doubled, like I'd just dunked my head in a bucket of ice water, and my vision went spotty.

A voice—hideous and croaking—sounded from behind me, bringing with it a cold that singed my earlobe like frostbite. "*It's not a dream.*"

Losing my footing, I made a drunken half-turn and clutched reflexively at the back of my arm, ready to face the horror behind me.

There was no one there.

A scream was born in my throat, but I couldn't draw the breath to voice it. Choking on the sound, I whipped back around to the woman in the living room.

The chair was empty.

She was nowhere to be seen.

Considering what happened next, I'm inclined to consider it no small wonder that I stopped to grab my keys and wallet from the living room table before running out of the house. No sooner had I discovered the living room empty of any presence did I hear a swell of laughter in the upstairs. Doors began to slam, footsteps charged along the floors of the upper level, and countless voices—all of them infernal—screeched in delight. One by one, all of the lights in the house were put out. The light in the kitchen blinked off, then the other living room light. By the time the dining room and stairwell lights went out, I was racing through the door, into the fog.

I struck the van head-on, knocking the wind out of myself, and had to limp into the driver's seat.

When I'd made it into the vehicle, I backed out immediately. Bouncing over the curb, I shifted into drive and put the pedal through the floor.

TWENTY

Everything in the motel smelled like cigarette smoke.

Even the ice from the ice machine tasted like Camels.

I'd made quite a scene when I'd rolled into the motel the night before. Shaken, barely coherent, I'd only gotten a room at all because I'd thrown a fair bit of cash at the tired guy working the counter. He'd asked if everything was all right, made sure I wasn't drunk or violent, and then helped me to a room, where I'd confined myself. It was only at noon that I finally emerged, taking a tentative glance down the hall and finding my way to the vending machines.

I hadn't gotten much sleep, and what little I had gotten had been awful. Burrowing into the crusty bedclothes, I'd tossed and turned the whole night, plagued by what I'd seen and the burdensome knowledge that I had, in fact, seen it. For hours I'd been able to feel cold fingers pinching the back of my arm. The voices of guests carrying on in nearby rooms sounded, at times, like that low, croaking voice I'd heard back at the house. Laying in bed with a pillow pressed over my face, I feared that I'd find myself back in the living room with the woman seated nearby the moment I dared remove it.

I checked out of the motel at almost one in the afternoon, looking like roadkill. When I walked to a small bar across the street to order some stiff drinks, the bartender almost refused to serve me. Once more, it was only because I had a fair bit of cash on me that he acquiesced and poured me a few glasses of Jameson. Thankful that the bar was quiet this early in the day, I enjoyed my drinks in near silence, listening occasionally to the oldies playing overhead. Roy Orbison's "Crying" came and went; by my third glass, it was Simon and Garfunkel.

The Jameson felt like it was going to burn a hole in my stomach, but it gave me the courage—or reinstated the necessary naivete—to ask some tough questions about what had transpired less than twelve hours ago in that forsaken house.

A ghost. I'd seen a ghost. Specifically, the ghost of the woman I'd found buried in the wall. The resemblance was undeniable. Her reasons for haunting the place and her identity were a mystery to me. Up until that point, I'd preferred it that way. My go-to plan had been to renovate the house as quickly as possible and then to dump it. I hadn't cared an iota about its history. The sooner I could forget about the corpse, the look of that abandoned neighborhood, the better.

And yet, so long as I had any dealings with the house, this spirit wasn't going to let me off the hook. I could feel it in my gut. Every time I'd set foot in that house, *something* had happened. If I continued hanging around, I was going to keep inadvertently recording things, would be plagued by visions of the dead every time I set foot there. The clear solution to all of this was to simply stop working on the house. If I never went back, the problem would be solved, no?

Perhaps that was true, but I'm the kind of man who likes to both have his cake *and* eat it. Why, I like going back for seconds if the mood strikes me. Despite all I'd been through, I wasn't ready to just abandon the project. I was scared, but I was *angry*, too. Angry that this thing had scared me away from my own house; angry that I'd gone running like a child. There was a lot riding on this renovation, and I wasn't quite ready to call it quits. Not until I was sure this ghost problem was insurmountable.

The voices. There was something about this woman—or this phantom that had been a woman, once—that really terrified me. She seemed capable of speaking in many voices. On the tape, and in my dreams, I'd heard an assortment of foul voices coming out of her—and last night, too, I'd heard a number of them in the upstairs. It was like she had a whole town living inside of her—like her body was home to a whole cast of characters.

Could she harm me? Were ghosts capable of injuring the living? Aside from the psychological torment she'd been putting me through with her frightening appearances, I hadn't incurred any physical harm yet. If the spirit was capable of hurting me, it probably would have done so earlier in my tenancy. I'd slept there, would have been a sitting duck on numerous occasions. There'd been no shortage of opportunities.

A fourth glass of Jameson—and my last, if the bartender's stern look was any indicator—instilled me with a bit more bravado.

My father wouldn't have been scared off by some ghoulish thing. He'd have laughed in its face, gone on working despite it. I didn't look to my father's example for a whole lot in life, but if there was any time that it made sense to emulate him, then this was it.

I was close to landing that TV show. And I wanted it. *Badly.* If I turned my back on this house, it was possible I'd never get an opportunity with the Home Improvement Network again. Of course, even if I bailed on the project and said goodbye to stardom, I'd be able to find work elsewhere, but ultimately I wanted to level up, to take my career to new heights. I didn't want to waste the rest of my life doing low-key renovations for clients like my father had done. I wanted to be a star, and pursuing my dream would require sacrifice.

It would require a TV show.

I thought about sobering up and heading back to the house, but the whiskey alone wasn't enough to ratchet up my courage.

It became clear that I was going to have to go into this project with a plan if I was going to do it at all. You don't just march into a building full of asbestos without planning ahead; so too would I have to prepare to deal with this house's particular problem. While funneling cocktail peanuts into my mouth, I tried thinking of ways I could make peace with the situation. *How can you fix the house* and *get your videos made, while minimizing your contact with this thing?*

Why, I wondered, were spirits sometimes leashed to places after death? The dead woman in that wall had likely been a victim of murder; even the detectives had said as much. Did she carry some sort of grudge towards her murderer that kept her soul tethered to the property? Or, did she linger on because she wanted to reach out to the living—to let them know what had really happened to her? I tried, believe me, but I couldn't envision this hideous spirit in the house as some innocent ghost in search of closure. In all my dealings with her, it seemed her main focus had been to scare the life out of me. I'd detected nothing but malevolence in her from the very start—malevolence directed at *me*.

Without knowing who had lived in the house previously, or what had transpired there during its years of abandonment, I had no way of knowing who or what I was dealing with. If I did some digging, learned about the house's past and managed to uncover something about this mysterious woman, then maybe I could turn things around. I didn't have a lot of time for that, however. The renovations were going to dominate my schedule for the remainder of the month.

Realizing that I had no intention of sleeping there ever again, or even spending time there after nightfall, my plan began to take shape. Each day, bright and early, I'd dive in and do as much work as possible until sundown. When evening came, I'd head off to a hotel to work on my videos, and spend the rest of my nights trying to get to the bottom of things. Returning to the house at all was a terrifying proposition, and yet I felt confident in my ability to work there by day. The greatest horrors—the nightmares and manifestations—only seemed to take place at night. By keeping to this schedule and not staying after dark, I could effectively minimize the threat.

I still didn't want to go back.

Most of my valuables, including my phone and laptop, were still at the house. I hadn't thought to pack a bag when running scared at 3AM. If I wanted to check my messages and get a new video uploaded, I had to at least get ahold of those and bring them back to the hotel with me. I had an extra video, comprised of odds and ends, that I could upload for the day, thus keeping up my streak. I could restart work tomorrow and spend the remainder of my day looking into the house's past.

What would happen if I actually figured out who the dead woman was? Would it be like the movies, where the vengeful spirit happily goes onto the next world because the truth of her murder has been revealed? It was doubtful. The way I looked at it, digging into the history and finding some answers—putting a name to the hideous face—could only help matters, though.

I idled in the bar until I could walk a straight line and then ate about fifteen dollars' worth of McDonald's across the street. When I was finally sober enough to drive, I went looking for a nice hotel—one with a bar and strict no-smoking policy, for starters—and reserved a room for the night.

All that was left then was to go back to the house.

The day was wearing thin, though. By the time I got there and grabbed up all of my most valuable things, the sun would be perilously close to setting, and I realized that my odds of coming face to face with something horrifying would increase substantially.

I'm not proud of this, but before heading to the house, I used the phone in my hotel room to call the non-emergency police line. I introduced myself, explained that I was an out-of-towner renovating a house on Morgan Road, and that I was fairly sure there was an intruder inside. I asked that an officer come by to accompany me while I gathered some of my things. The dispatcher promised that an officer would be by in the next hour, and I immediately set off for the house.

I was parked outside 889 Morgan Road much sooner than I

expected. I parked far enough up the drive to allow the cop car room behind me, but not so far that I was close to the house. Until I had someone else beside me, I wanted to give the place some distance.

The house looked undisturbed. The Callery pear swayed, the windows were all empty—at least, for the moment—and the sun was beginning to dip.

I waited for roughly half an hour before the police cruiser drove up and parked at the curb. As I'd sat waiting, I'd stared at the house expectantly. Its ghostly occupant didn't show, though. Nothing horrific reared its head.

Even so, I hated that house, and I wished I'd never laid eyes on it.

TWENTY-ONE

Officer Tanner met me half-way up the drive. He was a young guy, perhaps younger than me, with a blond crew cut and a bit of acne scarring on his cheeks. With a severe, narrowed gaze, he looked to me and then to the house. His first words to me?

"You're the guy from the video!" Tanner cracked a smile. "This is the house where they found the body, right?"

Embarrassed, I tried laughing it off. "Yep, that's me. Luckiest guy in the world. This house is a gift that keeps on giving." Shame hit me square in the cheeks, leaving them red. I imagined this officer—along with the rest of his department—watching the video I'd given to the detectives. They'd probably laughed long and hard at my freak-out. I'd become a department-wide joke, as I'd feared.

Mercifully, Tanner changed the subject. He pointed to the house, asking, "So, what's the story here? Something about an intruder?"

The truth was that I hadn't called him over to help me deal with a run-of-the-mill intruder. I simply hadn't wanted to go into the house alone since my last encounter with its resident phantom. Of course, I couldn't let him know that, and so I fed him a half-truth, leaving out all of the paranormal bits. "Yes, last night there was a strange woman in my house. An older woman. I don't know how she got inside. I've been seeing her around the property for a little while, in fact. I thought she might be homeless, that she was looking for shelter, but she's gotten more and more insistent. It's like she's committed to living here, no matter what. I changed the locks and put in this motion-activated light outside the front door, but it hasn't deterred her. I'm at wit's end with this."

That last part, at least, was entirely truthful.

Tanner scratched at his ear, walking up to the house until he was a few steps from the porch. "Pretty weird," he replied. "Why didn't you call last night?"

Not wanting to admit that I'd run from the house in terror, I offered another lie. "W-Well, I meant to call, but she disappeared. Snuck out of the house, I guess. I just came back to grab some stuff tonight, but it's possible she's returned, so I wanted to have a police officer with me before entering."

"OK," said Tanner. "I'll do a quick walk-through with you." He stepped aside, inviting me to open the door.

I hadn't had the presence of mind to lock the front door before fleeing, and I opened it with a mere push.

Tanner clicked his tongue and stepped inside behind me. "Now, I'm going to have to recommend that you lock your doors if you want to keep out intruders."

I ignored him.

Together, we walked through the downstairs, and I was relieved to find that nothing much had changed. My valuables were still there, and there were no clear signs of the woman. I spent some time staring at the folding chair where she'd materialized the night before and the back of my arm tingled for the memory of her spectral pinch, but I eventually snapped out of it and focused on gathering my things.

Tanner whistled now and then, remarking on the house's decrepitude. "She's a real heap, isn't she? Renovating this house is going to be rough. I commend you for it, but I have to wonder why someone would bother with a house in this part of town. There's hardly anything you can call a neighborhood for miles around—"

"The house had good bones," I replied, effectively cutting him off. By this point, I was tired of explaining my reasons to perfect strangers.

We went upstairs together. Tanner was a good sport and went into each of the rooms, the closets, turning up nothing of note. Not that I'd expected him to; somehow, I felt sure that the ghostly manifestations in this house were my own private show to witness.

Having cleared the house, Tanner accompanied me back downstairs as I hurriedly packed my valuables. I stuffed a backpack and duffel with my laptop and camera gear and snatched my clean clothing as well. As I did so, the cop proved more talkative, and leaning against the bannister he drummed a beat against the wood with his fingers. "No sign of an intruder. Make sure to keep your doors and windows locked from here on out. That should keep people out. Say, they found the body in there, right? Behind a wall? An old woman?"

I nodded. "That's right."

Tanner chuckled. "Well, if nothing's out of place, then maybe you aren't dealing with a flesh and blood intruder at all," he joked. "Could just be the old girl's spirit coming by to make sure she didn't leave the stove on."

I paused in my packing of the bags just long enough to curse under my breath. "Say," I went on to ask him, "do you know if anything ever came of that? The body, I mean. Did they manage to identify her?"

Tanner crossed his arms. "Dunno. That's not under my purview. Last I'd heard, she was still Jane Doe. If you call the station and speak to the detectives working the case, they might be able to fill you in. Then again, they might not. They don't often comment on ongoing investigations."

I'd packed up all of my important belongings and was taking a look around the living room in search of anything else I might need at the hotel when my gaze settled on the wall behind the folding table. I'd printed and taped up the exciting email I'd received from Mona Neeb at HIN there, but as I scanned it blankly, I realized something was wrong.

Someone had written on it.

No, not written on it, exactly.

Someone had taken a pen to it, had crossed off large portions. The few sections that remained legible spelled out a very different message, and for a time I couldn't hear Tanner's voice as he rambled on from the stairs.

Mona's email had been pleasant and thrilling to me; I'd printed it to remind myself of the potential reward that might await me after the job's end. In scratching out the bulk of it, the vandal had left behind a brief message, quite unlike the original in tone. Only these three chunks of readable text were left. The rest had been blacked out in gouging lines of ballpoint that had marked up the drywall behind:

WE WANT YOU

MANY OF US

The last line of the email had been left mostly intact, but taken along with the previous unblocked passages, it took on a sinister, rather than encouraging, air:

ALL OF US WILL BE WATCHING

Tanner walked into the room just as I tore the paper from the wall and stuffed it into my pocket. "You all set in here?"

"Yeah." I slung my bags over one shoulder and tried to hide my unease. I don't know if I fooled him—my hand shook as I clutched at the straps—but I did my best to look calm.

"Like I said," continued the officer, starting for the door, "just try and keep the doors and windows locked."

As if I *didn't*.

I followed him out onto the porch. "Thanks for coming by, I appreciate it."

"No problem. You have a good evening, now." Tanner marched back to his cruiser, but I stopped him before he left the drive.

"Officer?"

He turned and looked at me tensely, like he loathed the idea of assisting me any further.

"If I wanted to... to learn about who owned this house before I did... where would I look?" I asked, dropping the bags into the passenger seat of my van.

"Oh," he said, pausing. "If I were you, I'd look into contacting the Wayne County recorder's office. They're bound to have something. In fact, it's all automated these days. You can print files online for a small fee."

"The Wayne County recorder's office," I echoed. "All right, I'll look into that. Thanks."

Relieved that I had nothing further for him, he waved and hurried back to his cruiser. Moments later, he was gone.

I didn't waste any time, either. When I was sure I had everything I needed, I backed out of the driveway and tore down the street. I didn't dare look back at the house as I left for the hotel.

TWENTY-TWO

My favorite amenity at this hotel wasn't the super-plush bed, nor the in-room jacuzzi—although I enjoyed those both a great deal. The best part of staying there was the hotel bar, which was staffed by a friendly and seemingly inexperienced guy named Chas. I say inexperienced because he allowed me to order glasses of Glenfiddich 16 for the same price as a Johnnie Walker Red, and he poured them extra tall. His boss would probably throw a fit later on when he realized the barkeep's costly error. I played dumb and thanked him, sitting in a corner and drinking like a king behind my laptop. When I was through, I made sure to tip extra well.

The hotel bar was a nice spot; dimly lit, quiet and—perhaps most importantly—almost empty. Save for a middle-aged man in a corduroy jacket who sat in the corner opposite mine, smiling into his third or fourth long island iced tea, I was alone in the place. There were ten or twelve tables spread out before the well-stocked bar, all of them covered in neat, white tablecloths. The wi-fi was very good here, and free. Nursing my scotch, I got to work.

The first thing I had to do was upload a video to my VideoTube channel so that I could keep the challenge rolling. I'd had one video in reserve that I could use on just such an occasion, and I got it uploaded within a few minutes. Up to this point, my viewers had no idea of the trouble behind the scenes, and I intended to keep it that way.

The next order of business was more involved. Pulling up the website for the Wayne County recorder's office, I whipped out my credit card and began looking for files in their database pertaining to 889 Morgan Road. I had to pay a few bucks just to access their database, and when I found some files minutes later—a deed for the property dated to 1975, along with some tax filings—I had to pay a few more to access them. So long as the documents contained something useful, I didn't mind getting nickeled and dimed to death.

I had Chas pour me another criminally cheap Glenfiddich and then returned to my laptop to study the paperwork. It was all contained in a single PDF file, somewhat grainy and difficult to read. Or maybe it was the scotch that was making it hard to focus. I paged through the document, four pages in total, and made some notes on a napkin.

According to these official documents, the house had been built in 1975. The first—and only—owner listed was one Willard Weiss, who'd purchased the lot and had the house constructed between May and August of that year. I jotted down the name "Willard Weiss" and underlined it, but aside from that the deed didn't offer much info.

The attached tax documents were more illuminating, but just barely. Property taxes had been routinely payed on the house until 1990. Judging by the lack of other names or any further tax payments beyond that year, I supposed that the house had been vacant since around 1990 or 1991. *It's likely been almost thirty years since anyone's officially lived in the house,* I thought.

These documents hadn't given me much to work with, but I did have a name now—Willard Weiss—along with a pretty good guess of how long the house had sat empty. I took this name to Google, searching "Willard Weiss, Detroit", in the hopes of finding more information on the house's previous owner. This search spawned a number of results that ultimately furthered my investigation—and also left me with more questions.

The first result was for an individual named Willard Weiss who —as of the year 2010—had been listed as living in Detroit. There was a phone number listed, and for a second I got mighty excited, but an attempt to call said number got me nowhere. It was disconnected. The site listed an approximate age of eighty years for Mr. Weiss; given that his most recent listed contact info dated to nearly eight years previous, I presumed he was no longer among the living. And if he was, then it was possible he had an unlisted name and address. Considering his age, it wouldn't have been a stretch to say that he'd moved out of the area to live with family, or was in a nursing home somewhere.

A second search result helped me to fill in some blanks. It was an obituary dated to 1991—not for Willard Weiss, but for an Irma Weiss. Willard Weiss was listed as the husband of the deceased, who had passed in January of 1991 after "a brief illness" at fifty-four years of age. There was no photograph accompanying the obituary, and the listing itself was sparse. It made mention of a sole daughter—one Fiona Weiss, age 29—who at the time of the writing was reportedly some years "estranged".

For a time, I felt like I'd hit a dead-end. I took a sip of scotch and read through the brief obituary once more. Only then did I notice something. It was a small detail, probably inconsequential, but something about the name "Fiona Weiss" stood out to me. The initials for that name were "F.W". In the crawlspace to the house, I'd discovered a chalked handprint accompanied by those very initials. This Fiona, then, had probably been the one to leave that marking behind as a little girl. *Well, thank goodness* that *mystery has been solved,* I scoffed.

Without any other working leads, I took what I'd learned from my various sources and pieced together a timeline of events. This, I wrote down meticulously in a Word document.

The house had been constructed in 1975. Willard Weiss (born approximately 1938), Irma Weiss (1937—1991 according to the obituary) and their daughter, Fiona (born approximately 1962), had presumably lived in the house. At around the time of Irma's death in 1991, the house was abandoned, and by then Fiona was no longer speaking to her parents. There was no telling whether Willard Weiss was still alive; I couldn't pull up an obituary for him, which was encouraging, and yet I couldn't find anything else on him, either. Searches for Fiona Weiss were a dead-end. Depending on the nature of her estrangement, it was possible she'd moved out of State. Maybe she'd even changed her name.

OK, so I had a rough sketch of the house's history. *Now what?*

There were, as I'd initially suspected, almost thirty years since the house had last been occupied in any official capacity, and those years were all unaccounted for. The body in the wall—and the spirit that now haunted the place—didn't necessarily have anything to do with the Weiss family. It was more likely that the murder and hiding of that Jane Doe I'd found had taken place in that dark, thirty-year period.

I made some half-hearted searches for missing people in Detroit over the past thirty years, but the sheer volume of listings made it impossible to sift through them all. Moreover, if Jane Doe had been on a lower rung of society's ladder—a homeless woman, for instance—then it was unlikely she'd ever been reported missing in the first place.

I reviewed my notes once more after closing my tab at the bar. The timing of the house's abandonment—roughly at the same time as Irma's death—struck me as meaningful. Had Irma died *in* the house after this "brief illness"? The specter that haunted me, that turned up in my dreams and spoke in terrible voices—was it the spirit of Irma Weiss? The more I considered it, the less likely it seemed that this was the case. Irma had died at 54. The body I'd found had looked *far* older than that. Then again, the body *had* been sickly...

No, that didn't make sense. Irma's death had been reported—there'd been an obituary and everything. Unless her body had been scooped up after the funeral and stashed behind the house's walls, rather than receiving a proper burial, the Jane Doe had to be someone else. Still, I wished I could just name the ghost "Irma" and call it a day. It would have been so much more convenient that way.

I sighed a great, whiskey-soaked breath and packed up my computer. The detectives had been right; the way things were going, the body—and the spirit roaming the house—was likely to remain a Jane Doe.

TWENTY-THREE

I was up before the sun, and couldn't remember the last time I'd slept so peacefully.

You're getting started early today, I thought as I rolled out of bed. *Dad would be proud.*

I awoke with a nasty headache thanks to all the scotch I'd imbibed the night before, but thankfully it was nothing that a strong cup of Tim Horton's couldn't handle. I showered, dressed and headed out to the house before the sun had fully risen, but I didn't go straight there. Instead, I found my way to the old graveyard on Morgan Road and enjoyed a couple of breakfast sandwiches amidst the tombstones while the sky brightened.

The morning was pleasantly cool, and the peacefulness of the graveyard was a welcome start to what was sure to be a busy and exhausting day. It was funny that I found more comfort in a grave-yard than in the house I was set to work in.

The overgrown paths between the graves and the crumbing of the monuments, however depressing, had started to draw me in. There was sadness there, no shortage of dereliction, but there existed some-thing like intrigue, too. Maybe I just liked wondering about the people who'd been buried there so many years before, but as I paced through the lonely stretch, the dew leaving my pant legs wet, I couldn't help feeling that I was *supposed* to be there. Something was calling out to me, and I needed only to listen to find out what.

With the sun out, I—*barely*—found the courage to head to the house and begin my work. I'd already decided that today I was going to work to get the bathroom squared. I'd work through lunch to get as much of the tile torn up as possible, and get rid of the toilet and sink. When the shower had been razed and I'd replaced the undoubtedly damaged wall behind it, I'd call it a day.

Pulling into the driveway and idling out front for several minutes, I eventually grabbed up my camera gear and moseyed to the door. I passed by the dumpster, its rusty exterior flecked in mist, and peeked over the edge at the refuse I'd thrown in previously. I hoped there would be enough room for everything; I still had to dispose of the bathroom fixtures and all of the cabinetry. The busted kitchen appliances, too, if there was room.

I stood outside the entrance for another minute or two, fiddling with my keys like I didn't know which one to use. Finally, I went inside. The door eased shut behind me, and when the deadbolt clicked I couldn't help but feel trapped. The light through the window seemed less bright than it had a moment ago; the fresh, cool air had been replaced with the house's musty air, and my nostrils itched at the change.

I threw on my tool belt, and tried to act natural.

It was early in the day, and I reminded myself that there was no reason to feel jumpy. Pacing back and forth between the living room and dining room as I screwed together the parts of my tripod, I looked constantly for anything out of place, for signs of the ghostly woman. Then, when I'd hauled my camera and tripod up the stairs, setting it up in the bathroom doorway, I made a quick trip to each of the rooms along the hall. They were empty, undisturbed since my last visit with Officer Tanner.

I returned downstairs and began gathering my tools for the job.

Breaking up the old tiles on the floor and shower with a crowbar would be easy enough, and once they'd all been lifted I'd bag them and run them to the dumpster. While looking for my crowbar I got distracted by my phone, and paused in the living room to check my email. What awaited me there took me by surprise, and I immediately plopped down into the folding chair to read more closely.

It was another message from Mona Neeb at the Home Improvement Network. She wrote:

Hello, Kevin! Just wanted to let you know I've been enjoying your daily uploads. One of the producers here, Jack Hearn, has been following your work too. He's expressed some interest in having one or two of our representatives visit you there in Detroit, to tour the house and see your work first-hand. Jack is looking to produce a new program for the network and is very interested in what you're doing. Would you be open to meeting some of our representatives on the job site? When would be good for you? I was thinking we'd send them in a week or two, that way you'd have more time to get the house ready. Drop me a line and let me know your thoughts!

When I'd calmed down and my thumbs were steady, I tapped out a short—and overly optimistic—reply. *Sure, Mona! That sounds great!* I wrote. *I'm free to meet with network representatives whenever is good for you. It might be best to wait a week or two so that I have more to show them, but the work is going smoothly and I expect the job may even be complete before the thirty days are up.* I included my cell phone number so that we might discuss the specifics later on, and thanked her for her support.

Obviously, the work had *not* been going smoothly. The renovation had been fraught with trouble since day one.

That didn't matter, though. I had a week—two weeks, tops—to put all of the unpleasantness behind me and get this sorry old house fixed up. If this producer wanted me to show him an impressive thirty-day renovation, then I was going to show him precisely that. It didn't matter if ghosts or demons started peeking out of every doorway to spew pea soup in my face. The work was going to get done. There was too much on the line for me to keep dithering.

As I regarded this new message, I was reminded of the old one—the one I'd printed off and left hanging on the wall. I'd found it defaced the evening before during my walkthrough with the cop. It'd been a chilling message, potentially a threat. It had read, "WE WANT YOU. MANY OF US. ALL OF US WILL BE WATCHING." What that meant specifically was anyone's guess. It certainly seemed to clash with my admittedly limited understanding of the haunting. Were there *multiple* spirits in the house, or was the specter simply fond of referring to herself as a plurality? She had spoken in multiple voices, hadn't she? So, maybe...

"Nope," I said aloud. "I don't care." Raising my voice so that any unseen occupant of the house might hear, I shouted, "I don't care what you want. Leave my stuff alone, let me do my work, and maybe we'll manage to get along. How does that sound?"

Plucking my crowbar from a nearby box, I practically skipped up the stairs. I adjusted the camera, did a quick test, and when I had the shower in focus, I broke out my narrator voice. "Hey, there! This is FlipperKevin, here to continue this thirty day renovation challenge. Thanks for tuning in!"

THE TILES in the shower came down very easily. Many of them had barely been hanging on, and I soon discovered why.

The wall behind the shower was water-damaged.

I clicked my tongue and turned to the camera, tapping the mold-stained wall with my crowbar. "Ah, that's a shame. This wall is no good. Whoever installed this shower didn't know what they were doing. They used plain old drywall here when they should have used something water-resistant, like concrete backboard. I'm going to knock this drywall out of here and have a look at the space behind it. Fingers crossed that there's no serious damage."

I wrenched the toilet from its place and pretended to strain comi-
cally for the camera before lugging it downstairs and hoisting it into
the dumpster outside. When I'd managed to loose it from the wall, I
did the same with the bathroom sink. With those out of the way, I
had more space to work with, and I began ripping up the floor tiles.
All told, it took me just over two hours to pry up the tiles and dispose
of them in the dumpster. The maniac pace of the work left me
drenched in sweat, and hungry, but even as the afternoon wore on I
didn't allow myself a break for lunch. Chugging a water bottle and
munching on a handful of protein bars was all the break I needed.
When it came time to use the bathroom, I relieved myself in the yard
and got right back to work. I was determined to get as much of the
work done as possible before dark.

Throwing on my dust mask and safety glasses, I started on the
next phase of work; replacing the damaged drywall with something
water-resistant. "Let's see what's behind this wall, eh?" I said as I
began tearing down the drywall around the shower. *Better not be
another dead body,* I thought as the mold-blackened material began
hitting the floor.

Thankfully, there wasn't any corpse there. There wasn't even any
mold or damage to the studs. I was so pleased at this that I actually
cheered. "Yeah! Would you look at that!" I told the camera. I lifted it
from the tripod and took a slow pan of the exposed wall. "Not a bit of
mold. I keep lucking out with this house, I tell you what. All I'll need
to do for this is hang some concrete backboard. When that's up, I can
tile it just like it was before, and it should last for many years without
problems."

I took some measurements of the space and wrote down the
dimensions of the backboard I'd have to buy. I planned to pick it up at
a hardware store on my way to the house the next morning, where
they'd be able to cut it to size for me. After cleaning up the fallen
drywall and hauling it to the yard, I then brought the camera downstairs with me to the kitchen. Feeling energetic and wanting to get
some extra footage I could use in a later video, I took a sledge to the

kitchen cabinets, knocking them to pieces with a few well-aimed blows. I carried out the splintered cabinets and heaved them into the dumpster. Making sure that the camera captured my struggle, I dragged the stove and refrigerator out to the front lawn—the latter taking me more than half an hour of breathless starts and stops.

With hours of footage to sift through and a serious stink on me, I started packing things up for the night. The sun was beginning to dip in the sky and I was keen to light out before it was lights out.

When the cleanup was finished, I shouldered my bags and prepared to lock up. "OK, Irma," I said with a seasick smile, glancing around the downstairs. "Don't burn the place down while I'm gone. And maybe consider moving out, will ya?" I don't know why I called the spirit by that name—it seemed convenient, I guess. For that matter, I don't know why I insisted on calling out to her at all. Joking around about the situation made it an easier pill for me to swallow; maybe if I talked to her we'd build up some rapport.

I clocked out and headed for the hotel.

It'd been a good day, for once.

TWENTY-FOUR

The hotel shower felt amazing. I lingered in the hot water till my skin was red and savored the steam as I toweled off. After a hard day's work, there was nothing like feeling clean again.

I'd have liked to crawl into bed right then, when my relaxation was at its zenith, but unfortunately I still had a video to put together. When I'd thrown on some sweatpants and a T-shirt, I hiked down to one of the restaurants located beside the hotel and brought my laptop with me. There was a quaint Chinese place that served hot tea with every meal, and though I got a weird look for setting up my laptop at the table, the server didn't give me any fuss. I ordered steamed pork dumplings as an appetizer and two dinner-sized portions of chicken and broccoli. Hungry as I was, I wondered if I shouldn't preemptively order a third.

I threw on some headphones and sipped at my Oolong while reviewing the day's footage. I'd recorded for several hours, and there was a lot of fluff that would need trimmed. I started with the first scene of the day, my work on the shower, and cleaned up the sound as best I could during the muffled portions where I was wearing a dust mask. Pleased with this scene, I skipped ahead some to the part where I'd started carrying bags of tile out to the dumpster.

That was when I first heard it.

I didn't think anything of it, at first. In fact, I thought I was merely hearing the chatter of some other patrons in the busy restaurant. It wasn't until I cranked up the volume on my headphones that I became sure it was coming from the recording, rather than my immediate surroundings. And with that realization, one of the pork dumplings I'd scarfed down began a slow climb up my esophagus.

There were voices on the recording.

And they weren't mine.

I sometimes talked to myself, muttered, when at work. But that wasn't what I was hearing now. The recording featured a few unfamiliar voices in low conversation, and from the sound of it they'd been just a few feet from the camera—so close that they echoed somewhat throughout the cramped bathroom. I hadn't heard them at the time of the recording, though, which made no sense.

The longer I listened, the more I realized they weren't *wholly* unfamiliar.

One, high and wheezy, sounded like the air escaping a punctured balloon.

Another, coming in reply to the first, was a low, painful groan like a frog that had just been stepped on.

I dropped my fork onto my plate and sat upright, moving a little ways into the recording.

There I was, on screen, dropping more tiles into a garbage bag. I complained to myself about the weight of them as I lifted the bag off the ground. There were no other voices, no noises save for the jangle of shattered tiles as they settled in the bag. I walked off-screen. My heavy footfalls faded as I descended the stairs. From far-off, I could be heard to open the front door.

Before I could write off the hushed voices as a mere coincidence, they started up again. The moment I was out of earshot, the moment I'd stepped out of the house, the eerie chatter continued.

"What the—?" Though my binging on Chinese food was at least partly to blame for the perspiration forming across my brow, it was in listening to those voices that I really began breaking into a cold sweat. I'd heard them before, these voices. I'd managed to push them out of my mind for a time, to convince myself that they hadn't been real. But here they were, captured on tape.

And they were frightfully clear.

"*It's not a dream,*" said the croaking one with a sickening laugh, and I was sure at that moment that I wasn't listening to anything remotely human.

One voice, so low that it hurt my ears to listen to it, droned, "*Can you hear me, Paula? This is your Edward—Edward Franklin Ames.*"

Another voice entered the picture, this one disturbing in its echoey androgyny. "*Let me in. I won't hurt you...*" A growling laugh followed. "*It's me, sweetheart. Bradford from Annapolis. I just want to talk, Sarah.*"

I paused the footage and removed my headphones. There was soothing instrumental music playing overhead, and for a time I let it flow into me.

The waitress came by and asked if I was all right. "You look pale," she said, handing me the bill.

I choked down a cup of lukewarm Oolong and handed her a pair of twenties, shaking my head so fervently it was hardly convincing. "I'm fine. Fine."

Having had my fill of video editing, I shut my laptop and tucked it away. The waitress came by with my change and I hurriedly left the restaurant, my head swimming and my entrees abandoned half-eaten. I had more video to edit—there'd be no way around that—but I needed some time to think.

Starting into the cool evening, I stopped by a coffee shop across the street for a flat white. Rather than getting sloshed at the hotel bar like I'd done the night before, I sought the alertness caffeine would grant me. Maybe, with a little espresso in my veins, I'd be able to figure out what I was hearing in the background of these recordings.

THE HOUSE OF LONG SHADOWS   147

The laptop in my backpack seemed to weigh more than usual, as if the horrors I'd just discovered on it had real mass to them.

I'd watched enough ghost-hunting TV shows in my time to know what it was I'd captured. These were electronic voice phenomena—EVPs. The capture of voices that shouldn't have been there at all. Aside from videos or photographs, EVPs were about the best evidence of the supernatural that existed, though I'd never run across any so clear as these. Usually they were hard to make out, nonsensical, and could be attributed to radio interference.

Not these.

These were the real deal.

I rushed back to my hotel room, hung up the "Do not disturb!" placard and set my laptop on the bed. Without stopping to listen to the demonic little conversations in the margins, I managed to pare down the day's footage to the necessary tutorials and pieced together a video that was—I admit—sloppier than the norm. I uploaded it to VideoTube before I remembered to add in the intro animation, and unlike my recent uploads, this one didn't have any music in it.

With the day's work out of the way, I turned my attention to the other matters that quite literally haunted me. Even with all of the lights on in my hotel room the place felt awfully dark. As I pulled up the raw footage and got my headphones ready, I felt increasingly nervous, like I was about to do something illicit.

Sitting on the edge of my bed, I looked down at the carpet and found that my shadow was spreading across the floor like spilled ink. *What the—?* I shuddered, recalling the way the house on Morgan Road distorted shadows, and flopped onto the other side of the bed so that I wouldn't have to look at it. This whole city was beyond help, I decided. When I was done with this project, I'd go to some other State, far away, where shadows knew how to behave.

For a little while, I reviewed the day's footage with my headphones on, skimming the conversations that took place when I was off-camera between numerous unseen speakers. The croaking voice was a staple, and I seized up every time it spoke—though the others weren't necessarily less disturbing.

One, a gasping voice like someone on the verge of suffocating, recited a series of nonsensical rhymes that went something like, "*In the town where I was born, there was a boy who had a horn. And with that horn he drew the blood, the blood that nourished every bud. Deep in the marrow, a raven pleads; and in the marrow, the raven breeds.*"

I Googled this and some of the other bits I could comprehend, but nothing came up. The voice on the recording was apparently a real original, then.

I thought to search for something else before I lost my taste for the recordings and shut down my computer altogether. An earlier voice had claimed to be that of an "Edward Franklin Ames", reaching out to "Paula". A search for "Edward Franklin Ames" did produce a result, and upon reading it, my confusion—and revulsion—only multiplied.

There was a brief writeup on a website dedicated to historic Detroit. Specifically, Detroit's most notorious *murderers*. Listed among them was one Edward Franklin Ames who, in 1919, had murdered his wife, Paula Ames. His method? While she slept, old Eddy had taken a thick glass bottle and knocked her in the skull until it caved in. After getting locked up for this heinous crime, he'd been murdered by a fellow inmate in 1921.

I tried sourcing the other name I'd heard in the recording, that of "Bradford and Sarah from Annapolis". At first, I hit a wall, but taking a wild guess, it turned out that adding the term "murderer" to the search produced a hit. In 1952, a man by the name of Bradford Cox butchered a woman named Sarah Cantor a few miles from St. John's College in Annapolis. He'd killed her with an axe and had reportedly kept her dismembered body in the trunk of his car, only to be apprehended days later in his search for a new victim. A separate story, also archived on the Annapolis Messenger Journal's website, detailed Cox's suicide in 1958, while serving a life sentence.

I was disgusted by these discoveries, and at the notion that the spirits of such monsters should still linger in the world. And yet I was also curious why the voices of these men—one from far-off Maryland —had turned up in my recording. The article on Ames listed the site of his crime, and it was in a part of town some twenty minutes away from Morgan Road. He hadn't murdered his wife in the house I owned, so why had his voice been captured on tape? Bradford Cox had lived all the way out in Annapolis, Maryland. Why was I hearing *his* voice now, some sixty years after his suicide?

Maybe it was a coincidence.

It's no coincidence, you fool. More likely is that the house you bought is some kind of portal to Hell...

I tried not to think about it, returning to my previous stance of complete neutrality. *Doesn't matter. It's none of your business. Just get the work done. Fix the house, get your TV deal and never look back. This has nothing to do with you.*

Putting out the lights, I dove into bed. Sleep played hard to get, and while courting it my mind went all over the place. As I'd been doing lately when things got tough, I thought about my dad and whether he'd ever had a weird or frightening experience in any of the houses he'd worked in. His reaction would have been much different than mine, surely; he'd have been cool and disinterested. Unflappable. He'd even stared down the specter of death without flinching, and had been absorbed to his dying breath with the work he'd been hired to do.

If you listen to that tape long enough, you'll probably hear the old man make a cameo, I thought, and that brought me the closest thing to a laugh I'd had in hours.

I closed my eyes and tried to enjoy the soft mattress, the quality bed linens beneath me. All I could think about was the house, though.

889 Morgan Road was supposed to be empty right now, but if I focused hard enough I could practically see that frail, white-haired specter sitting in my chair, or pacing between the rooms. I knew she was there, and that she'd probably been there every night now for a

very long time. The dusty air was likely filled with horrible voices, all of them pouring out of that drooping maw of hers.

Irma, I thought. *These are Irma's prime hours. She's up and about, I'm sure of it.* I wasn't sure that the spirit really was of the house's previous tenant, Irma Weiss, but the name seemed to fit and I went with it. It felt better to give her a name, even a wrong one, than to simply refer to her as "the ghost". Doing so made it easier to humanize her.

Once, my dad had given me a piece of advice. It was rare for him to impart gems of wisdom, so I'd paid attention when he'd told me, *"Don't shack up with a woman unless you're married to her. You're asking for trouble if you let a girl into your life like that and you're not serious about it."*

I laughed aloud, thinking of the dead woman who was stalking around my house at that very moment.

Somehow, I didn't think that this was the kind of arrangement my father had been warning me about all those years ago.

TWENTY-FIVE

My alarm went off at six in the morning.

By seven, I was in the van, ordering a McMuffin and a large coffee.

A half hour later, I was at the abandoned graveyard in what was fast-becoming a daily ritual.

It had rained the night before, and little pools of standing water existed in spots where the ground naturally dipped. Being careful to keep my boots dry, I stepped over the puddles and walked along the grassy path, studying the grave markers and trying to read the faded names on them. Spending time in the graveyard daily, the occupants of the tangled plots were getting to be like the acquaintances one usually makes on their daily commute. There was Roger Smith, who'd died in 1922, and then there was Roderick Kemp who'd gone ten years before that, and who'd had a little cherub carved into the top of his tombstone. I felt like I was getting to know the whole crew.

I was eager to get to work, but in no rush to enter the house until the morning sun had had a chance to reach its every nook and cranny. It was while idling in this way that I made an inadvertent discovery among the toppled stones. I'd been preparing to loop back around towards the van and was in the rearmost section of the field when one stone in particular caught my eye. It was the marker's relative small-ness and simplicity that made it stand out among the rest, and taking a closer look I found it to be in rather good condition considering the ruination of those adjacent.

It was a tombstone for an Edward F. Ames, who'd lived between 1888 and 1921.

For a moment, I wasn't sure why the name rang a bell.

And then, startling, I remembered where I'd first heard it.

Heard the *voice* of Edward Franklin Ames, that is.

"*Can you hear me, Paula? This is your Edward—Edward Franklin Ames.*"

Pushing away the overgrown grass, I knelt down beside the grave marker and stared at it a long while, like I expected the name on it to magically change. The man—the infamous Detroit killer—I'd heard on that recording the night before had been buried *here?* Just minutes from the house I'd bought?

Without knowing how many graveyards there had been in the city of Detroit at the time of Ed's burial, I couldn't say whether this was as remarkable a coincidence as it appeared on the surface. I *could* think of something that would help me clear the matter up, however. There'd been another killer who'd identified himself—a Bradford Cox from Annapolis. If Cox was also buried here, then the voices of those two men in the recording couldn't be chalked up to mere coin-cidence.

But, what would it mean?

Had the spirits of these two brutal men gone walking from the cemetery one night and found themselves at home at 889 Morgan Road? And if that wasn't the case, then what rational explanation was there for the voices of these two men—separated by decades and geographical distance—being heard in my house just yesterday?

I knew as I started marching through the rows of graves that I was well beyond a "rational" explanation for what was happening. Reason wasn't even a part of the equation anymore. I'd moved beyond that. The best I could hope for would be to hold onto my sanity for the remainder of the renovation.

For an hour, I plodded around in the muck, looking at tombstone after tombstone.

As it turned out, there was no Bradford Cox in the lot. Some of the stones were too faded to read, but these especially weathered specimens were dated to the pre-war era. Cox had died in '58, and all of the markers from that period were more or less legible.

I wasn't sure whether the lack of such a tombstone was reason for relief. On the one hand, Edward Ames' presence in this graveyard, located a quick walk from my house, could very well have been a coincidence. On the other, I'd just burned a precious hour of my morning trudging through the swampy graveyard, obsessed with finding the resting place of a killer who'd died six decades ago.

Pacing around my van until my boots had begun to dry, I made a promise not to dig too deep into all of this. Something strange—no, singularly *supernatural*—was definitely going on back at the house, but it wasn't my business to meddle with. If I picked up on a real threat to my safety, I'd reevaluate, but no good would come from my wandering graveyards and reading stories about savage murders. For that matter, I had no reason to listen to any mysterious voices I accidentally caught on tape. I had a feeling that listening to such voices— voices that the living had not been intended to hear—was somehow unwholesome, if not entirely reckless. Like the cold water that had seeped into my boots and now left my socks soaked, the voices on that recording had gotten into me, left my nerves in tatters. It would be unwise to let the specters behind those voices live rent-free in my head, and I vowed to cool my jets in the search for answers about the house.

The work had to come first.

If I didn't complete the fix, the whole thing would be for naught.

The producers at the Home Improvement Network didn't care about Ed Ames, or the body I'd found in the wall, or my bad dreams. They just wanted results. If they didn't get them from me, then they would go looking for another handyman to star in their new series—one who could get the job done.

Upon returning to the van, I received a call from a local delivery service. Apparently my kitchen cabinetry was on its way, and would arrive that afternoon between the hours of one and two. I agreed to meet the deliverymen there at that time and then pulled away from the curb. The graveyard soon disappeared from my rearview, but as I got closer to the house the creeping fear I'd picked up amongst the tombstones remained. My unease was such that I decided to go driving through the neighborhood for a time. I felt guilty about it, knowing how much time I'd already wasted that morning, but—thanks to the puddles—I had cold feet both literally and figuratively.

Driving through the time-pummeled streets with the windows down, I saw something I hadn't expected to find.

A living, breathing person.

I was rolling along Telluride Road, roughly a mile and a half from my house, when I saw an old woman in a rocking chair. She was taking in the morning air on the porch of a one-story home, leafing through a newspaper and rocking gently. Her hair, a dark grey coil, fell over one shoulder of a threadbare shawl. The houses along Telluride were mostly in shambles, but this one appeared reasonably well-kept. The grass had been cut recently, and there were curtains in the windows—none of which were broken.

It may not sound like much, but in this part of town that was really out of the ordinary.

She looked up at my van as I passed and spared me a brief smile before looking back at her paper.

I was a minute or two past this anomalous, tenanted house, when I suddenly got the urge to turn back. I'd been looking for justifications all morning to postpone my work, and in this woman, I'd found one. It occurred to me that she had probably lived in the area for some time, and that she was likely to know the neighborhood. Perhaps she could even tell me something about the house I was currently fixing up. It wouldn't have to be a time-waster; if I recorded a little interview with the woman, I could use it in one of my videos. Viewers would love that—capturing more of the local color would make my video series all the more authentic.

I reversed, sped back down Telluride and singled out the house where the woman still sat, reading. Parking across the street behind a rusted-out car that looked as though it had been there through several winters, I went rifling through my bag for my camera. Not wanting to waste time switching batteries and adjusting the tripod, I opted to use my phone to record the video instead. I stepped out of the van.

The woman looked up at me as she heard my footsteps. The smile she gave me was kind, but guarded, and she set her newspaper on her lap so that she might give me her full attention.

"Good morning," I said, putting on a Colgate smile.

She nodded in greeting.

"I'm sorry to bother you, ma'am. My name is Kevin Taylor. I'm new to this area." I paused halfway up her yard, not daring to approach the porch unless I got her say-so. "I'm actually shooting a series of videos about my work here—a kind of documentary—and I was wondering if I could interview you."

The woman blinked at me hard, like the sun was in her eyes. And then her eyes widened in delight. "Interview?" She brought a trembling hand to her hair, smoothing out the silver locks. "I... I've never been interviewed before." Her coy smile told me she wasn't lying, and that she was excited at the prospect.

I took another step towards the porch and grabbed my phone. "My phone here can shoot in high definition and I can clean up the footage further when I go to edit the video. Do you have a few minutes to talk?"

Her nod was endearingly eager, and I started up the steps of her porch. There was a large, empty flower pot across from her, left upside-down, which she offered as a seat. I eased myself down and pulled up the camera app on my phone, sizing up a shot of her where the light was good. Now that I was within arm's reach of the woman,

I was able to inspect her features more closely, and I admit to being somewhat alarmed at her agedness.

To put it indelicately, she looked old as dirt.

Her face was gaunter than it had looked from the van, and her eyes were more sunken. Her hair was thinner from up-close, too. What *really* gave her the look of someone well into their twilight years were the deep creases that marked her skin. From head to toe, her flesh was plagued by tiny furrows; this made her look like a well-worn leather wallet. Her movements were slow—not feeble, necessarily, but noticeably slow, as though the muscles in her body didn't function so well as once.

Before I could begin, she leaned forward slightly, gaze narrowing. "Say... what channel did you say you were with?" She ran bony fingers through her hair, preening further. "I'll have to call my grandkids so that they'll know to tune in!"

I offered a conciliatory smile. "W-Well, it's not actually for TV. I'm a popular user on a website, called VideoTube. I create videos and post them online for people to watch. I have a lot of subscribers who watch my videos—millions of people. Maybe someday I'll get a proper TV show, though."

This all seemed to go over the woman's head. Before she lost interest or asked me to elaborate on the intricacies of VideoTube, I dove into my questions and began recording.

"What's your name, ma'am?" I asked.

"Lillian," she replied, her face brightening. "Lilian Davis."

I decided to banter with her a bit, break the ice. "All right, Lilian. Now, I've been told *never* to ask a woman her age, but would you think me a brute if I asked you how old you are?"

"Not at all," she laughed. "I'm sixty, going on sixty-one this September."

I put on a smile, but this answer of hers took me off-guard. The stereotype that women liked lying about their age might have had some merit, but this woman wasn't fooling anyone when she claimed to be sixty. She looked closer to a hundred. If she was sixty years old, then she'd had a very rough six decades by the looks of it—must have prematurely aged.

Wanting to test her answer further, I asked, "What year were you born?"

"1957," she said. Her reply was effortless, required no suspicious pause. Perhaps she was telling the truth and really was sixty, then. I couldn't wrap my head around such premature aging, but wasn't going to get hung up on it.

"Wonderful. So, I bought a house close by. It's on Morgan Road. Do you know it?"

She nodded. "Oh, yes, I know it."

"How long have you lived in this area?" I chanced. "Do you know it well?"

"About as well as one can know it," replied Lilian, grinning. "I moved into this house in the early 80's, with my husband. He's been deceased some years, God rest his soul."

"I see. So, what was this area like when you first moved in?" I looked around at the other houses along the street, most of them crumbling. "Was it a busy neighborhood? I can't help noticing that most of the houses around here have been abandoned for a long time."

With fondness in her eyes, Lilian leaned back in her rocker and fell into reminisce. "Yes, it was very nice, once. Lots of children. Families. Up until the late eighties or so it was a fine place to live. The houses started emptying out around then; the economy went into a slump, people lost their jobs and some industries pulled out of Detroit altogether, which put a pinch on people. It didn't happen overnight, but now there's hardly anyone living out this way. It's a shame. Some lovely houses hereabouts." She eyed me curiously. "You say you just moved in close to here? A house on Morgan Road?"

"That's right," I said. "889 Morgan Road. Do you know the house?"

She shook her head. "Can't say I do. Why did you move out here, of all places?" she asked. "Not much for a young man to do around these parts. Do you have a family? Any children?"

"No," I replied. "No family. I'm actually fixing up the house I bought. That's what this video series is all about. I do renovations, construction work, and show people how to fix their own houses online."

A silence grew up between us for a time. I felt a bit disappointed that she didn't know my house, that she couldn't tell me anything about its past. When she finally spoke again, it was to share some banal tidbit about the winters. She asked where I was from, and when I told her Florida, she claimed to have some family down there she hadn't seen in some time.

Wanting to steer things back to the subject of my house, I tried another line of questioning. "Were the families who lived out here close-knit? Was it a friendly place?"

"Yes," she replied. "All the kids used to play with each other. We'd have neighborhood parties and garage sales. Things were safe enough for a family back then, too. Didn't have to worry about people running off with your kids, or about suspicious types getting up to no good in empty houses."

"Right. I wonder if you might have been acquainted with the family that used to live in my house. It was owned by a man named Willard Weiss and his wife, Irma. I believe they had a daughter, too. Fiona?" I paused, waited for her to say she hadn't known the Weiss family, or to trot out another chestnut about neighborhood barbecues.

What she did instead threw me.

She chortled. "*Will Weiss?* You bought *his* house? Boy, he was a real character, you know that? And you ended up with his house?" She laughed again, patting the arm of her chair as if for mercy. "Oh, the stories I could tell about that man."

I perked up. "Tell me some more. Who was Willard Weiss?"

"Just about the greatest source of local gossip you could ever hope for," she said. "There's too much to tell. He was something else, that man. Not a *good* man, mind you, but he gave the rest of us something to talk about back when the area was more lived-in. I myself only met him a couple of times—used to see him around town. Friendly enough, but..."

"But...?" I prompted.

"Like I told you, he wasn't a good man. He and that wife of his never got along. Lots of fights. He was stubborn as a mule, but she didn't help things with her howling and screaming. Between you and me, I think she had a screw loose. I don't mind saying that because she's long gone, that woman, but she wasn't a pleasant sort of person even on the best of days. She hardly ever left the house. And when she did, it was only to stand under some tree—the one with white flowers."

"The Callery pear tree?" I asked.

She waved her hand as if she didn't know. "Not sure about what type. Some of the neighbors used to talk about how, on those rare days when she did come out of the house, she'd spend the daylight hours beneath that tree, playing with the flowers and whatnot. The rest of the time..." A flash of color hit her cheeks. "It's probably indecent to air a family's dirty laundry like this," she said, nodding to the camera.

"Not at all," I was quick to answer. "If there's anything too sordid, I'll make sure not to include it. I'm not trying to tarnish anyone's reputation here. I'm mostly recording this for my own benefit, and I'll only use the tamer parts of our talk for the actual video. Sound good?"

With license to spill all the beans she wished, Lilian leaned forward and did so. "Will Weiss, yeah... Like I was saying, he and his wife didn't always get along. I guess shortly before I moved in here with my husband, they had a daughter who went missing. She was pretty much grown—don't remember how old. Would have been in '79 or '80... something like that... when she ran off on 'em."

"Right, Fiona? I understand she was estranged from the family."

Lilian nodded. "Never met her; she was gone by the time I moved in, like I said, but to hear others tell it she'd been a weird girl, seldom-seen. Like her mother, she was almost always kept inside. She didn't socialize with the other kids in the neighborhood, even the ones close to her age. They homeschooled her, I think, and it made her anti-social. Eventually, I guess she got tired of dealing with her mother and she ran off when she came of age. Never sent her folks so much as a Christmas card after that. Just lit out one night. Can't blame her, considering. Her mother was overbearing, too hard to deal with. And I think that Irma had some real issues. I remember a rumor went around that she used to hear voices."

My heart stalled for an instant, and I found myself wanting to ask a load of questions about these supposed "voices" Irma Weiss had heard. What kinds of voices? Were they the same hideous voices I'd been picking up in my recordings, or were we talking about some kind of mental illness here? I resisted the urge to probe further and let Lilian keep talking.

"People used to talk about how Will's daughter would go out to the graveyard—sneak out at night, and just sit there. Will and Irma would complain about that, and would have to drag her home. I think the girl just wanted to be alone, to breathe the fresh air. A lot of kids in the area used to hang around that graveyard, so it's not like there was anything too weird about it. But they'd force her into the car and take her back home every time, screaming and hollering at her like they were going to kill her.

"So, without the daughter at home, I guess Irma just lost it. Poor woman; looking back on it, I really do feel bad for her. She'd been a controlling mother all those years, and when her daughter walked out the door she was left with nothing. Her condition got worse then, and the poor thing looked absolutely ragged. I think she was only in her fifties when she died—must have been almost thirty years ago now. Throughout the 80's, though, her husband, Will, made a real name for himself around town.

"Will was pretty broken up about his daughter flying the coop, and more than once over the years he moved out of the house out there, on Morgan Road. He started drinking, too. While he went out on his adventures, living in a bottle, Irma was left in that house all by herself, and I think that's what eventually killed her. He'd pop by to check on her now and then, but he'd never stay. Always had some place better to be. It was a midlife crisis like so many middle-aged men tend to have, but as always, it isn't the men who suffer, it's their wives. He couldn't be bothered to care for his sick wife, not when he felt he had so much life to live. It's possible, too, that he blamed his wife for their daughter skipping town—Irma always *had* been too controlling. All in all, it's a sad story. A very dysfunctional family."

Sensing that Lilian had nothing more to tell about the Weiss family's history, I thanked her for her time. I could think of no less than a dozen questions to ask someone like her, including: "Why are the shadows in my house so long?" and "Know anyone in town who might have stashed a dead body in my house?" or even, "Is there some place around here where I can get a good deep dish pizza?"

"One last thing," I thought to ask before stopping the recording, "What happened to Willard Weiss? Did he die? Move out of town?"

Lilian frowned as she searched in her memory for an answer. "Well... I wanna say I was still seeing him around town—at the grocery store, or the liquor store—up until a couple of years ago. He wasn't looking well when I last saw him, whenever that was. Barely recognized him. A life of drinking will do that to you." She paused. "Now that you mention it, I had a friend who lived around these parts until just a few years back. She kept in touch with some people, and I think she must have run into Will in town, had a chat with him. She said something about how he wasn't doing so well. I think he was planning to move into assisted living or something like that. Was having trouble getting around, couldn't see so well—you know..." She pointed to herself, grinning, "The kinds of problems us old folk tend to deal with."

"Any idea what assisted living home that might have been?" It was a long shot, but they say you miss all the shots you don't take, so I didn't see the harm in asking.

She shook her head. "No clue. For all I know, he's passed on."

"I see." I reached out and shook her hand. "Thank you for your time, Lilian. And for your candor. If I include any of this footage in my videos, I'll be sure to let you know."

She thanked me and seemed genuinely pleased to have engaged in conversation. Maybe, in a small way, it had felt like the old days for her, gossiping about the goings-on in the neighborhood with old friends. By the time I got to the van, she was already back to her newspaper, the shawl tightened around her shoulders and the rocking chair moving slowly.

Without rewatching the lengthy video I'd just shot, I already knew I wouldn't be using any of it in my uploads. I think, from the very start, I hadn't planned to use such footage to further my work. It had been all about my dogged curiosity from the beginning, and I cursed myself for going back on my promise not to dig deeper into the house's history.

Still, I was glad to have met Lilian. The details she'd given me had painted the house on Morgan Road in a new light—a more sympathetic light. The people who had lived there had not had easy lives. I knew a thing or two about growing up in a broken, dysfunctional family, and so I could empathize with Fiona Weiss.

Aside from quenching my curiosity, there was an added benefit to having learned about the people who'd once lived there: I found my fear surrounding the place had largely abated. I also had some new working theories about the spirit I was seeing in the house.

Irma Weiss had allegedly heard voices. It seemed to me that she'd struggled with some sort of mental illness, and had been largely confined to the house. The spirit of the frail old woman I'd been seeing—the woman who seemed to speak in strange, inhuman voices —was almost certainly Irma. Ignoring the fact that two of the voices I'd heard had identified themselves as notorious killers, the idea that the spirit of a mentally ill woman might wander a place after death, still mimicking the voices that had plagued her in life, was as feasible an explanation as I could muster, given the circumstances. It was heartbreaking, too. Decades after her death, Irma still hadn't found peace.

THE HOUSE OF LONG SHADOWS   163

There was one big detail I wasn't considering, though.

The corpse I'd found.

Was it Irma's? My gut told me that it wasn't.

To my mind, the spirit haunting the place almost certainly belonged to Irma, but the body was someone else's. I thought back to what the detectives had told me—that the body was probably a homeless woman. Since the house had become unoccupied after Irma's death in 1991, the house had sat vacant for nearly three decades. That was a lot of time no one could account for; a lot of time for someone to hide a body in the walls to cover up a murder.

I couldn't totally rule out the possibility that the body in the wall had been Irma's, but provided that she'd had a normal burial, how had her body ended up in the house? Had someone dug up her corpse and stashed it behind the wall as some sort of sick joke? No, it *had* to be someone else's body. There was no other explanation I could come up with that convinced me otherwise. The way things were looking, the woman who'd been walled up had nothing at all to do with the haunting; she'd merely been an easy scapegoat...

But, could I really be sure of *that?* The spirit I was seeing *looked* like the corpse.

My head was starting to hurt.

Maybe the spirit was Irma's.

Or maybe it was actually Jane Doe's.

Who could say?

I made my way to the house and pulled into the drive.

The morning was just about gone and I hadn't even been inside yet. My stomach rumbled and I thought about running out to get some lunch before starting my work, but recalling that HIN was planning to send some reps out to look at the place, I decided to stop playing games. The clock was ticking; if the network came by to look at my progress and found it underwhelming, it was possible they'd lose interest in me, and I wasn't willing to risk that.

I pulled up my VideoTube channel on my phone and was delighted to find that my latest upload—the one I'd done a poor job editing the night before—was actually trending on the front page of the site. It was amassing thousands of views by the minute.

I looked at myself in the rearview. "All right. You've got this. And just think—after this month is over, it'll be surf and turf every night. Get to it!"

With my pep talk out of the way, I started towards the house. Pushing open the front door, I gave the downstairs a tentative scan from the entrance and then, relieved to find nothing terrifying, summoned my sense of humor. "Irma, honey, I'm home!" I called out.

My voice echoed up into the house and my smiled faded.

The resounding silence was just plain unnerving. There was no way around it.

TWENTY-SIX

I nearly missed the deliverymen.

After making a quick run to the store for the concrete backboard I planned to install in the bathroom—something I should have done earlier that morning—I was getting it in place, talking at the camera, when there was a pounding at the front door that scared the daylights out of me.

A pair of big guys met me on the porch, and once I'd signed for the delivery I watched them drag the crates of stained hickory cabinetry into the house. Beefy as these guys were, they had a rough time with it. I gave them each a few bucks' tip for their time and made some casual chit-chat while they caught their breath.

The new kitchen cabinets had been a steal. I'd ordered them from a local company at almost half the usual price. The reason for this steep discount? The color hadn't been popular with consumers and they'd discontinued it. This set of cabinets had been taking up room in their warehouse and they'd marked it way down to hasten its sale. They'd even thrown in free delivery after I name-dropped my Video-Tube channel.

As the delivery truck rattled down the road, I went back up to the bathroom and apologized to the camera for the holdup. An hour later —after some minor difficulties—I got the concrete backboard up, as well as a moisture barrier. The next day, I'd probably start tiling it. I moved the camera into the bathroom proper after that and got some detailed shots of the shower drain. I removed the rusted cap around the top and shined a light into the opening to make sure there were no obvious defects. Previous tests had proven the drain free of leaks, so that was good enough for me. I measured the width of the opening so that I could cut the tiles to a snug fit and filed away the notes for later.

I was done working in the bathroom for the day and brought the camera with me downstairs, where I unveiled the new kitchen cabinets and graciously thanked the supplier. It would take me an afternoon to install them, at least, and I tentatively planned to begin that job when the bathroom was finished.

The rest of the daylight hours were spent tearing up the ugly linoleum in the kitchen. I cut it away in strips with a utility knife, but getting it un-stick in certain places took a good deal more effort than I'd expected. Carrying out armfuls of the flooring to the dumpster, I was surprised, by the final load, to find the sun slipping out of view.

That was my cue to get out of the house.

I'd gone about my work more or less happily that day, not stopping once to think about the house's history or the spectral presence that, even then, was probably watching me from the shadows. But when the daylight began to wane, I found it hard to think of much else, and I hurried to get my things in order for the next day.

Standing proudly in the kitchen, I took a little bow for the camera and stamped on the stripped floors. "Voila!" I said. "What kind of flooring do you guys want to see in this kitchen? New linoleum? Tiles? Hardwood? Let me know in the comments!"

I shut off the camera and broke down the tripod, stuffing both into my duffel. After that, I spent some time chasing dust bunnies with my ShopVac in the kitchen. All the while, the light coming in through the windows steadily dwindled.

I almost lamented the fact that I had to go. I knew the risks in spending time in the house after dark, but I was on such a roll I hardly wanted to quit. If I worked into the night, I could have the bathroom fully tiled in no time. The thought of working ahead appealed greatly, but the dying light made a good argument for clocking out early.

Still, it felt nice to get some work done, to make actual progress. Up to this point, my work in the house had been fraught with all kinds of delays. This was one of the only days I'd really had a good time working. I'd been *in the zone*. As I gathered my keys and phone and prepared to leave, I thought back to my father, and the way he'd worked with perfect focus all those years. The man had never been more at peace, more accessible, than when he'd been hard at work. Was this the kind of joy, the kind of accomplishment he'd felt in his long career of fixing houses? He wasn't around for me to ask anymore, but simply ruminating on the question made me feel a little closer to him.

My night wasn't over yet. When I'd showered and eaten, I'd stop by the hotel bar for drinks while editing the night's video. Then, if I got to bed early enough, I'd—

I paused at the front door, tracking movement in my periphery.

I'd been reaching out for the knob when something had shifted subtly to my left. An old, familiar dread imposed upon my good mood as I eased away from the door and withdrew a step or two into the dining room. It had probably been nothing. I *hoped* it had been nothing, anyway. I glanced around the dining room, then up towards the stairs.

That was when I saw it.

When I saw *her*.

At the sight of the phantom, I clutched my keys so hard that they dug into my palm.

A thin, pale figure dressed in a milky garb stood at the very top of the stairs, long tendrils of white hair fluttering in the draft like knots of cobwebs. She had her back to me, but I could still feel her eyes fixed on me as though they were embedded somewhere nearby. It was like the walls themselves were a part of her sensory network.

It appeared as though she'd paused in her ascent of the stairs. One thin, veiny leg was perched on the uppermost step; the other was frozen on the step beneath it. She stood completely still there, like she'd been caught in the act of something—or like a dangerous animal basking in the scrutiny of an onlooker before lashing out.

I was paralyzed, my mouth going dry and my knees buckling.

To an onlooker, it would have seemed like an easy thing to simply walk out that front door, to leave the house altogether. There was enough awareness in my fright-stalled mind to further complicate my situation however, and that's exactly what I did when I chose not to escape, but made an attempt at dialogue instead.

"W-Who are you?" I asked, my voice breaking like a teenager's.

The woman on the stairs didn't move a muscle. As though reality itself had glitched out, she remained cemented there.

Several moments passed before I found my voice again, asking, "Are you... are you the ghost of Irma Weiss? Tell me, who are you?"

The reply came not from the figure atop the stairs, but from elsewhere in the house—the kitchen, from the sounds of it. As though the house's passageways were mere extensions of her throat, the woman croaked in a bone-chilling voice, "*I am a raven that seeks to nest in your skin.*"

Dumb, mammalian conditioning required me to trace the source of the voice to the kitchen with my sight. When I saw no one there, I glanced back to the top of the stairs, where the woman—hitherto frozen like a statue—was now moving. With quick, rigid steps, she was coming down the stairs.

Backwards.

Bony hands against the wall and bannister, the woman kept her back to me and rapidly descended. Watching her jerking movements was like watching footage of someone walking on a VHS tape, but in reverse.

That was enough to get my legs working, and without hesitation I reached behind me and grasped the doorknob. At roughly the same moment the specter reached the foot of the stairs, her white hair swaying and the edges of her leathern face entering into view, I rushed outside and slammed the door shut behind me. Lunging out into the yard from the porch, I failed my landing and gave my ankle a solid twist.

I had to crawl through the grass to get to the van.

Even as I fled, I could hear the fleshy smacks of her white hands against the kitchen window. In the corner of my eye, I glimpsed her sinkhole of a mouth falling open, and from inside the house there erupted a racket like the roar of a crowd.

The pain in my ankle didn't really get to me until I was a mile down the road and the initial shock had passed. I could barely feel the accelerator beneath my swelling foot, and I nearly ran into a slow-moving bus. I grappled against throatfuls of bile and white-knuckled the wheel until I managed to double-park in the hotel lot.

When I finally went into the hotel, I didn't head straight for my room. I paid the bar a visit, asking the bartender for a bag of ice I could throw on my pulsing ankle.

I also asked him for as many high proof drinks as he could legally sell me.

TWENTY-SEVEN

Ever been asked a stupid question by a buddy along the lines of: "Would you eat a bucket of live cockroaches for a million bucks?"

I was faced with that kind of scenario, and it went something like: "Would you finish renovating a house occupied by a terrifying phantom in the hopes of landing a TV show when all is said and done?"

Icing my ankle in my hotel room, I was struggling to decide.

Do you really want this? How badly? What risks are you willing to accept, and what are your lines in the sand?

I returned to this question off and on while absentmindedly editing video on my laptop. The result was going to be embarrassingly shoddy, but I made sure to include a shot of my red, swollen ankle at the tail end to garner some sympathy and understanding in case the next upload ended up a little late. I told the viewers that I'd tripped on my way down the stairs. They never would have believed the truth.

Already some hours into the night, I hadn't been able to yank my thoughts free from the house's jaws. That apparition had me in her clutches. I couldn't look outside the window in my room without seeing long shadows creeping along the nearby lot. There was something mocking and nefarious about the way passersby in the hallway conversed; I knew that I was only imagining it, but their voices seemed either too deep or too faint to be properly human, and I felt like they were all talking about *me* as they passed by the door.

For all my terror, for all the fiery pain in my ankle whenever I hobbled around the room, I still wanted to woo the people at the Home Improvement Network. Call me stupid—I wouldn't disagree with you—but with so little keeping me from the opportunity of a lifetime, I was determined to see this project through.

Somehow.

I hadn't figured out the "how" yet.

My first thought was to call a priest to bless the house. If I could get a kindly old priest to splash some holy water around the premises, then perhaps Irma would get the hint and leave. Over time—and as I tried deciding on which priest to call from the diocese of Detroit—I grew impatient and I started considering something faster.

What if I went back to the house and talked things out with its spectral tenant? Her spirit was hanging around for reasons unbeknownst to me, but if I could zero in on them, then maybe I could ease her into the next life and off my property. This struck me as the most sensible thing, save for one vital detail.

The ghost of Irma Weiss was not especially talkative.

When asked, "Who are you?" the ghost had replied, "*I am a raven that seeks to nest in your skin.*" The very thought of that exchange made my guts writhe. Whether this was meant to be taken as a literal warning of possession, or as some kind of darkly poetic metaphor, I was unsure. Any further dealings with the house and its resident spirit would require a good deal of caution, though—more than I'd previously realized.

There'd been that note, too—her vandalizing of the email I'd posted on the living room wall. "WE WANT YOU", it had read.

I still wasn't sure how many spirits I was dealing with here, but having encountered the presumed ring-leader of this haunting operation, I had reason to suspect that this note, like the raven comment, was meant as a threat. The spirit in that house wanted me. *Why*, or *what* it hoped to do with me was unclear.

What would Irma have done if she'd caught up to me in the house? I'd asked myself before if she was able to harm me, but hadn't been able to answer the question definitively. I *still* couldn't answer it, but recalling the way she'd pinched me in the arm I had to concede that she was capable of certain physical acts.

Perhaps I, too, could physically interact with *her*.

If this situation could be dealt with by punching her in the head, I'd let it rip. Of course, it wasn't going to be that easy, and I suspected that Irma could throw some haymakers of her own if she so wished. Direct confrontation was unwise.

Hopeful that I could source some aid elsewhere, I busied myself with research. There were a few people who could potentially help me with this matter; the two living members of the Weiss family. If Willard Weiss and his estranged daughter, Fiona, still lived—and I *hoped* that they did—then they were among the only people on Earth who could shine some light on what was happening back at the house. I began searching for the two of them in earnest.

I started with Irma's daughter, Fiona. According to Lilian on Telluride Road, Fiona Weiss had left home sometime around 1980 and had never spoken to her parents again. I Googled the name, and there were some hits, but none pertained to the Fiona I was looking for.

I *did* find several pages listing the lyrics to artist Fiona Apple's 1996 hit, "Criminal", however.

The only search result that actually dealt with Fiona Weiss was Irma's obituary, dated to 1991. I'd suspected before that Fiona had gone on to live under an assumed name, probably so that her parents wouldn't be able to track her down, and I felt more certain now that this was the case.

That left only the family patriarch, Willard Weiss. I'd already tried finding his contact information online, and had only dug up outdated phone numbers. Lillian had shared with me a rumor that Mr. Weiss had been set to enter assisted living, and I figured that was my best lead. I Googled "Detroit assisted living facility" and prepared to make a list of phone numbers. I'd call each one and ask to be connected to Willard Weiss, pretending to be some long-lost nephew or something. I mean, how many such facilities could there be in the metro Detroit area?

Turned out there were more than fifty.

"You've got to be kidding me…"

It was possible that Willard was still alive, and that he was a patient at one of these facilities, but it was going to be difficult to track him down with so many to sift through. Moreover, if he was on some kind of no-call list for privacy reasons, it was possible I'd never get anywhere even if I *did* call all fifty on the list.

I'd emptied out a small cooler and filled it with ice from the ice machine down the hall. Plunging my bare foot into it and cooling my ankle, I racked my brain for another angle. Right now, I was alone in all of this. I had no one I could look to for assistance. My only desire was to see this renovation through to the end so that I could possibly land a TV gig. Was that too much to ask? When the work was done, Irma could keep the house for all I cared. *What if I went back there and bargained with her? 'Say, Irma, if you let me finish this video series, I'll surrender the house—fully renovated. You'll be able to shower in between all of the spooky stuff you like to do, even wash dishes, how does that sound?'*

Another hour ticked by as I remained mired in indecision. I felt an overwhelming urge to hit up the bar downstairs before it closed, to drown myself in liquor and call the whole project off.

I also thought about reaching out to Mona Neeb and explaining myself. I wouldn't tell her *exactly* what was going on, but could tell her that the house was actually filled with deadly mold, or that I'd been attacked by local gang members who insisted on turning the house into a meth lab, and that I'd have to pick another house to work on—a house far, far away from this one.

Would she—and the producers at HIN—be understanding if I backed out of the project?

Maybe.

Maybe wasn't good enough, though. The more I thought about it, the less I wanted to risk it. The folks at the network could just as easily label me a quitter and lose interest.

Hours of inaction saw me entertaining the avenue I most feared. Perhaps, I thought, I could go back to the house and try reasoning with Irma. It was a terrifying prospect, not to mention a reckless one, but if I could somehow figure out what the spirit wanted from me, then perhaps I could forge a diplomatic solution to the haunting.

But how would I protect myself? If I entered the house and she came after me again, how could I stay safe long enough to escape? My ankle was in no shape for running.

She touched you, once, which means she can interact with the physical world. At least, to some degree. There were plenty of blunt tools in the house. If diplomacy failed me, I could take a wrench to her. It was the only thing I hadn't tried yet. If nothing else, I hoped that swinging a wrench around would give me enough time to escape the house if talks went south.

It wasn't much of a plan, but I stood up and stepped into my boots.

And then I sat back down, because I realized how stupid it was.

Until the sun was up, there was no way I was going to explore that house on my own. I needed someone to come with me. Having no friends in the area, no one I could lean on at such an hour, I returned to my previous solution, that of getting a priest involved. I punched some search terms into my browser and went looking for a Catholic priest who could accompany me to the house for a blessing. It was late—closing in on midnight—but my distress was sufficient to compel me to call.

I called a few numbers and ended up hitting voicemail boxes. There was one voicemail recording, though—that of the St. Thomas Aquinas rectory in downtown Detroit—that offered a special number for *urgent* calls. The recording explained that a priest was always on duty for pressing matters, such as the Anointing of the Sick.

I wasn't sure if the blessing of haunted houses fell under the umbrella of "urgent spiritual matters", but I dialed anyway.

Three rings later, a man answered. "This is Father Kaspar."

I began by apologizing profusely for the lateness of my call, and it wasn't until repeated assurances that it was "no problem" that I finally explained my reasons for disturbing him. "Father, my name is Kevin Taylor. I'm in a bit of a bind. I hope you won't think me crazy, or feel like I'm wasting your time, however I've been having numerous supernatural experiences in this home I'm working on. It's getting to the point where I can't set foot in there anymore, and I'm in need of some help. Could you bless the house for me? Maybe sanctify the place and urge out any spirits that linger there?"

The priest did not mock, and he didn't appear to need convincing that otherworldly entities sometimes meddled in human affairs, however he *did* want to know why this was so urgent that I had to call him at quarter to midnight. "I'd be happy to come by and bless the house. Why don't we arrange something later on this week? I can call you tomorrow and depending on my schedule, I'd—"

"I know I'm asking a lot, but this is a matter of grave importance, Father. You see, I'm on a strict deadline to get this house renovated and I can't afford to put off my work. I no longer feel as though I can enter the house safely, however. Truly, I believe that whatever is haunting that house presents a real threat to my safety. I wouldn't normally insist on something like this, but I'm set to return there in the morning to continue work. If there's any way you could meet me there tonight, I'd appreciate it immensely." I paused. "Again, I'm sorry for the hour. I'd be happy to compensate you for your time, or buy you a drink. Under the circumstances, I just don't know who else I can turn to, Father."

Father Kaspar sighed and gave a grunt of assent. "I'm actually on my way back to the rectory right now. I just finished visiting a parishioner of mine in the hospital, so I'm already on the road. If you give me a few minutes to gather my things back at the rectory, I could meet you at the house in..." He mulled it over. "If you're sure this can't wait, I could be there within a half hour. Maybe forty-five minutes, depending on where the house is at."

My heart swelled with relief. "It's at 889 Morgan Road," I explained. I gave him a description of various landmarks near the house and he seemed confident that he could find it. "I appreciate this, Father. Thank you."

"No problem," replied the priest. "I'll meet you there by 12:30. Please, don't be late."

"Of course. I'll be waiting in the drive, in my van."

"All right. See you then." Father Kaspar hung up and I immediately pocketed my phone. Putting on a jacket and lacing up my boots, I hobbled out of the hotel room and to the van.

It was time to settle the matter.

Hope you're ready, Irma, because this time I'm not coming alone.

TWENTY-EIGHT

I made the drive quickly, running all of the yellow lights and some of the pink ones. Fifteen minutes later I was on Morgan Road, driving up and down the street and looking out for the priest. More than once, I passed the house. The lights in the lower story were still going, and from a distance, with its major flaws hidden by darkness, it almost looked *cozy*. I wondered if Father Kaspar would show up and be disappointed at its lack of conspicuous spookiness.

A few minutes past midnight, I finally eased into the driveway, waiting there with the doors locked and engine running. I left the brights on, too, painting the whole front of the property in brilliant light.

I draped my arms over the steering wheel and waited.

And *waited*.

Now and then I peeked at the rearview, hoping that the priest's headlights would appear further down the road, but 12:30 came and went with no sign of him. I was in no position to complain about his tardiness after calling him out so late at night, and if for some reason he decided not to show up at all, I knew that I wouldn't be able to blame him. My request to meet here at this hour had been more than a little unreasonable. Still, perplexed by his lateness, I reminded myself that the tangle of roads in this part of town could be hard to navigate with so many of the streetlights out, and I resolved to give him more time before freaking out.

Several minutes ticked by. I watched them pass on the clock like grains of sand in an hourglass.

Had he really gotten lost? Decided not to show up after all? I left my phone sitting on the dash, expecting a call that never came. They say a watched pot never boils; was I psychically warding off the priest's calls by staring at the phone?

It doesn't work that way, you imbecile.

Even though I was surrounded by tons of metal, I didn't feel secure in the van. Night had fallen hard over the property, and it occurred to me that this was the first time I'd really been *outside* the house after dark for a prolonged period. Usually, I marveled at the dense night from within the house, and without the benefit of bright headlights. Now, I was on the outside, looking in. It didn't feel right.

The yard felt alive. Blades of grass shifted in the wind, each of them looking like tiny fingers making a come-hither motion. Pressing my head against the window, I watched the blades bend then ease back into an upright position, bend and then straighten, as if to beckon me towards the house. There was something hypnotic about it.

When next I looked towards the house, I noticed an intermittent dimming of the lights in the windows. The light waned briefly, then brightened in perfect time with the susurrations of the breeze. Sinking into my seat, into the dark recesses of the van's cabin, it was like looking across a small body of water at a beachside property. The wax and wane of the yellow light was something akin to the turn of a lighthouse beacon, or else a bit of morse code intended by the occupants to reach someone situated on the opposite shore. The signal it was sending me seemed to indicate a message of "all clear".

The house was calling out to me, in a way.

Flying insects kamikaze'd against the windshield as I slumped in the driver's seat, eyes burning with a sudden desire for sleep. I'd been up since early that morning and hadn't planned to stay up this late. It was only the undercurrent of anxiety, and the need to keep searching for the priest's headlights, that repelled the Sandman whenever my head got too heavy. When this was finally over with, I'd return to the hotel and sleep well into the morning. I wouldn't even bother setting an alarm.

The fuel gauge appeared to tick down a notch as the minutes went by. It was 12:45 now, and there'd still been no sign of any other car. *It's no big deal,* I reiterated. *He's running a little late. So what?*

When 1 AM threatened to rear its head, I had to think long and hard about calling him—not out of impatience, but worry. *What if something happened to him? What if he isn't coming over after all?*

Finally, at ten after one, I broke down and called Father Kaspar.

It rang three, four times, and then went to voicemail.

OK, I told myself, *he doesn't like talking on the phone while driving. No big deal.*

Increasingly, I felt the desire to exit the vehicle. My fatigue was getting to be too much, and unless I got some air I was bound to nod off in the driver's seat. My legs were sore, and my back started to act up, the seat positions leaving much to be desired.

The only thing holding me back was a small voice in my head. Each time I went to reach for the car door, it spoke up. *I wouldn't do that if I were you. If you leave the car, you're going to be out in the open. That's just what the thing in the house wants.*

I chose to ignore that voice.

I powered down the van and stepped out to take a leak in the grass. I promised myself I'd only be outside for a few minutes—just long enough to wake myself up. Marching up and down the driveway, hoping that the priest was *just moments* from arriving, I stretched my legs and batted away a number of big, dive-bombing beetles that zipped through the air near my head. *There are some bugs, but this isn't so bad, is it? You're safe out here until Father Kaspar arrives.*

Without the headlights on, the property was miserably dark. To ameliorate the dimness I made frequent trips towards the porch, repeatedly setting off the motion-activated light. Every time the LEDs flashed on, I panned across the entire yard and sighed with relief at my solitude. *See? There's nothing out here. Irma's inside the house. You have nothing to worry about.*

What I was really trying to do as I marched in circles was muster the nerve to go in alone.

It was getting close to 1:30—a whole hour past the planned meeting time. I was tired of feeling helpless in the face of this threat, and started considering my options in dealing with it if the priest didn't show. On top of all that, I was just *plain tired*. The night air wasn't refreshing me like I'd hoped it would, and more than once, while spacing out, I felt dead on my feet. Recalling that I'd left the air mattress in the living room, I toyed with the idea of slipping inside for a brief power nap. I could inflate the thing and lay down for a minute. Just until the priest arrived. In fact, I didn't even have to sleep—merely laying down would feel wonderful.

The bugs were getting to me. A large moth drifted over from a thicket of tall grass and nearly used my shirt sleeve as an air strip. I batted it back into the yard with disgust and stood on the porch's lowest step. There, a red, buzzing beetle the size of a dime found its way into my hair. Clawing it out and leaving my greasy hair a mess, I stomped on the pest and retreated further onto the porch.

But the insects kept coming, and I noticed something in common between their flight paths. They were coming towards me because I stood directly in the path of their target—the house. The bugs should have been drawn to the light, but I watched as several fluttered past the glowing LEDs only to land upon the exterior walls, or the front door. Observing this, I couldn't help feeling that there was some subtle migration taking place, and that I was the only animal in all of creation that hadn't gotten the memo. If I didn't follow the insects to the house, I'd be left behind completely.

I eyed the van and considered returning to the driver's seat, but was immediately repelled by the thought of confining myself. With every passing moment, the siren call of the air mattress became harder to ignore. My ankle was beginning to throb and I wanted to take off my boots for a spell.

Would it be so bad to go inside on your own?

Time and weariness went a long way towards eroding the terror I'd felt earlier that evening. I'd spent hours looking for ways to put a stop to this haunting, or at least to rationalize it. At that moment, I was just tired enough—and maybe still buzzed enough from my trip to the bar—to feel dissociated from it all. Ghosts began feeling very much like abstractions in the face of my very real ankle pains and growing sleepiness. My courage was further goosed by the fact that, in all the nights I'd slept in the house, nothing bad had really happened to me. Irma had never actually hurt me—this sore ankle was my own doing.

Perhaps I'd pop inside for a second to rest my ankle. Where was the harm in a quick break? I absolutely wouldn't sleep, of course. I'd stay alert, perhaps snack on some of the granola bars I'd left behind. Yes, suddenly I was feeling hungry, and the granola bars sounded like the greatest treat on the planet. From one of the windows I'd keep a lookout for Father Kaspar—who, surely, was just having a lot of trouble finding the place. At the first sign of trouble, at the first disembodied voice, I'd lace up my boots and get out of there.

That small voice in my head had completely changed its tone. It seemed to say, *Come on in! Pull up a chair! Make yourself comfortable! A man should be able to relax in his own house! Welcome home, Kevin!*

Having paced around for an hour, I hadn't seen anything from the outside to ward me off. The house was still. The resident ghost, once so fond of looking out the windows, hadn't made a single appearance yet. Close as I was to the door, I'd heard no demonic mumblings.

To a first-time visitor, the house would have looked like any other work in progress. It would've seemed innocent, inviting.

I should have known better, but the closer I got to the door, the louder that voice in my head cheered me on. *YES! COME ON IN, KEVIN! REST THOSE TIRED FEET! JUST OPEN THAT DOOR AND LAY DOWN FOR A SPELL!*

I wondered if maybe the ghost was gone for the night. "Maybe Irma went out to the club," I said with a snicker. "There's still time before last call, I guess."

A cold wind left the flowers on the Callery pear rustling noisily, and it carried my little remark off into the distance, too. I instantly regretted saying anything and hoped that no one—either within the house or lurking outside it, in the shadow—would hear me.

It was with an unusual torpor that I stepped away from the door. I felt leashed, reeled in, and the fisherman on the other side of the front door wasn't keen on giving me too much line. The air was thinning and I looked anxiously to the van, felt my keys in my pocket.

Another moth drifted by. The grass took a bow as if to motion me towards the door.

Swept up in the current, the fisherman began to crank the reel, and I lost my fight.

I limped back to the porch, turning to survey the road.

No headlights. No priest.

With withering hesitance, I peered in through the dining room window. Nothing stirred.

Another nervous glance at the road.

Still no sign of the priest.

I pressed a hand to the door.

COME INSIDE, KEVIN! COME INSIDE, KEVIN! COME INSIDE, KEVIN!

I turned the knob. It was warm, as though it had been held within another palm just moments prior.

YES YES YES YES COME IN COME IN COME IN

I pushed open the door.

The rustling of the Callery pear sounded like a mess of thunderous applause. All of nature was delighted at my return; I was getting a standing ovation for reentering the house!

I stepped through the threshold, the familiar scent of dust and construction striking me as comfortable, even sweet. My pulse quickened as I beheld the downstairs of my home from the doorway.

You're home! I thought with a flash of rapturous joy.

I eased the door shut with my back.

At hearing the mechanism click, my pulse shot up further. The joy had been fleeting, though. The sound of the door closing had cancelled my inner parade and now something else was surfacing. It clawed its way through my guts, played hopscotch on my nerve endings.

Fear.

I felt fear because I understood where I was—where I *really* was.

It dawned on me all at once.

"You've been fooled."

TWENTY-NINE

The house possessed all the stillness of a crypt, and the dust-riddled air—so sweet to my nostrils only a moment ago—now smelled every bit as rarified.

Had I been of sounder mind then, and not bolted to the floor by terror, I might have done the sensible thing and gone right back out the door. Instead, I stayed put, waiting for something in the scenery to change and subsequently confirm my worst fears. I was held back, too, by a sinking and irrational dread that I might turn around only to find the door gone. The dining room, the stairwell, the living room, were all painted in soft light from the fixtures I'd left aglow, and in each of them I watched closely for the unseen painter to make some subtle mark in the canvas that would herald a nightmare.

Calm was in short supply, but as I stood there I rewound my thoughts and went looking for reasons not to panic.

Father Kaspar will be by soon.

Irma hasn't managed to hurt you—probably because she can't. You aren't in any danger.

Maybe the ghost just wants to talk.

Nothing emerged as I stood there, struggling to cram breath into my lungs. My initial fright waned sufficiently that I took some hobbling steps towards the living room, all while thinking up other pleasing fictions.

Maybe the ghost isn't in—maybe Irma's spirit isn't here anymore.

Maybe... maybe there never was a ghost at all, and you imagined everything.

What if there's something wrong with you, Kevin? What if you've been hallucinating?

I bumped into a toolbox and a mess of odds and ends spilled across the floor. I didn't bother picking them up, but as I continued towards the chair in the living room, one item in the bottom of said box captured my attention. A clawfoot hammer. I picked the thing up; it felt right in my hand. However useless a weapon might be against the force that filled this house, I was comforted by its weight in my palm. I focused on the tool's heft and my feelings of helplessness withdrew somewhat.

In my hotel room, I'd considered all kinds of ways I might communicate with the spirit—provided, of course, that she wished to talk in the first place. Feeling I had nothing to lose as I waited for the priest, I dragged my pounding foot across the living room, turned the folding chair so that it faced the front door, and sat down.

I was going to try diplomacy.

"H-Hello," I squeaked, setting the hammer down at my feet.

Upstairs, the floors could be heard to settle. Old timber popped and groaned as the building braced against the wind. It was a very normal kind of sound, and there should have been nothing unsettling about it whatsoever. But there *was*. Hearing the house vocalize in that way, I couldn't shake the impression that it had done so in reply to my salutation. By using my voice in this place, perhaps I'd attracted the attention of whatever forces prowled behind the scenes. I'd chummed the water. I could sense dark eyes locked on me, dissecting me.

"I... I want to talk," I said, jaw clenching tightly as the words left my lips. It wasn't true; I didn't want to talk to the thing in this house. I wanted to pretend it didn't exist. But it was listening now, I was sure of it, and since I had its ear, there was nothing to do but state my case. Whether the phantom could be swayed from its terrifying course was another matter, but I spoke as earnestly as I could under the circumstances. "I want to know who you are. I've been seeing you all around the property for awhile now, and it seems you've been trying to get my attention. If there's something you want, I *might* be able to help you. Want to talk about it? If you're a spirit that's stuck here, maybe I can help you move on..." I trailed off, annoyed by my own rambling.

There was movement across the floor. A long, ebon shadow that was *not* my own spilled out across the living room. Studying its length and watching its spread with a tightening of my shoulders, I realized that the person casting it stood a mere foot from the back of my chair. My sighting of the shadow coincided with a feeling of great pressure, as of someone leaning over me, bearing down on me with an intense stare.

She's right behind you, I realized.

I wanted to reach for the hammer, but I didn't budge. I folded inward the way a mouse might cower in the shadow of a looming snake. In the shadow I could see the phantom's sickly limbs, her tangles of hair. The apparition brought with it a repugnant scent, something like the tang of warm earth in a spot where an animal has been buried—and has only just begun to decompose.

She could have touched me. She could have responded to my questions in her multitude of voices. Instead, she just lingered. My gaze slipped along a track with only three stops; the hammer on the floor, the shadow of the horror that stood behind me, and the front door.

Finally, the shadow withdrew. I took this as a gesture of goodwill —she'd detected my discomfort and was giving me space. Thankful that the specter wasn't planning on lashing out, I found the boldness to ask, "Are you the g-ghost of Irma Weiss?"

The first loud snap made my heart palpitate.

The second drew my gaze to the right, into the kitchen.

By the third, I knew where the snapping was coming from, and I grasped the legs of the chair beneath me till my joints locked up.

The mouse traps. I'd set a number of mouse traps along the baseboards in the kitchen, and they were all being set off now. One by one. A small, white hand emerged from behind one of the tall boxes of new cabinetry, and three of its skeletal fingers wore the sprung wooden traps around the knuckles. Another hand reached for the top of the box, and then the figure raised itself up from the floor and stood to full height.

White hair obscured most of the withered face, but I could make out the empty sockets that lived behind the veil. The cavernous hollows where eyes had once been widened and narrowed expressively. The sockets puckered like throbbing wounds, and from those depths, looking like so many filaments of ground beef streaming out of an extruder, came masses of red, thrashing worms. I heard individual worms strike the ground with a fleshy smack as still others reared their heads.

Up to that moment, the phantom's lips had been shut, but as it reached over the box, a black maw came into view. Within that gullet—mouth opened so wide that the chin dragged against the top of the box the specter leaned upon—were small, trembling orbs, like pustules sprouting from the tissues of the mouth and throat. I saw those orbs for what they really were as the thing crawled over the box and found sound footing on the stripped floors of the kitchen.

They were eyes; countless, staring eyes.

There was an almost deafening outpouring of voices. They issued not from the apparition's mouth, but from the air all around me. Inarticulate shouts, curses and hissing laughs erupted from every direction. The upstairs boomed with voices and, soon thereafter, pounding footfalls entered into the mix. Trembling in my seat, I suddenly felt myself at the center of a very crowded room. The air was thick with presence, and the hairs on my arms registered movement as unseen lodgers brushed past.

The white-haired monstrosity grew nearer. Her steps were plagued by erratic jerks in the upper body, as though the limbs were being yanked in different directions; yet somehow, progress was still made, and within moments I knew she would be upon me.

This was the closest look I'd ever gotten at the specter, and as she advanced I realized, with a roiling in the pit of my stomach, that my feeble attempts at outreach had been insanely misguided. Without thinking, I fell to the floor and scrambled for the hammer, which I then threw as hard as I could. The tool whipped past her, taking a few strands of white hair with it as it came to rest in the living room wall. From all around came the shouts and murmurs of an invisible crowd, and I felt the jostling of unseen hands as I prepared to run.

Rising to my feet, I set out for the front door.

I hadn't taken two full steps before I encountered a problem, however.

Though I couldn't see them, the room was packed with people. They moved and shoved and grabbed like the members of a proper mob, and my attempts to rush past them were just as fruitful.

A deep voice, scarcely recognizable as human, chanted, "*LET ME IN, LET ME IN, LET ME IN,*" from close-by.

From what my eyes told me was open space, a sequence of piercing wails rang out.

I felt an elbow in my ribcage.

A cold hand pinched my cheek.

The floors beneath my feet rattled and strained as though a hundred men were standing upon them.

All the while, the phantom continued its pursuit.

The mouse traps tumbled from the specter's outstretched hand, a shower of red worms lurching out after them. Convulsing as though pained, and only capable of a wet, labored gasping, the figure shuffled towards me briskly, unfazed by the other presences in the room.

Backing away as quickly as I could through the packed space, I sought out an opening in the crowd, which led to my bolting from the living room altogether in a search for cover.

My first instinct had been to run towards the front door, or to one of the windows, but the density of unseen bodies blocking the way to the exits was immense, and I was forced to flee further into the house, towards the stairwell. To do otherwise would have allowed the specter to catch up to me. She followed at my heels, moving as quickly as her toothpick-thin legs would allow, mouth agape. The hundreds of eyes studding the inside of that mouth all stared unflinchingly at me, and with seeming delight, and I understood then that this white-haired woman was being commandeered by the scores of eyes within her. All those eyes shifted independently of each other, but were united by the same mind, the same cause. They wanted *me*. The woman was merely a host—an animal given over to the control of parasites. The machinery of her body had been rearranged for the benefit of those interlopers. She was not in control of those stamping feet, those searching hands. The parasites were.

A keening scream burst from the upstairs as I clawed my way along the bannister. I was shouldered and kicked by others on the stairs, felt unseen fingernails dig into my flesh. The blood they drew was real; rivulets of red cascaded down my forearm and dripped from my fingers as I fell upon the landing. Sighting a small toolbox I'd left near the top of the stairs, I took hold of its handle and cast it at the oncoming nightmare. The box clattered against the wall, showering the apparition in tools, but this didn't slow it down a jot. I kicked against the floor and gained my feet, racing down the hall and bursting through the door of the rearmost bedroom.

The air in this room was different, and from the moment I ran inside and slammed the door behind me, I felt reasonably sure that I was alone. The pushing and prodding of foreign bodies ceased here, and for the first time in minutes I was able to draw a proper breath. The room was dark, lit solely by the paltry moonlight coming in from the cracked window. Leaning against the door, I felt a savage pounding on its other side, as if ten men were trying their hardest to kick it down. I don't know how I managed to hold it closed, but I poured everything I had into the effort, and it held.

There'd been a thin band of light coming in through the underside of the door from the hallway, but as I defended against the violent blows, I saw it suddenly snuffed out, and I knew then that the house had lost power.

The blows eventually ceased, as did the footsteps and voices. Even so, they never completely cut out—attempts to enter the room were simply quieter. Stomping was replaced by quiet creeping along the hall; unseen hands took turns fiddling with the doorknob. Demonic yells became furtive snickers and pleading whispers. "*Let me inside. Let me inside, won't you please?*"

I don't know how I managed to keep them out of the room as long as I did, or what kept them from materializing within the room, through the walls, like ghosts in stories. But for awhile, things were quiet, and I came to feel something akin to hope—hope that I would escape the house. I wouldn't dare leave the room until morning—only when the sun was out, and its light had reached every corner of the place, would I be safe. I didn't know this for certain, of course, but it felt right, and I reckoned that a safe escape would be possible in five hours if only I could remain strong and repel the specter until then. I would have jumped from the window, but I sincerely doubted that I could make it to the yard without breaking a leg—or worse.

Somehow, I'd have to stay in this room until daylight. That was my only option.

I stood against the door in that dark room, trembling. The moonlight was so watery thin that I could hardly make out anything in my shadowed surroundings. There was a closet somewhere to my right, but I could only see it when the moonlight grew strong and was unimpeded by clouds. It felt like I was in a holding cell. There was nothing to do, nothing to see. One could only sit and await judgement.

My standing in this dark room, frightened out of my wits, reminded me of the time my mother had left me locked in my bedroom with the lights out. Decades had gone by, but here I was, still the same, scared child. I was shivering in the dark just like I had that night, afraid that something would get me.

I called out to my father, knowing all the while that no good would come of it. No good had come from doing so in my childhood years, either. I yearned to leave the house, and would happily forfeit any fame and fortune that might have come with renovating it. I was concerned only with my life, and felt a stinging regret for having played with fire. I'd been so obsessed with finishing the job and landing an offer from the people at the network that I'd chosen to ignore all the warning signs. I'd put the possibility of success ahead of my wellbeing, and now I was paying the price.

You deserve this, I thought.

The house remained still for a time, and I slumped onto the floor, keeping my back pressed against the door. I hoped that Father Kaspar would make a sudden appearance and clear out the evil that now ran riot over the property. It was a comforting mental image, if nothing else.

Then, there was a metallic sound. *Ca-clink.* Startled by the noise, I tried to place it, wondering what the apparition was up to. It had almost sounded like a lock being thrown—a deadbolt. Unable to figure out what I'd heard, I'd been about to write off the sound completely when I recalled what room I was in.

This was the master bedroom. On previous studies of the upstairs, I'd found peculiar locks on two of the bedroom doors. This one had a lock on its exterior—a lock, I'd fancied, that had been put in place to keep someone in the room. I'd thought it strange, had puzzled over its purpose, then.

Now, *I* was the one locked inside.

I gave the knob a tentative pull.

It didn't budge.

I was going to have to kick the door down if I wanted to get back into the hall. Either that, or I'd have to wait for the warden...

While tampering with the door and testing the lock, I heard a voice from nearby. It was not, as I first thought, coming from the other side of the bedroom door, the hallway. The voice, croaking and infernal, crooned from the other side of the unseen closet door, to my right.

Probably, the presence had been in the closet the entire time, but had chosen to wait before announcing itself. It had waited until I'd calmed somewhat, till I'd had some time to foster hope. Now that I knew I was locked in and my despair was soaring, it was ready to make itself known.

It spoke. *"In the town where I was born, there was a boy who had a horn. And with that horn he drew the blood, the blood that nourished every bud. Deep in the marrow, a raven pleads; and in the marrow, the raven breeds."*

Every muscle in my body seized up. With all the force I could muster, I sent my fists into the bedroom door. I took a step back and kicked it, too. It creaked, but it didn't break. Perhaps if I worked on it awhile I'd manage to bust through, but I had a feeling I didn't have that much time to work with.

I couldn't flee the room and I couldn't risk a jump from the window, so I stood my ground, shakily. I felt on the verge of collapsing, and the pounding in my temples had me feeling dizzy. My strength was sapped further as a sinister laugh issued from the closet. Said closet was coming into view gradually, as the veil of clouds slipped off the moon's face.

The closet door was sitting ajar.

I could make out the dim shape of something standing inside. Inch by inch the door opened further, as if prodded by a draft, but before the whole shape of the figure came into view, the moonlight died out again.

I'd seen enough.

There was someone looking at me from within the closet. The

space was alive with that croaking laugh, so reminiscent of a baying amphibian.

It greeted me with a mouthful of eyes.

My legs gave out and I hit the floor. I heard a scurrying as of dozens of feet, and felt as many cold hands groping at my flesh as I lay prone. There was time enough for only a single scream before my wits revolted and I spun into unconsciousness.

THIRTY

The chirping of birds.

From far-off, the steady rapping of a woodpecker.

The reek of that miserable tree was what really woke me. The pungent scent crept up my nostrils and shook me violently awake as I realized where I was.

I blinked the sleep from my eyes and tried focusing on my surroundings, hoping that it was a mistake—a stubborn nightmare that hadn't run its course.

I was in the house. In the living room, specifically. Beneath me was the metal folding chair. Somehow, I'd spent the night in it, sleeping peacefully. The ache in my neck attested to that. But I hadn't started the night in this chair. *You were upstairs... in the master bedroom... And there was...* With every incremental gain in cognizance, I recalled more of the horrors I'd witnessed the night before.

I scrambled out of the room, burst out the front door, and began dry heaving on the lawn.

I retched so hard that I feared my organs would come spilling out of my mouth, and when I finally regained control of myself I was unable to sit up. I rolled onto my side, clutching at my abdomen, and stared into the blue sky. It was a warm, pleasant morning. Even so, I couldn't stop shaking.

What happened last night?

I'd gone into the house—been lured there—while waiting for the priest. To my knowledge, Father Kaspar had never shown, though. Then, that thing had appeared—the woman. Irma. She'd come after me, chased me into the upstairs. I'd taken refuge in the master bedroom, but she'd been waiting for me in the closet. I'd passed out after that.

I eased myself up onto all fours and then shuffled to the van. I dug my cell phone from my pocket—the battery nearly dead—and locked the doors as I dialed Father Kaspar. I wanted to know why he hadn't come.

The priest picked up, sounding a bit tired. "Hello?"

"Father Kaspar," I began, clearing my throat and trying not to sound viciously angry, "this is Kevin Taylor. I called you last night, asked you to come to my house?" I paused. "You never came."

"Oh, Mr. Taylor." The priest took a deep breath. "I'm sorry about that. You see, I *did* come by the house last night, though I was delayed due to some unforeseen car trouble. It was past 2AM when I finally arrived, and though I saw a van in the driveway, I did not find anyone inside. The door was open. I came in, called out for you, but there was no reply. I figured that you'd grown tired of waiting and had left the premises. I'm sorry—I would have called you to inform you of the delay, but I left my phone at the rectory."

"But..." I grit my teeth, wondering if the priest was trying to pull a fast one. "But I was there. I was in the house," I said. "I didn't see you, didn't hear you. I kept an eye out for a while." There were several hours I couldn't account for after passing out in the upstairs. It *was* possible that the priest had shown up, but why hadn't I heard him? If he'd really entered the house, he would have seen me sleeping in the chair—why hadn't he woken me up? And on the off chance that the house really had been empty upon his arrival... then where had I been?

Father Kaspar chuckled impatiently. "I'm sorry, Mr. Taylor, but when I entered the house I saw no one. I didn't walk through the whole house, but I waited for about ten minutes and called out loudly. There was no one there. The door had been left open, and I thought that maybe you'd gone out for a walk. I went around the property but didn't see you in the yard, either. I thought you'd packed up and gone. If you'd like to arrange something for a later date, I'd be happy to pencil in a blessing sometime this week." I could tell by his tone that he was rather annoyed at having to recount his visit, and he seemed to be implying that I'd wasted his time. "In the future, I'd recommend not calling so late at night for these matters."

I apologized to the priest for his trouble and hung up.

I buried my face in my hands and thought long and hard about the night before. Just what had happened after I'd lost consciousness? Could I have possibly left the house without remembering it—gone sleepwalking? No, I'd never done that before.

Then again, I'd come to in the living room, and had no memories about how I'd ended up there. The door to the master bedroom had been locked from the outside—I'd been a prisoner—and yet I'd woken up downstairs.

I worked over my furrowed brow with my palms. *Think! Why weren't you here when the priest arrived? Where could you have gone? And how did you get out of a locked room? Did the spirit let you out?*

That was when I noticed it. My jeans, which had been a bit stained with paint the night before, were absolutely filthy. Long tracks of mud ran up and down the legs. My shoes, too, were muddy and damp. I pinched off some of the dried mud and felt it between my fingers. *What did you get up to last night?*

Having had my fill of horror, I decided it didn't matter and powered up the van. When I'd reversed onto Morgan Road, I stamped on the accelerator and left the house behind.

I decided then and there that I'd never go back.

THIRTY-ONE

A shower and change of clothes did much to refresh me on the outside, but the filth that persisted within would not be washed away so easily. Lounging in the hotel room, desperate for answers, I feared the darkness would sully me forever. The events of the previous night were wedged deep within my psyche like a splinter, and I knew there'd be no removing it. It would heal over, eventually, and the body would break it down, but some trace of it would always remain.

I was thankful to be out of the house. Seeing the outside world again was a pleasure I hadn't expected to ever partake in just twelve short hours before. And yet, the fear and stress remained a constant, almost as though the world could offer me no comfort. I may as well have been carrying around the house itself, balancing it across my shoulders.

Though I was determined not to go back to the house, I still craved answers. The terrors I'd experienced in the last twenty-four hours required some sort of explanation, lest I spend the rest of my life puzzling over them. I turned to the only resource I had—the web. The house had scarcely been lived in since it had first been built, but recalling my conversation with Lillian, the woman who'd lived on

Telluride Road, I had some reason to believe that the house's first and only owner, Willard Weiss, might still be among the living. Could Weiss, probably in his 80's and living in assisted care—if he lived at all—assist me? Was there anything he could tell me about his time in the house that would shine light upon the hideous things that filled it?

For awhile now, I'd thought of the eyeless specter in that house as the spirit of Willard's deceased wife, Irma Weiss. I wasn't so sure anymore that the presence in that house had ever been a human being, though. It had seemed too nightmarish, too bizarre an apparition to have been a human soul. Perhaps Irma hadn't figured into it at all, and this thing—whatever it was—had more to do with the body I'd found in the wall. Even that seemed like a stretch; how could a human soul become so positively hideous in death?

I sat on the bed, scanning a list of care homes in the metro Detroit area and writing down phone numbers. As I did so, my attention was repeatedly drawn elsewhere—to the walls I shared with adjacent rooms. From the room to my right, I heard something like a woman wailing. It may have been someone actually crying, or else it may have been coming from some television drama. I tried tuning it out, but other sounds began entering the fray shortly thereafter, which only added to my distraction.

There were air vents on both sides of the room, near the ceiling, the slits in them half-open. Through them, while I worked at my computer, I occasionally heard strange sounds. Furtive tappings and scrabblings, as of unseen fingertips; then voices in hushed conversation. I knew that I was hearing the talk of people staying in nearby rooms, and that the sinister character of their voices must surely have been a product of their traveling through the vent system, and yet as I listened, halting in my work with a shudder, they seemed inhuman in their tinniness. Low and aberrant, the voices reminded me of all I'd heard in the house.

I'd put together a list of twenty-five assisted living facilities and their corresponding numbers, and was ready to start calling each in the hopes of being connected with Willard Weiss, but the voices coming through the vents waxed dominant and set my nerves on edge. I stood beneath one of the vents, closed it all the way with a push, but could still feel the voices reverberating off the metal shudder as I pulled my hand away.

It's impossible, I told myself. *You're hearing things. Those voices are confined to the house. There's no way you're actually hearing them here. It's just someone in the next hotel room—someone's TV or something. Stop fretting.*

I leaned over my laptop and started ringing up care facilities in the area. Even when the first few secretaries couldn't find a patient by the name of Willard Weiss in their registries, I found I was happy to talk to other human beings, and I tried prolonging my conversations with them by making small-talk. My list of twenty-five was whittled down to a list of fifteen, then seven, as I called and received word that there were no patients admitted under the name I sought.

When only five facilities remained on my list and I was beginning to fear that I'd never find the man, I struck gold.

The secretary who answered the phone for Tremainsville Meadows, an assisted care facility in nearby Auburn Hills, put me on hold while searching the patient registry, and then informed me cheerfully that there was, in fact, a patient by the name of Willard Weiss staying there. After I lied, claiming to be the man's nephew, she supplied me with his direct number in what I assume was probably a breach in protocol. I jotted it down hurriedly, and then she connected me.

In the eighth grade, I'd once called a girl I'd liked to ask her to a movie. Back then, I'd thought my heart would give out while waiting for her to pick up, I'd been so nervous.

The stress and anticipation as Weiss' line rang were easily triple that. The phone stuck to my sweaty palm, and I couldn't keep from rocking anxiously as I sat at the foot of the bed.

Finally, there was an answer.

Willard Weiss sounded gruff, bothered, as he picked up the phone. The secretary, who'd remained on the line, told him that he had call from his "nephew" before she signed off, leaving Weiss to mutter, "Nephew? I don't have any nephews. This has gotta be a mistake."

I swooped in before he could hang up. "Mr. Weiss? This is no mistake. I'm sorry to disturb you, but I'm calling because I need your help with something. I've been looking for a way to reach you for a while now."

Weiss grunted, his voice tinged in confusion. "Eh... you need *my* help with something?"

"That's right," I replied. "You see, I've been living in your old house—889 Morgan Road. I understand that you and your family lived there through the seventies and eighties. I have some important questions to ask about the property."

There was silence on the other end.

"Mr. Weiss, I'm sorry if this is a bad time, but I've been having... well, some major difficulties in that house. I've been renovating it, you see. The house is in surprisingly good shape, but ever since I started staying there, I've been seeing things. Horrible things. And last night, everything came to a head. I understand that your wife, Irma, died in that house? There's something else, too. A while back, while fixing some drywall, I discovered a dead body—the corpse of a woman—ensconced in the living room wall. I was hoping that maybe you could shine some light on—"

The dial tone sounded.

He'd hung up on me.

Willard Weiss was alive and well, but he wasn't in a talking mood.

THIRTY-TWO

I looked out my window at the sun. It was dipping over the horizon, setting the dimming sky ablaze in furious shades of pink and orange. A beautiful sunset by any measure.

And I hated the sight of it.

I wasn't in the house anymore and should have had no problems with the night. Despite that, my hackles went up at the prospect of the day ending, and that sliver of unease I'd been carrying around with me began to metastasize into something more prominent.

I'd attempted to call Willard Weiss three more times since he'd hung up on me, and I'd spaced the calls apart by an hour or more. Unfortunately, he hadn't picked up for a single one, and I knew he was avoiding me. What his reasons were, or if he simply thought I was some sort of crank, remained to be seen. While passing the time between those calls, I'd checked my email and even had a peek at my VideoTube channel, where messages had poured in from users looking for my newest video. I didn't have the heart to tell them that there weren't going to be anymore.

If I was lucky enough to put this all behind me, it was possible I'd never make a video again. Fixing up old houses was a great way to stumble upon secrets that were better kept hidden, and I'd lost my taste for it all. Even becoming a TV star had lost its appeal. It was possible that I'd change my mind in the future, but somehow I doubted I'd ever put on a tool belt again. In fact, I got to thinking that maybe I'd never enjoyed it at all. Perhaps 889 Morgan Road had simply been the last nail in the coffin. A simple job pushing a mop or scrubbing toilets sounded mighty fine right about then. Better that than digging around in people's houses. There was too much history in those places. I'd gone into this renovation blind and was now caught up in a mess that, frankly, wasn't any of my business. I wasn't keen to run into the same trap elsewhere.

I ordered room service and ate disinterestedly, keeping the TV on for some extra noise. A few bites into a slice of pizza, my thoughts shifted away from the pawn shop program on the screen and back to the events of the night before. I'd spoken to Father Kaspar that morning, and he'd insisted that upon his arrival there'd been no one in the house. He'd claimed, too, that the front door had been open. I was almost certain—certain as I could be of anything that occurred on that terrifying, chaotic night—that it had been shut. Pairing this curious absence of mine with the mud I'd discovered on my jeans that morning upon coming to, I wondered where I'd gone in the night, and why I couldn't remember.

Had I gone into the yard? Somewhere else in the neighborhood? If so, why had I done it? I clearly hadn't been clear-headed in doing so. Possessed by fear, it was possible I'd run out of the house, delirious, and done all sorts of dumb things. Not being able to remember even a bit of it is what really disturbed me, though.

In case I really was getting up to nocturnal mischief without realizing it, I decided to set up my camera in the room. The battery would hopefully last through the night and capture any shenanigans in the event that I went on a nighttime stroll. It was a purely precautionary measure, probably a waste of time, but I set the camera up near the door of my hotel room and then prepared to go to bed.

It was still early, but the activity of recent days had left me ragged. If anything was going to help me sort this mess out, it was regular sleep. I slid into the bed and put out the light, draping an arm over my face to block out the last traces of day that seeped in through the blinds.

When next I looked out into the room, the darkness was nearly perfect. There was no more sun, and the only light came from imperfect sources—the slit under the door, the reddish glow of the boxy numbers on the alarm clock.

Prone in the darkness, I courted a now familiar discomfort. Like an itch was spreading across my entire body, I reacted violently to the lack of light and balled myself up tightly beneath the covers. It was impossible to feel comfortable in the dark. Without the lights on to convince me otherwise, I got the distinct impression that there was someone in the room with me—perhaps several people. Even as the air conditioner kicked on for a few minutes, the air remained too heavy to circulate, and its staleness clung to me like a sour syrup.

I switched on the bedside lamp three, four times before I called it a night, and each time I found no one sharing the suite with me. But I had only to turn off the light to reacquaint myself with dread and to suspect, with more intensity than I had the previous time, an unseen occupant. In fact, without the lights on, I couldn't even be sure that I was still in the hotel. My understanding of the world had been nudged so far off base that I couldn't rule out the possibility that the switch on the lamp mediated the flux of time and space itself. Maybe, when the lights were on, I was well and truly safe in my hotel room. And maybe, when the lights went out, I was transported to the house on Morgan Road. Could I really be sure either way? Wasn't the darkness that fell upon this room of the same species that packed every corner of that accursed house? In that sense, I'd never manage to fully separate myself from the house. Stepping beneath the shade of a tree, or venturing into a dark movie theater would be sufficient to unite me with it, at least in spirit.

I was too tired to philosophize further and mercifully drifted off.

THIRTY-THREE

I'd gone to bed in a pair of old sweatpants and a thin sleeveless T-shirt. The first thing I noticed when I awoke, aside from the chill that had dominated me from head to toe, was that the garments were sticking to my skin. It was like a fever had just broken, and before I could fully open my eyes the shivers and aches had their way with my limbs.

The bed had grown scratchy, the mattress soaked through with what I took to be my sweat, though as I planted a hand on it to lift myself up, the sensation that met my fingers was nothing at all like a mattress.

Blinking, mouth dry, I felt sprigs of something like grass feathering against my palms. The scent of moist earth struck me in a great wave, and the surprise it incited gave me the jolt I needed to properly awaken.

"What in the world?"

The stuff beneath me had felt like grass because it *was* grass.

I was outside, beneath a pre-dawn sky, my clothing soaked through with dew. All around me, jutting from the ground like broken teeth, were stones—grave markers—whose engravings were too difficult to make out in these minutes or hours before sunrise.

I was in the old graveyard on Morgan Road.

And I didn't know why.

"But... but how?" I raked a muddy hand against my cheek, the fingers feeling sore. A cold wind shot past me, almost knocking me onto my rear, and I reached for a nearby tombstone for support. I tried gaining my bearings and panned around the site. In the low haze that clung to the openings between monuments, I was able to sight out the road. Looking up and down it as far as I could, I saw no sign of my van. My gaze drooped to my feet, their soles tingling like I'd just waked across coals. They were bare, and in the places where the filth hadn't completely coated them, they looked a bit cyan for the cold.

I was dizzy, and had to drape both arms over the tombstone to remain upright.

Clearly, this was a dream. A *weird, distressing* dream. I'd been having a lot of those lately. This had to be another one. I gave my forearm as hard a pinch as I could with my shaking, mud-caked fingers.

The pain saw me inhale sharply.

It was a fluke. It *had* to be. I was hallucinating the pain. Everyone knows you can't feel pain in a dream.

I slapped myself in the face.

I did it *twice*.

The burning pain in my cheeks told me everything I needed to know.

Pacing slowly towards the road and carving a path through the mist, I looked to the brightening sky. Using the taller stones to pull myself through the graveyard, I eventually stumbled onto the shattered road and had a look up and down Morgan Road. The few streetlights that actually functioned had blinked off in anticipation of sunrise, leaving the world awash in an eerie twilight.

To my back, long shadows dipped between the stones. There was a rustling in the damp grass that, upon inspection, had no visible source. The wind struck me head-on and I felt myself becoming overwhelmingly nauseous. "W-What am I doing out here?" I asked between bouts of gagging. I stared across the mess of toppled monuments, waiting for an answer. "W-Who's there?"

There was no reply.

Hobbling like a zombie, I started down the road and hurried away from the graveyard. Every step was painful, but I trudged on nonetheless, my head too crammed with fright to dwell on the physical. I'd walked—not driven—several miles in the middle of the night to this remote, abandoned spot. And I couldn't remember a moment of it. One minute I'd been drifting off back at the hotel. The next, I'd come to like a feral child in the grass, surrounded by the dead.

This wasn't the first time that I'd woken up without knowing what had gone on the night before, and I had a suspicion that the mud I'd found on my jeans the last morning might have come from this same graveyard.

I'd been coming here in my sleep for two nights running.

I'd been *drawn* here, outside of my own control.

This time, though, I'd prepared for this possibility. Before going to bed, I'd set up a camera in my hotel room. What had it captured? Something told me that I really didn't want to know. It would be easier, funnier, to write this off as some kind of bizarre sleepwalking incident. If I returned to the hotel room and watched the tape, it was possible I'd find something terrible, something that would put a whole new face on the matter.

It was time to leave Detroit. Whatever was plaguing me, drawing me back to this derelict neighborhood, had its limits. If I drove out of the State completely, eventually I'd get far enough away that it wouldn't be able to claw me back.

At least, I hoped so.

But I'd learned better than to rely on mere hope, and knew that I needed to seek out some answers before permanently leaving Michigan.

I needed to see what was on that tape. Now that I knew I'd lost all control of myself after dark, I had to face to possibility that there was something wrong with me; that the house, or rather the thing lurking in it, had sunk its fangs in me. Had I been hypnotized by it? Possessed by that hideous specter I'd taken for the spirit of Irma Weiss? I felt the need to talk to someone with experience in these matters. Father Kaspar, the priest, might be able to do something for me. If there was something hanging onto my soul, maybe he'd know how to get rid of it.

There was someone else I'd have to talk to as well.

Willard Weiss had hung up on me, but I wasn't through with him yet. Until I knew for sure that he had nothing to do with the haunting of 889 Morgan Road, no insights to share, then he'd remain on my radar. I had a feeling that I'd have to visit him personally; if he had his way, he'd just keep hanging up the phone. A face-to-face talk, even if I had to strong-arm him into it, was my only option where the old man was concerned.

I made it into town within an hour, and though I looked like death, the locals—probably used to seeing the disheveled homeless wander about—didn't bat an eye. I slipped into a CVS and bought some first aid supplies before the cashier noticed I wasn't wearing shoes, and then caught a bus to a stop within a few blocks of my hotel.

When I returned, I was shaken—but not at all surprised—to find the hotel room in a disarray. To begin with, the camera had been repositioned. I'd set it up on the tripod, near the door, before going to bed. It had since been moved some feet to the right, so that it was parked in the doorway to the bathroom.

That was hardly the worst of it, though.

The blinds had been left open—dangling from the wall—and all of the faucets in the bathroom had been left on. The bedclothes had been thrown everywhere, and the cords to both the lamp and alarm clock and been knotted together. The air conditioning had been turned to its lowest possible setting, lending the room an uncomfortable chill and leaving beads of condensation forming on the window as the new day outside began warming the pane.

Most chilling was what I found scrawled across the bathroom mirror in soap. The bar of soap was still inside the sink, one of its corners worn down like a stumpy crayon. In rough letters, the following message had been left behind:

Deep in the marrow, a raven pleads; and in the marrow, the raven breeds.

It'd been quite the party, by the looks of it. A party I had no recollection of.

Once I'd soaked my battered feet in isopropyl alcohol and picked the crumbs of asphalt from my cuts, I limped out of the bathroom and retrieved the camera. I switched out the dead battery and powered it up, sitting on the bed with my feet up.

Nothing could have prepared me for what I saw on that recording.

SOME FAST-FORWARDING WAS necessary to get to the action. The camera had captured roughly forty minutes of content around all of the dead space. Curiously, the battery had packed up shortly after the action ended, almost as if it had been intentionally drained by some outside source. I'd had to switch it out before watching the footage.

In the first two hours of the recording, there was nothing to be seen but blackness. This blackness was eventually interrupted by a flash of the bedside lamp. The bulb didn't come on like it usually did, with a click and a flash. Rather, as though the light were a liquid being poured slowly into the bulb, the light had *gurgled* on, appearing less yellow and more orange than was the norm. And when it came on, I showed up in frame.

I was not sleeping in the bed, as I had expected, but *standing* on it.

Staring at the ceiling with a blank expression, my hands hanging limp at my sides, I stood there, completely still, for ten or fifteen minutes. Meanwhile, the bedclothes—previously balled up and gathered at the foot of the bed—began rising into the air as if on a strong gust of wind. The sheets and blanket circulated about me sluggishly, seeming to defy gravity, and as they hovered, their lacy borders came into contact with what appeared to be obstacles that were invisible to the naked eye. As the folds of fabric slumped over and became snagged on unseen fixtures possessed of real shape, the contours of what appeared to be heads, shoulders and outstretched arms appeared in their creases. The bed was surrounded by a dense, unseeable congregation, and I stood on the mattress at its center. As the swirling bedclothes washed over the members of this crowd, they at times looked like the generic ghosts one might see in television—figures draped in a sheet with holes cut into it for eyes.

The light flickered off for a moment, and when it returned, I was no longer on the bed, but floating *above* it. My head was not visible, but I appeared to be in animated conversation with someone nearby, perhaps on the ceiling. My legs swayed beneath me like the string on a helium balloon, and a number of hushed whispers sounded across the suite, which made the camera speaker crackle somewhat. I couldn't hear myself, couldn't make out the din of conversation among the other occupants, but that I'd heard these voices before back at the house was beyond doubt.

As if signaling a scene change, the light blinked off and on again, and the next bit involved me standing at the window, speaking to someone through the glass. I had my back to the camera, and my body was largely blocking the window. Even at this imperfect angle I could make out a reflection distinct from my own, and I was shaken by its deformity. Gaping black eyes of differing widths stared back at me as I mumbled. A gaping mouth opened in reply, and from within it there glistened a hundred quivering eyes.

Irma.

The light bubbled. When it came back on, the angle of the

camera had changed to capture me standing in the bathroom. Someone—I couldn't be sure who—had moved it. This new position was sufficient to capture me fully in frame, but whoever I was chatting to in the mirror was omitted. To my horror, some minutes into this whispering exchange, I picked up the bar of soap and began writing on the mirror with it.

I had been the one that left the writing on the mirror.

There was a garbled flurry of voices accompanied by a burst of static as I dropped the soap and left the bathroom. The look on my face was dreamy, stupid, and a litany of long shadows flashed across the walls as I passed—all of them stemming from my own. I bumped the camera as I walked out, and then the main door could be heard to open and close. I'd walked out in my pajamas, barefoot, and set out for the graveyard then. The reasons for it were unclear, but it was plain that I hadn't been forced; by the looks of it, I'd thought it a wonderful idea at the time.

The lights flashed off, and this time they didn't come back on. As darkness reigned however, there were occasional grunts and growls in the darkness, along with footsteps. Eventually, these petered out. Finally, the battery lost the last of its juice and the recording came to an end.

The recording on my camera, it could be argued, was incredibly valuable. It was the most convincing proof of supernatural phenomena ever put to tape. I didn't think of it that way, though. To me, it was only solid proof of how hopeless this was.

The spirits in that house had followed me out.

They were interacting with me after dark, when I should have been asleep.

I'd brought them out of the house and into the hotel room. They'd hitched a ride like head lice.

My skin crawled at the thought, and it took all my self control not to smash the camera to pieces. I didn't want to believe what was on it. I wanted to believe, as any ordinary Joe who might stumble upon it, that it was all fantasy—movie magic.

THE HOUSE OF LONG SHADOWS   211

With a shaky hand, I picked the camera back up and set it on the desk. Then, stepping into my boots and tugging on a sweatshirt, I tucked the device under my arm. There was someone who needed to see it.

Father Kaspar hadn't been too impressed when I'd called him to bless the house in the middle of the night, but if I showed him this footage he'd understand the severity of the situation.

If my hunch was right and I was currently carrying a number of spiritual hangers-on, then I was in desperate need of help. Showing him the footage would prompt him to take action.

I set out for the St. Thomas Aquinas rectory downtown, the camera rolling around in my passenger seat.

THIRTY-FOUR

As I stormed towards the rectory, I simply kept a lookout for a man
with a white collar.

The parking lot of the attached church was rather full, and a
handful of people emerged from inside. A grey-haired middle-aged
man in purple vestments stood outside the main door, shaking hands.
A Mass had just let out, by the looks of it.

I pushed past a few waves of parishioners, camera squeezed
tightly under one arm, and jogged up the steps towards the priest.
"Father?" I called, waving manically.

The man turned. He'd been speaking to an elderly woman about
making plans later in the week for brunch when I'd interrupted him.
He spared the woman a smile, and that same smile tightened as he
sized me up. I cut a rather deplorable figure in my mud-stained garb
and wild-eyed state. "Yes, how can I help you?"

The voice was the same I'd heard on the phone. It was him.
"Father Kaspar."

He nodded, waited for me to proceed.

"My name is Kevin Taylor. We spoke on the phone."

His eyes lit up and he looked at me with renewed interest—and possibly disgust. "Oh, yes. You're... the one working on that house. You wanted to make plans for a blessing, right?"

A few families with young children wandered past. For their sake —and because I was already embarrassed for looking like a hot mess— I tried to rein it in. "No, it's... things have gotten more serious than that. The house isn't the problem anymore, it's..." I brought a shaking hand to the camera, squeezed it in my palm. "C-Can we talk, please?"

Moved by the urgency and fright that was apparent in my face— or else wanting to get this encounter over with as quickly as possible —he nodded. "Yes, certainly. Let's... let's go inside, Mr. Taylor." He smiled at the remaining church-goers as they filed out and then motioned to the main door, leading the way.

I shuffled after him, shoulders tense, head low. "T-Thank you, Father."

"We'll speak in the sacristy, if that's all right with you." Passing through the narthex, we entered the church and then cut a sudden right, entering a small room that looked half like an office and half like a dressing room. A pair of altar boys were sitting around inside, shooting the breeze, and the priest gave them a quick nod that made them scram. Kaspar eased the door shut and began removing his purple vestments, revealing the black cassock beneath. "So, what brings you here today, Mr. Taylor? I don't mean to rush you, but I'm set to spend some time in the confessional this afternoon, so I'm a bit pressed for time."

I held out the camera and gave it a little shake, as if he was supposed to understand. He didn't get it, and instead looked at me like I was a total idiot.

"I, uh... I've been having troubles, Father. Serious troubles," I said.

"How may I be of assistance?" he replied, putting up his vestments on a hanger.

"Do you... do you believe in ghosts, Father? In demons?" I asked.

He arched a grey brow. "Erm... What is this about, Mr. Taylor? Specifically?"

I spilled my guts. "That house, Father. I've spent a lot of time in it. And all that time, there's been something in there with me. I didn't know it at first. I played it off, pretended like it wasn't there. Even when things got frightening, I... I ignored it, tried to work despite it. But... I can't ignore it anymore. Whatever is in that house—a ghost, a demon, I don't know what—is in me now. I think. I mean, it's... it's hard to explain. I have, uh... footage here, that..."

Father Kaspar's blue eyes narrowed and he leaned against a table, arms crossed.

"There's something in me," I reiterated. "I need it out. I... I need you to cast it out. I know how crazy that sounds, but I've... I've got proof. Can you exorcise me, Father? Please?"

Father Kaspar patted my arm, and for a moment I thought he was on the verge of acquiescing. Instead, he began to shake his head. "I'm sorry, Mr. Taylor, but that isn't quite how it works. Exorcisms are rather tricky things. One can't simply procure an exorcism from any old parish priest—there are hoops to jump through, and only certain priests are trained to carry out such rituals. What's more, the Church wishes to first rule out psychological reasons for—"

"OK, but... I have proof!" I interrupted, shaking the camera at him again like an angry fist. "I can show you!"

"I understand, Mr. Taylor," replied the priest, eyeing the camera. "But as I've just explained to you, an exorcism is not possible at this time. And while I'm sure that you think it a perfect cure for what ails you, I—"

I interrupted once more. "Father, you're not hearing me! I have an actual problem here! I've... I've been seeing the most dreadful things. And I've been going places late at night—without knowing that I've even left my bed. I've seen things in that house that you wouldn't believe. Please, you've got to help me! I've got nowhere else to turn."

The priest, more bothered by my meltdown than anything,

nodded to the door. "If you'd like, I'd be happy to bless you, Mr. Taylor. We can even pray for the intercession of St. Benedict." He eased open the door and pointed to a small, square fountain sitting between the pews. "Come, this is our baptismal font. I'll bless you with holy water."

"No, Father, please listen to me. I *need* an exorcism. I mean it! I can prove it to you!" My voice rose in pitch, echoing throughout the building. A number of stragglers remained in the church, kneeling in the pews. They were probably waiting for the priest to finish up with me so that they could meet him in the confessional. Now and then, they looked over at us; it was clear my noisy pleading was making them nervous.

Father Kaspar donned a warm smile and stood in front of me, tried urging me to the fountain. "Mr. Taylor, please... lower your voice."

Panic raced through me and I tugged like a maniac at his arm. "But Father! You're not listening to me!"

The priest's smile tightened and murmurs arose from the kneelers.

"Mr. Taylor, please let go of me," snapped Fr. Kaspar. "I'd be happy to bless you, but I can't just perform a ritual like exorcism without consulting the Bishop, and—"

"Please!" I shouted, thrusting the camera at him. "Please, watch! When you've seen this, you'll understand!"

Several of the people in the pews stood and began towards us. Father Kaspar eyed me firmly, shaking his head. "That'll be quite enough. I won't tolerate this behavior in the sanctuary, Mr. Taylor." He motioned to the tabernacle, to those still kneeling in prayer. "I know that you've come looking for help, but this is a sacred place and I'd appreciate it if you could—"

"Is he giving you trouble, Father?" asked a middle-aged man wandering up from the pews.

"But... but won't you just..." I sucked in a shaky breath. "There has to be someone in this city who can perform an exorcism, right?" I struggled to contain myself, but couldn't help grabbing the priest's arm once again. "Please, watch this and call the Bishop. I'll stay put here, and—"

Rattled at the vicious shake I'd given him, Fr. Kaspar shrugged me off and stepped back. "All right, that's enough. If this is how you're going to act, I'm going to have to ask you to leave. I'm sorry that I can't give you what you're asking for at this time, but this is no way to—"

"But, Father, please!" I shouted.

"Hey now," uttered the stocky parishioner to my back. "You heard him. Get outta here, or I'm calling the cops."

"Mr. Taylor, please. Calm yourself," urged Father Kaspar. "I won't have you jostling or threatening anyone here."

"But... but you're not listening!" I shot the priest a pleading look, tears in my eyes, but understood that he could not give me what I wanted. He wasn't authorized to perform an exorcism—perhaps he hadn't even been trained in the rite. I could stand here, screaming in his face all day, but I wouldn't get what I was asking for. "I... I'm sorry," I managed, stepping away from the fountain. "I'll leave. I'm sorry... for the disturbance." Priest and parishioner watched me closely as I left the premises.

I returned to the van, dropped the camera into the passenger seat and rested my head on the steering wheel. *What now?* I thought. *What should I do?*

I recalled that there was *one* other person I could contact for help in this. He'd been unwilling to chat during the first go-round, but perhaps he'd be more talkative during a proper visit.

I decided to go looking for Willard Weiss.

THIRTY-FIVE

I made a pitstop at the hotel to gather my things, because when this meeting was through I had a feeling I'd leave Detroit, never to return. I had no idea where I'd go from here, what actionable tidbits my conversation with Weiss might yield, if any, but as soon as possible I wanted to flee the Motor City for some place that felt safe. I thought about returning to Florida, to the little town I'd grown up in. These days, memories of a less-than-perfect childhood didn't bother me so much; in fact, they were rather a welcome relief from thoughts of where I'd been recently. The demons in my past were nowhere near as vicious as the ones that pursued me in the present.

I rushed into the hotel lobby and squared things with the clerk at the desk. From there, I went straight to the room to clear out my stuff. Everything of value got stuffed into my backpack and duffel. I did pause long enough to seek out the address to Weiss' home facility, Tremainsville Meadows, and in this lull I noticed a hunger that left me woozy. It'd been a long time since my last proper meal.

And it would be a while longer still. In a hurry to meet with Weiss while the sun was still out, I'd have to settle for whatever I could purchase from the hotel vending machines. I scribbled the care home's address onto a slip of hotel stationary, stuffed it into my pocket and then hauled my stuff into the hall.

The hallway proved noisy as the other guests on my floor went about their business. From the room across the hall I heard the fiery monologuing of a talking head on the news. Venturing towards the vending room where all of the soda and snack machines were, I heard all kinds of things. A baby whining. A pair of men in conversation, laughing heartily at some joke.

I envied them all. They were all living their lives—had things to look forward to. That wasn't the case for me. Not anymore. It was too early to sign my death certificate, but if I was even half-right about the nature of the evils that plagued me, my days were as good as numbered. I wished more than anything that I could laugh and love and carry on like these people. I missed the easygoing bliss of a lazy afternoon, the merciful ignorance of the common man. I'd seen and experienced too much now—too much for *anyone* to bear without gambling away a bit of sanity—and I grieved this new stage in my life. Even if I parted with these horrors, nothing would ever be the same.

The Coke machine in the vending room wasn't much consolation, but I scooped a handful of change out of my backpack and started hunting for quarters. I'd slid two coins into the slot when, from around the corner, I heard something else mixed in with the joyful sounds of daily life.

A whisper, low but insistent.

"*Let me in. I won't hurt you... It's me, sweetheart. Bradford from Annapolis...*"

The coins slipped out of my palm and struck the floor with a clatter. *No,* I thought. *Not here. Leave me alone. Just leave me alone!* I turned cautiously, peeked around the corner and surveyed the hallway. It was empty, silent.

I took a deep breath, braced myself, and knelt down to pick up the change. The spirits could toy with me all they wanted, but soon I'd shut them up for good. I wasn't sure how I'd do it, how long it would take, but I was on my way to meet with Weiss and it was possible he'd clue me in to some solution for all of this. I held this sliver of hope in my heart with a vise grip.

The coins had gone everywhere. Sliding my hand beneath the nearby ice machine in search of change, I brought out one dusty quarter after another. Reaching further, my fingers ran up against something I first took to be a thick power cord. It had some give to it, was smooth and cold to the touch. There were bumps in it, too.

I counted four of them before it dawned on me that I was grasping toes on a human foot.

I backed into the Coke machine with a thud that sent the bottles within it rattling.

Trembling now and maintaining as great a distance as I could in the cramped space, I lowered my gaze and peered into the gap beneath the ice machine.

Someone was standing behind the boxy thing, and their pale, vein-laced feet were planted in plain sight. One of the toes wiggled, as if in amusement.

She was here, in the room.

I forgot my hunger and thirst, and dove out into the hall. The bottoms of my wounded feet stung as I took hold of my bags and galloped towards the exit. For a second there, I wasn't sure that my bruised ankle was going to hold. I struck the walls as I went, the noises of other tenants swelling into a blur that sounded something like the joint murmurings of those invisible fiends. As I ran, glancing back towards the vending room, I noticed a long, humanoid shadow seeping down the hall. It tailed me all the way to the lobby.

I was out of breath by the time I made it to the van. Stuffing my bags into the passenger seat, I locked the doors and pulled out, nearly hitting some guy in a Mercedes. He didn't let off the horn until I was out of the parking lot, but I barely heard its bleating for the rushing of blood in my ears.

The spirits were following me everywhere I went.

In the daylight.

I swerved out into traffic, and as I fell into line with a number of idling cars at a red light I began punching my steering wheel. The thing was misshapen before I finally let up, my knuckles raw and eyes stinging with tears.

I wiped my eyes and stared at my sorry reflection in the rearview, stunned at what I saw. The circles under my eyes were so dark they looked like I'd applied them with makeup. My cheeks were painted in stubble and my skin was dry and flaking. There'd been a change in my hair, too. There was a streak of grey running through it where, last I'd checked, it had been dark. I'd thrown self-care out the window completely over the past several days, but I hadn't expected to look quite so rough as this. I looked ten, fifteen years older than my age.

This haunting was literally killing me.

Bolting into the fast lane, I set off for Auburn Hills to corner Willard Weiss. He was my only remaining hope.

THIRTY-SIX

I parked at the very edge of the visitor lot outside the Tremainsville Meadows assisted living facility. There were a handful of other cars, and I reckoned that most belonged to legitimate friends and family of patients there.

I was *probably* the only person who'd come here to shake down one of the tenants.

Making my way to the sidewalk and strolling into the community proper, I did my best to look natural. I was pretty hard on the eyes, disheveled, but hoped not to attract any undue attention as I went poking around.

And there was, unfortunately, a lot of poking around to be done.

I didn't know where Willard Weiss was staying, and couldn't exactly stop at the visitor's center to ask for directions.

The assisted living portion of the campus was more of a retirement village, comprised of one-story duplexes and staggered kiosks where staff members congregated. Neat, winding sidewalks wormed through the entire campus like veins. Every lawn was perfectly manicured, every tree expertly trimmed.

A pair of staff members dressed in olive green scrubs—Orderlies?

Nurses? I couldn't be sure—stepped out of one of the kiosks and eyed me with real curiosity as I stormed up the walk, reading the numbers posted outside each building. I held my breath, hoping that they'd lose interest in me, and sure enough they wandered off the next minute. The numbers on the duplexes—11-33, 11-40—meant nothing to me. I needed names.

Short of asking one of the staff members where I might find Mr. Weiss' residence and alerting them to my unwanted presence, I had no option but to seek out his location by other means. It occurred to me that the residents here probably received mail and, if I was lucky, that the last names of tenants might appear on the mailboxes of specific units. I hiked around for close to half an hour, dodging more of the wandering staff and getting strange looks from various patients and their guests. I must have looked homeless, or else mighty suspicious, skulking around like I did.

Eventually, I did stumble upon a bank of mailboxes situated within a gazebo. My hunch had been correct; last names were listed alongside the unit numbers. A moment's search and I'd found my man.

WEISS—UNIT 10-44

Several more minutes were spent trying to orient myself to the seemingly random ordering of the duplexes. Here was unit 12-10. Across from it was 09-13. Just when I was beginning to feel hopeless and was considering asking a kindly-looking old woman lazing on a bench near one of the kiosks, I located the unit I was looking for. Like all the rest, it was painted white with flaky brown trim and shutters. Peaceful though the retirement community was, some of the buildings therein looked in need of a facelift.

Maybe if I came out the other end of this fiasco unscathed, I'd offer to fix up Weiss' duplex as a thank-you.

The lights were on in the window, which was a good sign. Someone was home.

The trouble with showing up to a place unannounced is that you can never be sure how you'll be received. Actually, in this case, that wasn't entirely true; I had a strong feeling that my presence here would not be welcome, and so decided to rely on stealth rather than good manners to gain entry.

When the area had cleared of passersby, I approached the duplex above whose front door the numerals 10-44 were etched and peered in through the front window. I spied a television set, an easy chair, and a small, cluttered table. There was no sign of the unit's tenant, however. It was possible I'd caught Weiss on the toilet, or that he'd stepped out for a bit.

I tried the knob to the front door. Locked. Walking about the perimeter, I sought out another way in. Half-hidden by a towering pine on the other side of the building, I found it. A sliding glass door. A careful pull of the handle showed me it was locked, and the long, white blinds were drawn so that I couldn't see in. For all I knew, the old man was just inside the window, and would hit me over the head with something the moment I snuck in.

It was a risk I'd have to take.

In my years fixing houses I'd learned an easy way to circumvent such doors and went rummaging around in my pockets for the multi-tool I always carried. Kneeling in the grass and looking around the property, finding myself perfectly alone for the moment, I withdrew the flathead screwdriver portion of the multitool and carefully eased it into the seam where the door met the track. With a bit of pressure, I succeeded in bumping the door off the track, and could now slide it open and closed as I pleased.

I won't lie; my day had been a nightmare. Still, I felt mighty proud about that maneuver. It was like something out of a heist film. If life ever went back to normal, perhaps I'd record a video about this kind of stuff. "How to break into a house like a pro!" I could only imagine the comments I'd get on *that* video.

The door slid open and I slipped into the building quickly, so as to avoid being seen. The white blinds rattled as I brushed past them.

I was standing in a kitchen. There was a freshly-made sandwich on the counter and a frosty bottle of Diet Coke, too. This kitchen opened up into the living room I'd seen from the other window. A courtroom drama murmured from the TV. Directly across the small kitchen table was a hallway that appeared to lead to a single bedroom and bathroom.

It was from this hallway, with a stony gaze, that the tenant suddenly emerged.

He filled up the doorway as he paused in the hall. He was taller than I'd imagined and had a good bit of weight on me, too. A wreathe of white hair festooned the sides of his head; the top was mostly bare. His nose was long, his eyes green and sharp. Dressed in a pair of sweatpants and a white T-shirt, the man cut an imposing figure. He didn't look like the kind of man who needed help taking care of himself. Though I'd placed him somewhere in his early 80's, it was clear that the years had been kind to him.

"Willard Weiss?" I said from across the kitchen.

The man dissected me with a steely gaze. If looks could kill, he'd have spilled my guts across the kitchen floor.

"I just want to talk," I said, presenting my palms.

The man didn't move. He just kept on mad-dogging me.

"I tried calling before, but..."

Weiss' eyes shifted towards the counter. "I see you didn't get the hint, huh?" he spat.

I turned to the counter, eyeing the sandwich and soda he'd left there. "If you want to sit down and eat, I won't keep you. I just want to talk. I'll try not to take up too much of your time, sir. I just... I need your help. I wouldn't have come here otherwise."

He smirked. "Mighty kind of you, letting a man eat in his own home. Why don't you get out of here?" He took a heavy step towards me. The table stood between us, but his arms looked long enough to reach me even from there. I *really* didn't want to hit an old guy, and side-stepped towards the counter, where I noticed the cell phone that was sitting a foot away from the plate of food. *That* was what he'd been looking at. He wanted to call for help, get me kicked out of here.

I snatched the phone from the counter and shoved it into my

pocket, getting stern with him. "Let's cut the nonsense, OK? I don't make a habit of breaking and entering, so when I do it, you'd best believe I have a good reason. Now, you're going to tell me what I want to know, or else—"

"Or else?" challenged the old man. "What will you do? It doesn't matter what I tell you, kid. You're not going to like what I have to say."

"Let me be the judge of that." I motioned to the table. "Just tell me about the house on Morgan Road. About Irma. I've been seeing hideous things ever since I set foot in that place. There was a body stashed behind one of the walls—since unearthing it, I've been haunted by this devilish woman." I shook at the memory. "I can't say for sure, but I think it's your wife's spirit. Irma's ghost."

Weiss slid down into a chair. He was shaking now—judging by the redness in his cheeks, it was with anger, rather than fear. He stared at me, fists balled on the tabletop, as I continued.

"I bought that house from the City of Detroit. I'd planned to renovate it. Even after finding the corpse, I'd tried to keep fixing it. But..." I trailed off for a moment. "I just want to know if you can tell me why I'm seeing these things. I understand your wife died in that house. Is it possible that Irma's spirit is still lingering there—that she's the one I've been seeing? What about that body in the living room wall? Do you know anything about that, or was it put there after the house was abandoned in the early 90's?"

Weiss' shaking continued, but the color had dripped steadily from his face so that I could no longer attribute it to rage. The man still looked like he wanted to kill me, but he looked scared, too.

"I've done my homework," I added. "I know that your wife died in the house—that she struggled with mental illness. I know that your daughter ran off, too—that you guys didn't have a great relationship with her. I know that I have no business barging into your home like this, and believe me when I say I'm sorry to have done it. But until I get some answers... until I can understand what's happening to me... I don't have a choice. The way you're looking at me—the way you hung up on me before... why do I have a feeling that you know what I'm talking about? What can you tell me about the thing haunting that house, Mr. Weiss?"

There was silence as the old man leaned back in his chair. He smirked, lowering his gaze and giving his head a shake. When he finally looked up at me, his eyes had softened a touch, but his tone was as abrasive as ever. "Kid, you don't know what you're talking about. You don't know a thing."

It was Weiss' turn to take the floor.

THIRTY-SEVEN

"I wish you hadn't come here," began Weiss, sighing. "I would have liked to live out the rest of my days without having to concern myself with this. That house was never meant to be lived in again—not after what happened there." He looked wistfully to the living room, where the TV droned on, and for a second I thought he might make a break for it. The anger had gone from his face and there was only timidity there now. It looked out of place on his rough-cut visage. Dragging a palm against his smooth cheek, he fell into contemplative silence.

"What happened at the house?" I asked, crossing my arms. "There was a woman living nearby who told me some things about you and your family. She's lived in the neighborhood since the early eighties, and she shared some of the local gossip. I don't mean to be indelicate, but the impression I got is that you left your wife to suffer in that house. She sounded like an ill woman, probably in need of psychiatric care. After your daughter ran out on you two, it seems she only got worse. I've heard tell that you weren't around much in those days. Be honest with me: Is that why Irma is still around? Does she have some kind of grudge that's keeping her spirit anchored to this world?"

I thought my explanation was pretty thorough and rational, but Weiss threw me for a loop.

He grimaced, massaging a tightened jaw. The anger was back for a moment. "You think you've got it all mapped out, eh? Then why did you come here?"

I didn't back down. "Well, it's the truth, isn't it? Or, do you have a different version of events? I mean, why else would your wife's spirit keep wandering the house?" It occurred to me that there were other spirits to account for as well. Perhaps dozens of them. For a while, I'd been hearing queer voices in the house. The croaking, demonic voice I'd come to associate with Irma was the one that most stood out to me, but there'd been others. The voices of two murderers—Ed Ames and Bradford Cox—had been heard in the ghostly throng as well. Rather than bombard Weiss with all of my questions about the various aspects of the haunting, I gave him time enough to answer the queries hitherto posed.

And he did, but not in the way I'd expected.

"You really have no idea what you're talking about," replied Weiss. "The thing you're seeing... it speaks in a hundred voices, doesn't it? Terrible... *monstrous* voices..." He glanced up at me, cocking his head to the side. "It isn't Irma."

"What?"

Weiss shook his head.

"Well, who is it, then?"

Licking his lips, the man took his time in answering. "You say you found a body behind the wall in the living room. What did you do with it?"

"I called the police, obviously. They carried it off," was my reply.

Weiss glowered. "Of course you did. And that's why you're finished. That's why you're seeing it. You let her out." He planted his elbows on the table and folded his hands. "I can't believe you let her out."

My head was splitting with questions, and the first one that made it out was, *"You* knew about the body, then? Who is it? Whose body is that, if not Irma's?"

With distance in his gaze, Weiss sighed into his clasped palms. "It's my daughter's. Fiona's."

I let this sink in, and when it had, I chuckled derisively. "I don't have time for this. The body behind that wall was aged—an old woman's. White hair, shrunken body. I saw her myself. The spirit that's been following me is slight and bent like an old crone. Your daughter ran off in, what, 1980? '81? That isn't possible. At this point she must be in her fifties—"

The old man struck the table with a beefy fist. "You're going to march into my house, claiming to be haunted by terrifying things, and you're going to tell *me* what's possible? Why don't you shut your mouth and let me finish. You might learn something." He took a deep breath, reaching into the pocket of his sweatpants and pulling out an inhaler. His breathing had grown a bit labored, but after two puffs from the thing he was back to normal. "The body is Fiona's, yes. I know because I put it there myself." There wasn't any remorse in his tone as he admitted to this. If anything, there was a kind of stubborn pride.

I didn't believe him, figured he was jerking me around, but I let him keep talking.

"It was a joint decision, actually. Irma and I had no choice, and after much debate we decided it was for the best. We couldn't let her live. Not after what she'd become... And after we did it, we made sure to spread that rumor—that she'd had it with us and had run off, like kids that age are wont to do. It was believable. No one questioned it. But in reality, Fiona hadn't gone anywhere. She'd been in the house all along." He scowled at me again. "And she'd *still* be there, if not for your meddling. I don't understand it. Why would you want to live in that house? That neighborhood—the entire city—is a dump. You're young, you could live anywhere. Lots of houses to fix up in finer cities. Why come here?"

I didn't have an answer at the ready. I shut up and took my lumps, waiting for him to start up again. When he was slow to do so, I egged him on a little. "So... you murdered her, then? Murdered her and hid her body behind a wall? That's sick. What could have driven you to do it? And you talk about it like it was a perfectly natural thing to do. Didn't you love your daughter?"

He snorted. "Stop running that mouth of yours. You don't know me, or my late wife. You don't know what we went through, either. Seeing as how you're looking for answers, I'll fill you in, but you'd better shut your trap."

"All right," I conceded. "I'm listening."

Weiss sat up. "I'm a native of Maryland. Irma was, too. We tried for the first few years of our marriage to have children—to no avail. We decided to adopt, instead. In 1970, we adopted an 8-year old girl, Fiona, from a Maryland orphanage just an hour from our home in Annapolis."

"Annapolis?" I asked. The city name rang a bell—it was the place where Bradford Cox had killed a college student in 1952.

"That's right. The house had been my father's—and his father's before him. A gorgeous old German Colonial built on family-owned land in the 1800's. The plot it sat on, I guess, had once been a POW camp in the Civil War, but until we brought Fiona home, that had never meant anything to us." He drew a deep breath, chewing on his lower lip. "Not a few days had passed since we'd brought Fiona home when she began acting strange. Adopted children—especially orphans who've been tossed around in the foster system—often have trouble adjusting to their new homes. But this... this was different.

"From the very start, that girl didn't like sleeping at night. I used to joke, early on, that she wasn't a girl, but an owl. You know what she told me? 'No, I'm not an owl. I'm a raven.' Well, we tried everything, but we couldn't get the girl to adhere to a normal schedule. She had dark circles under her eyes all the time. She looked ill, though the doctor couldn't find anything wrong. He gave us some sleeping pills for her to try. They didn't work, and Fiona remained nocturnal.

"My daughter—no, it doesn't feel right to call her that after what happened. *That girl*, she wasn't a normal child. We set her up at two different schools, but she had trouble fitting in. She lasted a week or two at each before Irma insisted we pull her out and homeschool her. That wasn't such a problem, since my wife was overjoyed at finally being a mother. Sitting with the girl, teaching her... I'd never seen Irma happier. But the girl, though she kept on with her studies, just behaved more strangely as time went on.

"I'd come downstairs at night to get a drink of water, and I'd see her sitting alone in the living room. Most kids at that hour, if they aren't asleep, they're watching television or sneaking a midnight snack. Not Fiona. No, that girl would be sitting in a chair, facing the wall, mumbling to herself. This behavior concerned us. We asked her why she was doing this, who she thought she was talking to. She insisted she had 'friends' in the house, and that she had to speak to them every night.

"There's nothing weird about a kid having an imaginary friend or two, but this quickly got out of hand. It wasn't just a quirk with her— she kept doing it to the point where it was uncomfortable for visitors to the house. We disciplined her, warned her to stop, but she'd still do it. From dusk till dawn. She'd stand in corners sometimes, or in the basement with the lights off, just whispering with people that no one else could see.

"Therapists told us that this was just Fiona's way of coping with stress; that she'd stop on her own time. But those therapists never listened in on the conversations the girl was having with these 'friends'. Irma came up to bed one night, in tears, because she'd heard Fiona mumbling to herself about *murder*. She used to recite rhymes— strange, disturbing ones—that she claimed to have learned from her special friends. Ravens figured into a lot of them. It was getting to be too much. Irma was at wit's end. We even considered taking her back to the orphanage, figuring we weren't cut out to be parents.

"But, no. We kept her. We pressed on. Because that's what you do, right? You can't just send the kid back like a defective appliance or something. That's not how parenting works. It's *supposed* to be hard. If it isn't difficult, you aren't doing it right.

"I mentioned earlier that the house was built on a POW camp, right? Well, I got it into my head that—just maybe—there was something in the house that the girl was particularly sensitive to. Spirits... ghosts. An old place like that, where a war was fought, is as likely a place as any to host some otherworldly things, and some people, I think, are more sensitive than others. I loved that old house, had grown up in it myself, but because I wanted to be a good father and to separate this girl from whatever spirits might have been on the property, I decided to sell it and move far out of Maryland.

"At that time, Detroit was a fine city. Lots of cheap houses, not nearly so much crime. It was a good place to raise a family, I thought. Taking the money I'd made in the sale of the old house, I bought a plot of land there on Morgan Road, built the house you've been fixing up. It was 1975, and I was proud of it. I felt like I'd really made a good decision, like this was the start of a new chapter for us. Maybe it would have been, if only we'd adopted a different little girl."

"What happened when you moved to Detroit?" I asked. "Why didn't things work out as planned?"

"Because the girl brought her friends with her," Weiss replied flatly. "Like ticks that'd hitched a ride on her skin, the spirits—whatever they were—followed her to Detroit, to the new house."

I nodded, but was having considerable trouble understanding how such a thing was possible. "I don't get it. How could she bring spirits along? It's not like you can pack them in a bag, you know?"

"I couldn't properly explain it at that time, but I've had a lot of time to think since then, and there's one obvious explanation." He arched his feathery brows. "She let them inside," he said, patting his breast. "Invited them in."

"Fiona... allowed herself to be possessed by the spirits in your old house?" I asked.

"To put it simply, that's exactly what she did. But when you let something like that inside, you find it isn't keen on leaving. Hold it in long enough, and it begins to change you. Damage you. A human body is made for one soul, young man. Have you ever stopped to consider what might happen if you inserted a second? A third? What about ten? Twenty?" Weiss cracked his knuckles. "Fiona began to change—slowly at first, but then radically. She was thirteen years old when we moved to Detroit, a notoriously difficult age as it is, but her moods got more and more wild. Rude or outright obscene outbursts were not uncommon, and sometimes they were even delivered in interesting new voices. That is to say, Fiona began speaking in voices besides her own—masculine voices, elderly voices... and then voices wholly lacking in human character.

"She knew things that she shouldn't have known. Started talking about news items—murders—that had taken place before she'd even been born. Talked about the killers themselves as if she knew them personally, in fact. And it turns out that she *did* know them, better than anyone else on this Earth, because she'd invited them in. Allowed herself to become seeded by them, *infected*. That's what she became—an infection, a walking disease. And it showed.

"She'd always looked tired, sickly, like I told you. It only got worse the more of them she allowed in. Her hair started to change—got whiter than my own," said Weiss, tugging on his thin hair. "At some point, probably before the move, she'd been terrified at the prospect of losing her friends at the other house. So, in order to keep from losing them, she invited them into her own body. And it slowly killed her. She came to look so monstrous, so aged by the end, that she was unrecognizable."

"Why would she do that?" I asked. "Why invite spirits into her body? Why bring them from Maryland?"

Weiss shrugged. "I've thought about that. I might have asked her outright, but by the time we realized what was happening, only *they* would respond to us. I think that Fiona's early childhood was probably hard. She spent a lot of time alone, had always wanted friends.

Peculiar child that she was, she could see and communicate with things that the rest of us are usually fortunate enough to overlook. Having finally made a connection with someone, she didn't want to part with them when the time came to move. And when she became possessed by them, I think she liked the fact that they'd never leave of their own accord. They'd stay with her forever. It felt secure.

"But the ghosts she brought with her weren't enough after awhile. She started looking for more 'friends'. Though we kept her under lock and key, she'd run out some nights and go exploring. Sometimes, she'd go into the crawlspace and we'd hear her scurrying under the floors like an animal, chattering with the spirits. Other times, Irma and I would spend hours driving around the neighborhood looking for her, only to find her sitting in the old graveyard down the road, talking to the headstones. She found other restless souls there and brought them along. I don't know how many she absorbed into herself before all was said and done, but…"

I knew the tottering graveyard on Morgan Road very well. I'd woken up there that very morning, confused and soaked. Fiona had been drawn there, too—for the purpose of swallowing up new spirits. That was why I'd heard the voice of Detroit killer Edward Franklin Ames in the house. Fiona had spent time at that grave and had invited him in. She'd likely encountered Bradford Cox's spirit under similar circumstances, back in Maryland.

"Not that we didn't try a few things over the years," continued Weiss. "When our terror outweighed the shame we felt at having a monster for a daughter, we did seek help. Two Catholic priests came to the house under the cover of night to assess her. They wanted to rid our daughter of the spirits that had taken hold, but she wouldn't cooperate—wouldn't even allow them near her. She threatened violence against them and practically chased them out. She was no victim here—she was clinging to these evil spirits of her own free will.

"By the time she was about sixteen, we'd come to accept that Fiona would remain our private burden. We kept her hidden. She wasn't allowed out of the house. We kept her in her bedroom, the one with the lock on the outside of the door, and only went inside to deliver meals. Not that she ate them, mind you. By then, the girl was being nourished by *something else* and had no interest in worldly food or drink.

"On occasions where she'd get loose, we'd find her stalking around the property like an animal, staring into the windows of neighboring houses. The others along the street didn't know what we were going through. They thought the girl was homeschooled and that Irma was overprotective, yes. I think a lot of them thought that she must have been sick. They seldom ever saw her, except at a distance, and so it was easy enough for us to maintain those illusions. We stopped having company, stopped talking to our families once we got to Detroit. As out-of-towners, it was easy enough to keep to ourselves.

"We knew that we weren't going to live forever. That's why we decided that something needed done. We were afraid that she'd do something to us—she'd sometimes enter our bedroom and stare at us while we slept—and then escape into the world. We couldn't let that happen. We installed a padlock on the door to our bedroom to keep her out at night, but a person can only live that way, in constant fear, for so long.

"So, we hatched a plan. She *had* to be dealt with. In 1981, when she was 19 years old, I poisoned her. She proved susceptible to muscle relaxers. Irma had been prescribed some after a back injury she'd gotten after a tussle with Fiona. I injected the girl with twice what I believed to be a lethal dose and she went into a coma.

"The rest, I suppose, you already know. I hid her body in the living room wall. We told people we saw in town that she'd run off on us, and though they were sympathetic, none seemed particularly surprised. But Fiona didn't die." Weiss shuddered. He fished his inhaler back out of his pocket and set it on the table, preemptively. "Not right away."

"She'd been behind the wall for only a few hours when we first heard her stir. The voices—terrible, inhuman voices—started coming out of that wall, calling out to us all around the house. We heard her thrashing around in there, trying to break free. This went on for some nights. She died a slow death back there, and we heard every minute of it. And even when her body gave out and she suffocated, the voices kept going. Her corpse was still filled with them. Parasites.

"We'd hoped that the spirits in her body would move on, that they'd eventually leave, but they clung to her like wasps in a hive. And they went on to incorporate themselves into the rest of the house, too. You'd walk around after dark and see long shadows up and down the halls, or *feel* someone looking at you in an otherwise empty room.

"But those voices... Every night, you could hear them. Months had passed since we'd put the girl back there, and the voices kept on. I couldn't handle it, I moved out. Irma, though..." Weiss hesitated, jaw growing tense. "Nights and nights of this drove her out of her mind. She knew better than to listen to the voices and the terrible things they spewed, but even as she stuffed her ears with cotton or went out into the yard, the knowledge that the house was filled with them got to her. It began to affect her health, the constant stress and terror. The house was such a burden that it aged her and killed her years before her time. She'd wear earplugs after sundown, trying to drown them out." Weiss drew in a shaky breath. "She didn't want to leave the house for two reasons. The first, was that she thought—rightfully—that someone should live there and keep an eye on Fiona's resting place, lest it be disturbed and the nightmare start up elsewhere. Her other reason was that, frankly, she'd always wanted to be a mother. Fiona had been a monster, but she'd been our responsibility, and to her dying day Irma had committed herself to the girl."

The true monster in this story wasn't Fiona, as far as I was concerned. Her parents had been the real villains here. Listening to Weiss justify the murder of his own daughter left me nauseous. That he'd treated it as a duty and demonstrated so little remorse left me badly shaken, but I didn't interrupt him as he kept on.

"Irma's body gave out and she died before she could end up like Fiona. For that, I'm thankful. I abandoned the house after that. The neighborhood as a whole was on the verge of emptying out, and there seemed to be no chance of the area ever being spruced up. Maybe, far into the future, the houses would all be demolished and something else would be built there, but by then I reckoned I'd be dead and it wouldn't be my problem anymore.

"I have a theory about the nature of that house, based on the changes I saw over the years. After Fiona came to rest in the wall, after her physical body died, her spirit and all of the others she'd housed became something else. Transformed, if you will. They integrated with the house, possessed the *building*, so to speak. And they laid low, waiting for someone to come in there and give them a new body. They would have taken Irma if she'd only listened to them. That's how they get in, I think. If you start listening to the dead, open yourself up to them, they sneak in. Slowly at first, so that you barely notice. Then, when the floodgates open, all bets are off. And I guess that's where you come in."

"What do you mean by that?" I asked, though I already knew.

"The spirits," uttered Weiss, sizing me up with a frown. "They're in *you* now."

This news was not altogether new; I'd already suspected that the spirits had followed me out of the house. Nevertheless, I didn't believe that they'd made a home in me—that I was toting them around. I laughed nervously. "No, that's not right. They're tailing me, but... I haven't let the ghosts in. I would never do something like that. Fiona invited them, went looking for them, but I..."

Weiss stared at me a long while, toying with his earlobe. "I suppose it is up for debate, isn't it? I saw Fiona ravaged by these spirits that now accost you, saw her transformed into a monster over the course of years, but what do I know? You're probably fine. Perfectly fine." He waved as if to dismiss me.

"I've been seeing them—Fiona... the shadows... And I've been hearing the voices. Just before I came here, at the hotel I'd been staying at, I—"

"That's right," replied the old man, chuckling to himself. "You've been seeing them *outside* the house. Which means they've found a way to move freely beyond the bounds of that property. Tell me, how do you think they managed that? For twenty—no, *thirty* years—after I abandoned that house, they stayed put. They fell into a lull. Fiona's corpse sat behind that wall, undisturbed. But suddenly you come along and find the body. You let her out. And no sooner do you let her out, do the voices start. And the shadows, and the sightings. No, I'm sure that things happened before you found that body, didn't they? It didn't feel quite right in that house from the very start. But you stayed. You stayed." He laughed harder, shaking his head. "You gave them permission, kid. You made yourself at home there, and the pests that had laid their roots in the building descended upon you when you least expected it."

"No, no... That's..." I wanted to shut him up, to deliver some artic-ulate argument to the contrary, but came up short. Thinking back to my first days in the house, there *had* been the long shadows, the seeming malfunction of the porch light, the disembodied footsteps, the scratching behind the walls. Things had only gotten worse after my discovery of the body, but even before that day the house had indeed given me a bad vibe. And Weiss was right about one thing: Despite my feelings about the property, I'd stayed there. Even the night after finding Fiona's corpse, I'd stayed.

"Irma wasn't all there towards the end," continued Weiss, soberly. "She knew to protect herself from the spirits—not to listen to them. Whenever she did listen, they'd tell her, 'Let me in. Let me in.' Like the wolf in the Three Little Pigs story. 'Let me in'. My wife was unwell, but she wasn't stupid. She never listened to those voices. But you did, didn't you? And you did nothing to protect yourself. What did they say to you?"

I froze up at the memory of those strange and terrible voices. "At first, I didn't hear any voices. But then, when they did start up, they said all kinds of things," I replied. "There was one... it spoke in rhymes. Others would be snippets of conversation. Or sounds of laughing. Crying, too. I don't know... there were so many. After finding Fiona's body, I ended up capturing some of the voices on camera. I listened to them, tried to figure out what they were saying. It was hard, though. The voices are so ugly, so... inhuman."

Weiss nodded. "Notice how they didn't start up all at once. Things got worse slowly over time, didn't they? It makes sense. I'm sure that the house had been used by squatters and the like for brief periods, but no one had properly lived in it for a long, long time. The spirits aren't dumb. They won't suddenly awaken, start jabbering from the onset. They'll start up slowly, wait until you're comfortable there. Until you're willing to dismiss their murmurings as voices on the wind. You've got to hand it to them—that's the way a predator seizes its prey. You were like a frog in a pot of water. They boiled you slowly. By the time you knew what was going on, it was too late."

I wasn't sure what disgusted me more: The idea that I may be filled with malign, foreign spirits, or the amusement Weiss expressed. "OK, enough. I get it. Staying in the house was stupid. I've realized that for awhile now. But surely it's not too late. I'm still not inviting them in like Fiona did. Surely I can cast them out... right?"

"Maybe you can," said Weiss. "But those things take time... If I'm right—if those spirits have changed... coalesced into something more virulent—then time is the one thing you don't have. There's only one safe option."

"And that would be?"

Weiss spelled it out for me. "To die somewhere remote, some-where hard to find. From this day forth, consider your body a tainted vessel. Imagine it's filled with nuclear waste. How might you dispose of such a thing? I'll tell you how: You go out into the desert some-where, find a ditch and you die in it, hoping that no one ever finds you and catches the same batch of spirits that now cling to you. Maybe, in a hundred years, their presence will wane and they'll dissipate like a foul gas, returning to wherever they crawled out of. That's your best bet, and my only advice."

"You can't be serious," I challenged. "*Roll over and die* isn't going to cut it. I want to live, Mr. Weiss."

"I'm being completely serious. Do you think that I killed and hid Fiona for my own pleasure?" was his rejoinder. "It was the responsible thing to do. It *needed* done. As her father, I had to take responsibility for what she'd become. If I let it out of that house, then there was no telling what that ghost-filled abomination might have done. Despite her monstrosity, Irma loved the girl to the very end. Women are like that, aren't they? Sentimental. A mother can't help but love her child, no matter how awful they become. It wasn't like that for me. I suspect you haven't got any kids of your own, and so you don't know what it's like to be a father. In order to be a father, you have to be prepared to turn off your heart. To know when enough is enough. No, no... this is more than mere fatherhood. If you consider yourself a real man, then in situations like these you must set things right without hesitance."

"This is nonsense. As a father, your biggest job is to protect and care for your children. You gave up on her and killed her instead. Calling it a 'responsibility' and dressing up the matter in all this talk of manhood might help you sleep at night, but it's murder—plain and simple. You should feel ashamed of yourself. No father deserving of the title would ever think to do what you did."

Weiss frowned, tossed his shoulders. "You wouldn't understand..."

"Enough. How can I stop it?" I demanded, as if expecting him to suddenly come up with a new, more appealing solution.

He stood, his knees cracking as he did so. Shuffling across the kitchen, Weiss took the plate of food on the counter and brought it back to the table. Guzzling some soda, he burped loudly and sat back down. "I'm sorry to have to tell you this, but there is no way out. You did it to yourself. You stayed in the house, gave those things the audience they craved. Now you're a threat—not merely to yourself, but to others. Those spirits will warp you. If you truly value the safety of other people, then hide away in some hard-to-reach place and—"

"No! Don't even suggest it." I fumed, pacing around the kitchen. "There has to be something else. Maybe this has happened to other people. Or, you know, there could be some clue in the house. If the spirits are in me, maybe I can return them to the house. I'm not gonna go down without a fight!"

"You haven't listened to a word I've said," replied Weiss, choking down a bite of his sandwich. "I don't envy your position, but you know what needs done. You know what you have to do. If you don't do it soon, you'll end up wishing you'd never been born. Now, kindly leave. It's getting dark, and I don't care to see what you've brought with you."

Rage flowed through me. "Why don't I just call the detectives who collected Fiona's body, huh? Maybe I'll fill them in, tell them whose body that is and how it got there!"

Weiss shrugged me off. "Feel free. I did what I thought needed done."

"You killed your own daughter! You gave up on her—you were a monster and a coward!" I could've spat on him. "Killing myself won't fix this. I wanna live! Why don't you help me find some way out of this—an actual solution?"

Willard said nothing.

The old man wasn't going to change his tune. I'd learned everything I could from him. I returned his cell phone to the counter. Leaving him to his dinner, I slid open the door and stepped out into the lawn. Before I shut it behind me, I thought to ask him one last thing. "There's something I've been wondering about. There's a Callery pear tree growing in the front yard. Why? It reeks. I've hated it from the moment I first saw it."

At this, Weiss set down his sandwich and looked sorrowfully past me, into the dusk. "Oh, the tree." He sighed, wiping at his lips with a napkin. "I planted it for Irma. She loved its flowers, and I just wanted her to have something pretty to look at. She was a prisoner in that house towards the end. Tending to that tree was the only joy in her life."

I'd been planning a smart reply, but I swallowed it instead.

I took off, burdened with more than the ghosts I'd brought.

When I'd arrived, I'd hoped that Willard Weiss would be of help to me. I was now leaving his place, weighed down with leaden despair.

THIRTY-EIGHT

I sat in the van, staring down at my phone. I had a new voicemail message.

Though I couldn't bring myself to listen to the entire thing, the caller—a woman who spoke way too fast—was apparently affiliated with the Home Improvement Network. She'd been calling to "touch base" and wanted me to "get back to her", presumably to arrange for a visit to the house by network representatives.

I deleted the message before it finished playing and threw my phone into the passenger seat.

I didn't care about that anymore. I wished I'd never cared about it in the first place. It'd been my determination to see the job through, to secure a TV deal at any cost, that had gotten me into this mess. Now I had nothing.

No, not *nothing*. I would've much preferred to have gained nothing from the house, actually. But the house had given me quite a lot, and without my knowledge. The house had gifted me *multitudes*.

The sun was going down. Night was on its way, and I knew what that meant.

Weiss is right. You're absolutely done for.

Though I'd brought the camera with me, packed with horrid footage of the supernatural, I hadn't even shown it to him. Not that he'd wanted to see it; he didn't need visual proof to believe in monsters. In his days living on Morgan Road with Fiona, I reckoned he'd seen his fair share of such horrors.

To hear him tell it, I had no choice but death. You don't need me to tell you why I thought that was a bad idea.

I wanted to live. To make it through this somehow. Though Weiss had offered no solution, I still believed—or tried to believe—that there was a way out of this. Even after watching myself on tape, floating in mid-air; even after coming to in the graveyard, I grasped blindly for an escape hatch.

I was willing to concede the point that the spirits in that house had entered my body, that I now served as a kind of host to them. I couldn't feel them in any obvious way, but the not-so-subtle changes in my appearance made their presence hard to deny. My eyes and skin had changed, and my hair had started going prematurely grey, like Fiona's had. I was being transformed into something monstrous.

But life is precious. I couldn't stand Weiss' suggestion that I simply give in and accept death. I would try everything in my power to break free of this curse—but I wouldn't just roll over and die. Suicide would never be on the table.

Thinking back on the time spent in the house, I tried to look at things through a new lens, applying everything I'd learned from Weiss. What I most wanted to discern was the exact point when the spirits had taken hold. Figuring this out proved exceptionally difficult, however. After a bit of meditation on my earliest moments there, I found I couldn't be sure of anything. Had I been in full control of myself throughout that first night, or had my reactions been guided by an external force?

One easy case to look at was my own relationship to that abandoned graveyard near the house. I'd discovered the spot before I'd even found the body—before I'd even known the name Fiona Weiss. I couldn't have possibly known of its significance, or of Fiona's pilgrimages there to seek out new souls, but I'd found myself drawn to the spot, repeatedly, just the same. My gut told me I hadn't wound up there of my own accord. More likely, I'd been lured there by Fiona. Her influence, however subtle, was likely vaster than I realized.

Until I'd spoken to Weiss, I had been certain that the body in the wall had been that of an old woman. I couldn't have guessed at the truth—it was too unbelievable, too grotesque. A peculiar girl had taken to inviting spirits into her body, and the resulting strain had left her an aged husk. It had resulted, too, in a specter more terrifying and loathsome than any borne of a single human soul. Countless spirits had taken up residence in the girl's body, and for decades they'd merged within her corpse. In Weiss' opinion, they'd mingled behind the walls of that abandoned house, evolving into something new, more virulent.

Now, they were in me.

Weiss had told me that I'd brought this on myself, and I hated to admit it, but he was right. I should have left in those early nights when things had begun feeling off. After the first few incidents, the first suspicions of trespassers, or glimpses of long, unnatural shadows, I should have backed out of the project. I thought back to the note, too—the one that Fiona had modified. She'd spelled it out for me, plainly. *We want you. Many of us. All of us will be watching.* I'd chosen to ignore the warning.

I cursed my father, stupid though it was. I'd spent a fair amount of time wondering how my father would have handled the job, how my father would have fared in the face of such strange events. *"Don't give up on this job! Dad wouldn't have given up!"* I'd told myself. It'd been a terrible misstep to stick to my father's unreasonable standards, though. He'd been obsessed with his work up until his final breath. My father had been a perfect example of what I'd have done well to avoid in life. Instead, I'd clung to his memory and emulated his stubbornness.

I started driving. The sun was slipping and every hair on my body began standing on end as if to watch it set. The van was large, spacious, but it didn't feel that way as I took off down the road, racking my mind for a destination. With every passing mile, I felt like there were other people in the cabin with me. We were pressed in like sardines, barely any room to move, to breathe.

Thinking back to my talk with Weiss, something he'd said really stuck in my craw. *"I did what I thought needed done."* I wondered if Weiss would be so keen to follow that path if he were in my position. No matter his foolish ideas, there would be no peace or comfort in suicide. Throwing away my life wasn't in the cards—I refused to even entertain it. There *had* to be another way.

I rolled onto the highway and started going south. I wasn't sure where I'd end up. The tank was half-full and I just wanted to put Detroit behind me for good.

Food. It'd been a while since my last meal. Maybe I'd be able to think more clearly if I ate something. I couldn't think of anything that sounded remotely appealing, but every few miles, when the billboards for restaurants popped up, I took a gander and tried to decide which exit to take.

In the distance, stretching into the sky so that it was backlit by the final embers of the day, was a cathedral. The sight of it brought me a good deal of relief, and I assured myself that I wasn't alone in this—that there were still people in the world who could help me get rid of these things. My visit with Father Kaspar had gone sideways, but surely I'd find someone else who could cast these ghosts out of me.

Or, I wondered, *what if they aren't in me anymore? What if they've moved on?*

Now that I was speeding out of Detroit, there was no telling how the spirits would react. I rolled down the windows, let the fresh air wash over me. The feelings of stuffiness and occupation in the van immediately dissipated.

The further I drove, the more I wanted to believe that the spirits had never really been inside of me. *You never spoke to them... you never went looking for them. You never gave them permission.* Unlike

Fiona, I'd never formally invited the things into my body, and I'd never gone looking for them. She had been overrun by spirits because she'd courted them, "swallowed" them up. That was a big difference. Perhaps the spirits had taken an interest in me, but so long as I didn't want them there, they would never be able to stay in me like they had in Fiona.

I had a warm feeling right then. A feeling that, somehow, everything was going to be OK.

Glancing at the next set of billboards, I decided to take the next exit to grab some Arby's.

Before I could shift into the right lane, I felt a strong tickle in my throat and began to cough. My lungs ached as I hacked over and over again, a terrible itch running up and down my airway. Something needled my epiglottal flap—a tonsil stone? When I finally caught my breath, I hit the dome light and opened my mouth, inspecting myself in the rearview mirror.

What should have been a momentary glance became a full-on stare as I discovered a bump on the inside of my mouth, just beyond the soft palate. It was fairly small in size, looking very much like a boil that hadn't come to head. I kept one eye on the road, another in the mirror as I reached into my mouth and explored the new growth with my fingertip. It ached, and as I touched the angry flesh I felt something just beneath the surface that wanted desperately to protrude.

I pulled my finger out—to keep myself from gagging—and had another look.

In having nudged it, the lump had seemingly come to a head. A bit of white peeked out at me.

That was when I realized I wasn't looking at a pustule, or a tonsil stone, but at a *sclera*.

An eye—presumably the first of many—was starting to emerge from the inside of my throat.

As if the owner of that eye were delighted at my discovery, a loud, croaking laugh emanated from the van's rear compartment.

In my distraction, my grip on the wheel going slack, the vehicle had begun to list. Gazing with horror at my reflection, I failed to correct course in time. My eyes snapped back to the road as something grey loomed in my periphery.

It was too late.

After that, I only remember slamming into the median.

THIRTY-NINE

The nurse shook out a freshly laundered pillowcase and stuffed a pillow into it. Bringing it to the bed, she instructed me to sit up so that she might set it behind my head. "You weren't like this for the first few days," she said, smiling. "I was here the night they brought you in. You were like a different person."

I pushed aside my dinner tray, packed with unappealing, mass-produced foodstuffs, and sat upright. "First few days? How long have I been here, again?" I blushed. "Sorry, I'm still a little fuzzy on the details..."

The nurse was a chatty woman named Denise. She was in her early 30's, recently separated, and had two children—a boy and a girl. Her son, Daniel, was named after her ex—a drunk. She held out hope that they'd be able to save their marriage through couples therapy. One of her girlfriends, a hair stylist named Becca, knew a woman at her church who'd gone through marriage counseling with some local relationship specialist, and after just two sessions...

Why did I know all this? It was because every time the nurse had stopped into my room that day, she'd lingered ten, twenty minutes to chat. *All* of the staff here were like that, as if they were bored and looking for conversation. The one thing they *hadn't* talked much about was my arrival to the hospital, or how long I'd been there. It was like they'd all made a promise not to broach that subject. Even the doctors hadn't said much to me. They'd referred to my stay in "days", had discussed a certain difficulty with my care in rather vague terms, but that was all.

"Today is your fifth day," admitted Denise, opening the blinds and letting in a bit of sun. "When they brought you in to the ER, I was told you were non-responsive. They hurried you to the ICU, did a bunch of scans to figure out why you weren't regaining consciousness. They thought you were in a coma. The scans didn't find anything, though, and then you came around. It's pretty miraculous. You got some bumps and scrapes, but for the most part you came out of that wreck OK." She laughed to herself. "Though the scans didn't show anything, you probably bumped your head in the crash, and that's why you started acting the way you did."

"How do you mean?" I asked.

"Well, it's hard to describe. You've since told us you have no history of mental illness, and the toxicology panels all came back negative, so we know you weren't high. Trouble is, you acted very strangely those first few nights. You were in and out of it then, mostly sleeping during the day. At night you'd get up and walk around."

I tensed up. "I was active at night, huh?"

"Yeah. And you used to talk to yourself. We had a new girl, a nurse's aid, working three nights back who came in to check on you during the hourly rounds. You scared her half to death. She said you were standing in the corner, talking to yourself. We see that in patients who struggle with dementia or certain mental illnesses. I think the trauma of the crash probably shook something loose. You look too young to me to have dementia." She furrowed her brow. "Now, let me ask you something. Your license said that you were twenty-five, but that's a typo, right?"

"Uh, no, that's correct," I replied.

There was incredulity in her gaze, but she said nothing more on the matter. Turning towards the mirror over the hand washing sink and really focusing on my reflection for the first time in awhile, I understood her confusion.

I looked wrung out. My hair was more grey than brown now, and my skin was starting to sag.

"The third night you were here," continued Denise, "You *really* gave us a scare. You popped out of your room while the staff was doing shift report at the station. No one saw you leave. We had to call a code brown—a search for a missing patient. Security guards found you half an hour later, down in the morgue!" She laughed. "I don't know how you got all the way down there without being noticed. You even got inside! We ended up having to sedate you at night, to keep you from exploring. Now that you're with it again, it's funny, right? But when they told me they'd found you in the morgue, it was kind of freaky. Like a total horror movie thing, you know? That reminds me, my friend Becca, the hair stylist, she saw a movie awhile back that was *really* scary. I think it might have been one of those Stephen King movies. You like those? It was probably the one with the—"

My time at the hospital had been a blur. Since totaling my van and ending up on the intermediate care unit, my grip on the passage of time had loosened considerably. Days had bled into nights, nights into days, and the only thing that had really stood out to me was the constant churn of faces. If I focused hard, I could remember brief interactions, like scenes from a movie.

"*Hello, Mr. Taylor. I'm Doctor Florian. I just wanted to see how you were doing today.*"

"*What's that, Mr. Taylor? You'd like more ice water? Sure thing, I'll bring the cart by.*"

"*I'm sorry, Mr. Taylor, but the cafeteria only serves Pepsi products. Can I interest you in some juice instead? We have apple, orange, grape—*"

I could remember some of that back and forth.

What I couldn't remember was any of this "strange" behavior I'd exhibited. I didn't remember talking to myself. I didn't remember wandering to the morgue.

But that isn't to say I didn't believe it. There'd been a precedent for such behaviors in my waking at the graveyard. Sometimes, after dark, I wasn't in full control of my body, because the spirits would come out to play. Fiona had probably led me down to the morgue in the hopes of chatting up the souls of the freshly-deceased. For all I knew, there were now some former patients of this hospital in me, alongside Ed Ames, Bradford Cox and all the rest.

I'd been so out of it over the course of my hospitalization that I hadn't thought much about Fiona or the house on Morgan Road. My waking life had been consumed by banal interactions with staff, with routine medical procedures and preemptive rounds of sedatives that left me drowsy and uncertain. Whenever my thoughts did touch upon those terrible subjects, I tried dismissing them out of hand, hoping that a continued denial of the facts would be enough to save me.

But every time I looked in a mirror, I seemed a little older. And apparently, I'd been going out of my room for nightly walks, or standing around, muttering in odd voices. As much as I wanted to believe that everything before the crash was fiction, the reality was impossible to deny. The worst was yet to come.

Denise took notes on a clipboard after fastening a blood pressure cuff around my arm. She then hit some buttons on the bed. Sighing, she knelt down and looked at the buttons more closely, hitting them until they made a discordant dinging noise. "Not again..."

"What's wrong?" I asked.

"Can you stand up for me?"

I did as I was told—with a lot more difficulty than I'd expected. My legs felt brittle, my muscles shrunken.

Denise mashed the buttons once more, then invited me to sit back down on the bed. "Every scale in this building is trash! This is the third one I've tried for you, and I can never get an accurate read." She pointed to a little LCD panel on the right bedrail. "See? This is supposed to give me your weight, but even after zeroing it out, it's not giving me the right number. These bed scales are made to weigh patients up to six-hundred pounds, but it's telling me that you're over the limit!" She combed a hand through he hair, laughing. Tugging away the bedclothes, she asked jokingly, "You aren't hiding anyone else in bed with you, right?"

I shrank away from her.

Deep within me, I could feel an alien soul brushing against my bones.

Denise had to go see her other patients and excused herself. She stepped out of the room, closed the door behind her, and left me alone. Where I would usually have invited the silence, I wanted nothing more than to listen to her inane chatter.

The sun fell away from the window, hidden by clouds. I tried to distract myself by thinking about the weather—it looked like rain—but what I saw reflected in the glass bowled me over.

There was a chair across from the window, near the doorway, intended for visitors.

And there was someone sitting in it.

The frail body twitched. Snow white hair hung down past the shoulders like lumps of Amazonian vines. Skeletal hands sat limp in the figure's lap. Though she did not move, I could feel Fiona watching me. Not with her own eyes—those were gone, long decayed—but with the dozens that blinked behind her lips.

I sank into the bed, hyperventilated into a pillow.

Ignore her. She'll go away if you ignore her.

I felt the bed below me, the metal rails on both sides of me. These things were *real*. The figure sitting across the room wasn't real—not in the same way, at least. I was a part of *this* world, the physical world of hospital beds, of talkative nurses. Fiona had been a part of it once, but was no longer. She could interact with my world, wander through it, but her influence ended there. She was like a shadow peeking through from the other side—a memory.

This isn't her world. Ignore her. You never let her in, never gave her permission, so she can't affect this world. Ignore her and she'll disappear. The more you think about her, the more you focus on her sitting there, the more power you give her.

I cleared my mind, tried counting to three.

When I finished counting, she'd be gone.

I'd open my eyes at three, and I'd be alone again.

"One," I whimpered.

I heard a fleshy foot connecting with the waxed floors.

"T-Two..."

There was movement at the foot of my bed. Hands gripped the bedclothes tightly. The rails creaked as someone climbed over them. I felt someone's weight pressing down on my legs, felt something coarse—hair-like—tickling my arms. Even with a pillow pressed against my face, I could feel someone watching me from above.

To test the hypothesis I had only to utter "Three" and open my eyes, but I couldn't do it.

The pillow was pushed gently aside. There was someone laying next to me. I could feel their cold lips pressed against my ear. They parted, and from deep behind them there came a quiet, croaking voice, which counted, *"THREE."*

FORTY

It was no small feat, getting discharged from the hospital against medical advice the next morning.

A psych doctor had to come by and clear me mentally before I was allowed to sign the requisite forms, and I was warned that such a discharge would make it next to impossible to bill insurance for the cost of my care, which was by that time many tens of thousands of dollars. I'd be on the hook for every penny.

It didn't matter. I dressed in a pair of surgical scrubs and lit out with only my wallet and cellphone.

I'd stayed awake the entire night, fearful that Fiona might take me on another nighttime journey if I slept. When the nurses came around, I refused everything, not wanting their drugs to mess with my head. In that time, I'd struggled to come up with a plan.

I had accepted the miserable truth. I was possessed, colonized by the souls of the dead that had come to rest behind the walls of that house after Fiona's passing. She was in me, too, and nightly directed me in seeking out more souls to add to the collection. If I allowed it, she'd keep on goading me, leading me to fresh souls in need of a worldly vessel, and my body would eventually burst at the seams.

Already I had aged considerably, as she had. A human body is built to contain but one soul—the strain of hosting many was truly terrible.

My shaky plan was merely this: I'd try reaching out once more to Willard Weiss.

My talk with Weiss had not gone the way I'd hoped. He'd cleared things up for me, had provided me with all the information there was about the haunting of the house on Morgan Road, but hadn't offered a viable solution.

I called him first thing, while waiting for a cab in the shadow of the hospital building. I didn't expect him to come up with a solution, to save me from this, but before leaving the city and seeking out answers on my own, I felt the need to speak to him again. His closeness to the events that had created this haunting made him vitally important, and if there were any other details to be gleaned that might be of use to future investigators, I wanted desperately to know them.

I hadn't expected him to answer, but he did. "It's *you*, isn't it?" was the first thing out of his mouth.

I told him that it was, in fact, *me*. "Things are getting bad," I said. "I don't look my age anymore. I feel like I'm falling apart, man. I'm losing track of time, and I see her everywhere. Each night, she's guiding me to do things. I was in the hospital, and even there..."

Weiss was silent for a long while. When he spoke up, it was merely to berate me again. "I've told you this already, but you did it to yourself. You shouldn't have stayed in that house. I wish I'd burned it down. I wish I'd hidden her elsewhere. Maybe this wouldn't have happened, then." He cursed under his breath. "You shouldn't have stayed there, kid. You could have avoided all of this."

"That doesn't help me much," I replied. "And I didn't have a choice but to stay there. I was working on the house, fixing it—I mean, how was I supposed to know? No one told me about what had happened there, what souls were resting in the place. I've stayed overnight in a number of worksites before and never encountered something like this."

"No!" spat Weiss. "You *did* know, and that's why you're up the creek! Tell me again, how many signs did you ignore, huh? How many things did you pass off as 'coincidence'? You messed around in that house even when, deep in your heart, you knew you shouldn't have been there. You brought it upon yourself. I shouldn't feel bad for you. I do, but how I wish I didn't."

"That house was supposed to be my shot at something greater!" I shouted. My eyes ached with tears. "It was supposed to be a turning point for my career. I only had to fix it in thirty days and put out some stupid videos. People—*important* people—were interested in me! They wanted to put me on TV when I was done. I stuck it out. Even when things got scary, I kept working in there because I wanted so badly to succeed. But I couldn't have possibly known what I was getting into. No one could have known."

Weiss sighed. "I don't care about your reasons—they amount to nothing but greed, ambition. You didn't have a clear head, and so you chose to ignore the warnings. Now you're sowing the rewards of your carelessness. And for what? To fix up that accursed house? So that you could play at being Bob Vila?"

A taut silence grew up between us.

"In all these years, I've wondered if I couldn't have found another way to help Fiona," began Weiss, clearing his throat. "But the answer I've always returned to is a resounding 'no'. And I'll tell you why that is. Fiona didn't want to be helped. She'd gathered those spirits up, willingly invited them. She'd wanted them there. Even now, she doesn't want to be separated from them, which is why she's taken up residence in *you*."

"But... but I didn't invite them in," I said.

"No, you *did*. With your carelessness. But you do differ from Fiona in one crucial way. You don't want the spirits to stay. You want them out. So..."

I held my breath.

"Perhaps there is a way out." Weiss paused. "There may be something we can try..."

"*Anything*," I was quick to reply.

The old man took his time in responding. "I wasn't intending to do this," he began, "but I want to help you if I can. I'll make a phone call, get ahold of this friend of mine and let him know of this grave matter. He's got some experience with these things... I'll make an appeal to him, see if he can't help. It's been years since I've gone back to that house, but I suggest we meet there. Can you meet me there this afternoon? Say, at two? This is a delicate matter. We don't want the eyes of the world upon us while attempting to work this out."

"Absolutely, yes," I replied. "I can meet you there."

"Very good. I'll take a cab, bring my friend along. I don't want to get your hopes up, but... we may be able to turn this around yet. Tell me, is the house safe? Is it still stable after all these years?"

"Oh, yeah, the house isn't a problem," I replied. "I have all of my tools laying around, and it's a little dusty, but it's not dangerous."

"Good, good. Now, listen. Due to my medication schedule, I can't be out much past eight at night. It would be better to get this over with early, so I'll head over as soon as I can. If it takes me longer to get there, don't worry. Stay in the house until I arrive, lest we get separated and waste time. This nightmare started there. I'd like for it to end there, too."

"OK, I'll meet you there around two," I said.

The plan was drawn.

A cab rolled up to the curb and I dropped into the back seat. When the driver asked me where to, I told him to take me to the graveyard on Morgan Road.

Weiss had advised me not to get my hopes up. That was a tall order.

For the first time in quite a while, I felt like I had a fighting chance.

FORTY-ONE

I stepped out of the cab and was greeted by the graveyard. The driver hadn't said much on the way over, but when he had spoken, it had been to proclaim this area a "dump", and to express veiled interest in the reasons for my being driven out here.

I'd deflected each and every question.

Whether I'd wished to see the graveyard again because of my own affinity for it, or whether it had been Fiona's silent urging that'd brought me there, I couldn't say. Considering what was to come, I wanted to take a short walk to center my thoughts though, and figured that the five minute jaunt from the graveyard to the house would suit my needs nicely without holding me up longer than necessary.

I walked past the ramshackle houses, kicked pebbles down the battered street. I felt I knew this road much better now than when I'd first started my renovation project. Perhaps this feeling of familiarity with the area was Fiona's doing, too. There was no way to tell what thoughts were mine and which ones belonged to the spirits fluttering in my depths. I looked at a house and thought I recognized it—but was it simply because I'd taken notice of it on a previous drive, or was it because one of the souls in me had once lived in the place?

I'd fed solely on hopelessness and fear for so long that the concept of a happy ending was now foreign to me. Suppose that Weiss' friend managed to help. What would I do then? Would my life ever return to normal? Fondness may have been too much to ask for, but would I ever be able to look back on these days with anything like calm?

The staggered houses were becoming more familiar to me now. Up ahead, a few hundred yards away, the shape of my own house entered into view. The Callery pear swayed and beckoned. The sight of both the tree and house no longer disgusted me. Knowing that the tree had been put there as a kindness for Irma Weiss, who had been so in need of comfort in her miserable final days, made it hard to hate it. The house itself didn't scare me—without the dark souls that had walked its halls, it was nothing but an empty building now.

If Weiss and I succeeded at banishing these devils inside of me, what would become of the house? I was quite sure I'd never set foot in it after this. Without the long shadows, without the hushed voices, but with a bit more work, it would actually be a fine home. I studied it as I approached, tried to imagine a family living there in the future.

It wasn't as hard to imagine as you might expect. Someone else could fix up that house down the line and be quite happy with it. Just not me.

The house no longer had any power over me because I understood that I carried the worst of it inside my person. The property had transmitted every sinister characteristic into me so that only a house was left.

I walked up the lawn, and was surprised to see a black sedan winding up the usually quiet street. It slowed as it passed the house, the driver taking a look at me, before speeding off. The windows had been tinted, obscuring any passengers. Had it been Weiss? I watched the car disappear into the distance and figured they'd gotten lost in the web of potholed streets.

I unlocked the door and stepped inside. I was back. Somehow, it felt like I'd been gone from the place for a very long time.

For a while, I stood at the dining room window, monitoring the street and checking my phone compulsively. Then, with nothing else to fill my time, I began walking from room to room, recalling my brief tenancy in the house and picturing some of the scenes that Weiss had alluded to during our talk. His wife and daughter had both died in this house—a house which he'd intended as a fresh start for the family.

I walked through the upstairs, opening a few of the windows to let the fresh air in. Having learned all of the sordid details of the house's hidden life, I was struck by the tragic atmosphere. My previous stays in the home had been marked wholly by fear, but now that I knew something of the family who'd lived in it, I was moved by a great sadness.

While pacing, I had a look at my own work, too—in many cases the jobs left half-finished. Someone else would have to tile that bathroom.

Sorry, dad. This time, I'm ditching the job. You never realized this, but sometimes in life you encounter projects that you just shouldn't finish. This is one of them, I thought to myself.

Returning downstairs, I looked at the kitchen, so stripped and empty of its fixtures. Tall boxes of cabinetry still sat inside; maybe the next person to buy this house would like my choice of cabinets and would install them.

I heard the sound of tires crunching gravel. A car was inching up the drive.

"Thank goodness," I muttered, checking the time. It was a few minutes before two—Weiss hadn't wasted a beat. Car doors slammed shut, footsteps pounded up the yard.

This was it. My future hinged on this meeting.

I threw open the door, readying a greeting for Weiss and the friend he'd brought along.

Instead, what I found on the other side of the door was the butt of a rifle. I felt the weapon connect with my brow, and suddenly my legs turned into noodles. I crumpled, falling backward, and felt myself dragged deeper into the house. Before my vision went completely black, I noticed three figures standing around me. They all wore hooded sweatshirts. I couldn't make out their faces—they were indistinct. Their voices, too, coalesced into a blur of barking laughter.

One of the figures patted me down, pulled my wallet from my back pocket. He ripped the cash out of it, nicked a few of the cards. He took my phone, too. The others set out through the house, searching for things of value to take with them. I heard them muttering to each other, tearing open boxes and dumping their contents all over the floor.

I could taste blood. My body refused to move no matter how hard I tried to rally my limbs. Dazed and frightened, I felt consciousness slipping away. All the hope I'd felt just moments ago went with it.

Lights out.

FORTY-TWO

There was a deep wheeze.

Then the cracking started up again.

And the scratching. *Scratch-scratch-scratch.*

An eternity passed before I could open my eyes. The pain in my forehead made me wonder if my skull hadn't been split. I brought a hand to my brow, shocked that I was even able to manage movement, and felt a warm, sticky wound between my eyes.

I'd been hit in the head while answering the door.

The hooded men had come in, mugged me.

Awareness stole over me all at once. The air tasted dirty, full of dust, and I remembered I was in the house, surrounded by my half-finished projects. I tried to sit up, but it wasn't until my third or fourth attempt that I did so. And even then, I could only keep it up long enough to glance at my surroundings dizzily.

There was still daylight coming in through the windows. I couldn't say how much time had passed since the attack, but it was still daytime. That was a good sign. I spied a lone figure standing several feet away from me, in the living room. My vision was scrambled, but when I heard the shaking of an inhaler, I knew it was Willard Weiss.

"Oh, you're awake," he said from across the room. He walked over to me, carefully lowered himself to the floor and sat beside me. With great care, he supported my shoulders and allowed me to rest against him.

I wanted to communicate to him that I'd been attacked, that some muggers had left me for dead before he'd arrived. The result was word salad.

Thankfully, Weiss seemed to understand what was going on. "You were on the floor when I got here," he said. "It seems you were attacked by someone. They made a mess of the house. I wasn't sure whether to call an ambulance. I'm glad you're coming around. This neighborhood is unsafe; unsavory types probably took an interest in this house once they found out someone was working on it." He rummaged around in his pocket. "Here, take these. They'll clear your head." Weiss funneled a couple of bitter-tasting pills into my mouth. I had a hard time swallowing them. Eventually, I choked them down.

Weiss helped me back down to the floor, then stood up. My vision had cleared somewhat. I was better able to see him as he left my side. He was dressed in jeans and a long-sleeve shirt. Both were caked in dust. His neckline was ringed in sweat. I soon realized why.

Returning to the living room, he picked up my drywall saw and continued cutting into the wall.

Scratch-scratch-scratch.

Scratch-scratch-scratch.

That was the noise I'd been hearing—his carving away at the drywall.

"W-What are you doing?" I asked—or *tried* to ask. My tongue didn't cooperate.

Weiss yanked away a big chunk of drywall and let it drop. He then returned to his cutting, increasing the size of the opening by more than double over the course of the next ten or so minutes. He worked slowly due to his age, but his work was very careful. Whenever he felt overwhelmed at the job, he'd sit down in the folding chair for a breather, or take another puff from his inhaler.

The opening he was making seemed quite large. Large enough, I supposed, to fit a man.

"What are you doing?" I asked again. My speech was garbled, but I think he heard me.

Rather than answer my question, Weiss began to ramble. "Almost done now. You're a big fella, so I think I'll have to remove one of these studs. You're a handyman, aren't you? You probably know a thing or two about this sort of work. I was good with my hands when I was young. This gets tougher the older you get." He chuckled weakly, clearing more of the drywall. "It's probably been forty years since I last worked on drywall."

"W-What are you doing?" I asked for a third time. "Why are you..." I scanned the room, looked for the friend he'd promised to bring with him. The two of us were alone.

Noticing the confused look on my face, Weiss wiped his hands on his jeans and sat down. "There's no one else here. I didn't bring anyone else. Didn't see the need."

"But..." I began.

"My plan was to come here and talk things through with you—to convince you of what really needed done." He cocked his head to the side. "I told you before what you had to do, didn't I? And you called me up today, yammering about how you wanted another solution. There is no other solution to this problem, kiddo. So, since you can't man up and do this yourself, I'm going to do it for you. I'm going to set you up in this wall just like I did Fiona all those years back. It's my responsibility."

I tried to stand, but I only managed to raise my upper body off the floor.

"What you're set to become, well... we can't let that out into the world, can we? You know it, even if you don't want to admit it. You know what you're turning into. You've seen it with your own eyes. If something isn't done soon, there's no telling what'll happen, and so we don't have the luxury of time."

"No... you're wrong," I gasped. "You're not fixing anything by killing me... You're just... kicking the can a little further down the road...This isn't a solution..." I swallowed hard. With a grunt, I raised myself on my forearms and attempted to crawl towards the living room. As I did so, the pain in my forehead flared up again and my surroundings began to spin. I drooled all over the floor and rolled onto one side, the ache in my skull becoming unbearable. "No... I won't let you do this," I blurted. "I'm... I'm not going in there... You can't do this! You were supposed to help me!"

"I suspected you'd feel that way." Weiss stood, looked down at me. He whistled. "They sure did a number on you, didn't they? You won't believe this, but that break-in was sheer chance. I had nothing to do with that. It's just another consequence of your picking this old house in this busted-up neighborhood. I'm surprised you didn't get assaulted sooner." Weiss picked up a saw and singled out the stud he wished to remove. "Whatever fight you've got left will be gone once those pills kick in."

I swallowed hard. The taste of the pills returned to my tongue for an instant. "W-What? What were they?" I groaned.

He laughed, taking some measurements within the wall. "They weren't Aspirin, I'll tell you that. Sleeping pills. Many times over the recommended dose. I clearly haven't experimented with that kind of dose myself, but the warnings on the bottle tell me you'll slip into respiratory distress soon enough."

I retched, squirming on the ground and trying to spit the pills back up.

"Don't bother. I gave you those for *your* benefit, not mine. Once you get put back here, you're going to wish I'd given you a dozen more. Now, if you'll excuse me, I want to get this stud removed." He spared me a little grin. "We've got some time before sunset, but I'd prefer to be out of here before your friends start up."

"How... how could you..." I buried my face in the floorboards.

"You know, I've had a lot of time to think about this particular job since I first did this. I've been able to think of improvements. I'm not happy to do this, but if you'll excuse me, I *am* happy to do it *better*. You get that, don't you? The pride that comes from a job well done? Even a somber job?" He knocked some dust from the bald crown of his head and began sawing. "First thing… you've gotta pick a non-load-bearing wall. That way, you can take out one of these studs without causing a collapse. Once I've done that, there'll be plenty of room for you."

So dazed that I could hardly focus my eyes, I looked up at Weiss and watched him work. As he rambled on, I almost felt like he was doing a tutorial, and I even glanced around the room, wondering what his camera setup was like. *Didn't see that coming,* I thought. *Weiss gets to make the last tutorial in this series. What a twist.*

Weiss kept talking, but I couldn't keep his voice in my ears. There were intermittent blanks in my awareness as the head injury and sleeping pill combo wreaked havoc on my brain. When next I came to, I felt myself being dragged slowly towards the opening. He'd managed to carve the stud out of the wall, and was now getting ready to drop me into place.

Weiss was old as dirt, but the guy had muscle. Huffing and puffing, he grabbed me under the arms and hauled me like a sack of trash across the floor. He only set me down twice, and during one of those instances, palming sweat from his face, he sucked at his inhaler. I tried to put up a fight, to shake him off, but had no control over my body. "That isn't going to work," he said, stepping on one of my hands.

Hauling my limp body further, the towering man heaved me up and into the opening in the wall. I landed with a thud, the darkness fast-encroaching. When he'd massaged my limbs into position so that they weren't in the way, he trudged over to some boxes and found my pillow. He slit the thing open with a utility knife and grabbed up as much of the cottony stuffing as he could hold. This, he proceeded to stuff into my mouth, and then into my ears, explaining, "I'm sorry for this. I'm hoping that by sealing you up this way the voices will be silenced. Maybe dampened, at least. I'm doing everything I can to make sure you're never found. That the voices can't escape you. I hope it works." He packed the stuffing into my ears and I heard no more.

When I was aware of my surroundings, I was accosted by terrible pains from every quadrant. When I was not, there was only a soothing darkness. A darkness that looked more and more appealing as the minutes passed.

Now, Weiss was measuring the opening. Now, he was cutting one of my leftover sheets of drywall to size, and pressing it into the hole. It shook as he taped it into place. I couldn't hear, but I felt my surroundings vibrate as he began applying drywall compound, as he shifted his weight, as he spoke close to the new wall and his voice reverberated off of it.

He'd worked slowly all the while, but from the dark space behind the wall I could see that he'd done a very fine job. Age had robbed him of speed, but not of his skill. I was impressed with his technique.

There was no sound. There was no light. There was very little air, and more often than not, my tired lungs refused to fully expand. The pain faded; my limbs were filled with throbbing warmth. Eventually, I don't know how much time passed, the vibrations stopped, too. That meant Weiss had left.

I was alone.

And then I remembered that, from the moment I'd first walked into it, I'd never *actually* been alone in the house. Something like a laugh emerged from the pit of my stomach at this realization, and all of the cold, shadowed bodies pressed into the space around me laughed as well, like they were in on the joke.

FORTY-THREE

I'm walking up the stairs.

Light gushes in through every window. It makes the wood floor look slick with melted gold. The boards have been oiled recently. They look like new.

I'm drawn into the hallway. There are voices, calm and polite. Happy, even. Someone laughs about a joke, but I don't hear it. I'm in the hallway, which is a nice shade of eggshell white now. The trim is different, too.

No locks on the doors.

The big room at the end of the hall, nearest the bathroom; I step into it and find my way to the window, which glows with fiery sunlight.

There's no crack in the glass anymore.

Birds flutter by the window as I glance out into the yard. The road is black and looks to be baking in the sun. I can smell the freshly-laid asphalt from here. I remember summer. The grass has been trimmed back. There are hearty-looking peonies in a planter just below the window, and in the sun their pink petals look about to combust.

The Callery pear sways. The flowers are less white this year, more yellowish.

There's a girl standing beneath its blossoms, and she's looking up at me through the window. Blonde braid, pink jumper, pinker cheeks. She's shading her eyes from the sun, staring upward.

Then she's gone.

The Callery pear's scent rides the breeze.

I can't believe I ever disliked it.

THIS WAS the third showing of the day. The realtor stressed this point. "The offers are going to come pouring in any minute," she told the couple. "There's a lot of interest in this neighborhood, and I think you can see why."

"No doubt," said the husband. "But there's something I'd like to know. This isn't a new construction, is it?"

"No, it was built in 1975," replied the realtor.

"Was it empty like all of the other ones?" inquired the wife. "I mean... how long did it sit empty? That kind of makes me nervous, you know? What if it was used as a drug den? How have the bones held up?"

"Well, to be honest with you, this is the only house the developers were able to salvage in the whole lot. It's been empty about ten years. I don't have much information on the last owner. He was a younger man, and I think he put some work into the house. Frankly, his work may have gone a long way towards preserving it these past ten years. Unfortunately, he abandoned it. The State reacquired it, and then the development company bought it—along with the rest of these lots on Morgan Road—for a steal. They decided this house was worth fixing, and I'm glad they did. It has so much charm, doesn't it?"

The husband paced into the living room. "Absolutely. It looks brand new! I never would have expected that it was abandoned." He knocked on one of the walls, grinning. "It's held up great. Why did the last owner stop fixing it up? Any idea?"

"Hard to say," replied the realtor. "Possibly he didn't recognize its potential. Back then, the neighborhood had been in a disarray, barely hanging on. But the development project has been going on for the past two years, and in that short time, things have really turned around, as you can see." She led them into the kitchen, pressing a hand to the breast of her blazer in mock adoration. "Oh, and have you seen this kitchen? The cabinetry is real wood—stained hickory." She drummed her fingers against the cabinets. "It's timeless."

The wife beamed, pacing through the kitchen. "It is lovely. I can't believe how much care has gone into the renovation. And it's so spacious!" She turned to her husband. "There's actual counter space here. A lot more room for the coffee maker, chopping vegetables..." She laughed. "I'm still surprised that this falls into our price range."

The front door flew open. Tiny footfalls filled the house as the daughter raced inside. Pausing in the kitchen beside the trio of adults, she cleared her throat and tapped the realtor's arm.

"Yes, sweetheart?" asked the realtor, peering out the kitchen window. "Did you like the yard? It's spacious, isn't it? And isn't that a lovely tree?" She spared the parents a glance. "An ornamental tree of that kind usually costs a lot of money. It's gorgeous."

The girl spent only a moment sharing her thoughts on the tree. "It smells funny," she declared. With that admission out of the way, she asked the question that had brought her into the house to begin with. "Who is that man in the window?"

The realtor smirked, glanced at the girl's parents. "Man in the window?"

The girl nodded. "In the upstairs window. I was outside, by the tree, and I looked up. There was a man in the window. His mouth was full of cotton. He looked very sad." She frowned. "And kind of scary."

The adults in the room had a good laugh.

"A man with cotton in his mouth?" asked the realtor. "I can't say

I've seen anyone like that roaming around, but I'll make sure to keep an eye out." She looked back to the girl's parents, fanning herself with her hand. "Though, on the subject of *cotton mouth*, I could really use a cool drink. Do you have plans for lunch? If not, I'd love to take you to the Mexican restaurant down the road. They make the best margaritas in town."

"Oh, that sounds amazing," said the wife.

The realtor fished the keys from her pocket and led them back to the front door. "It's within walking distance, actually. They've got a kid's menu, too..."

The group started onto the newly-paved sidewalk, heading in the direction of town. Before leading everyone to the restaurant, the realtor had paused at the Callery pear, glancing into each of the windows.

There was nothing to be seen in any of them.

She laughed to herself. Of course there wasn't. The little girl had been mistaken, or else goofing off. A man with a mouth full of cotton —what a strange thing to imagine!

No, the house was empty.

But if she had her say, it wouldn't stay that way for long. "If you'd like to put in an offer, I'd be happy to draw up the paperwork after the meal," she told the prospective buyers, much to their delight.

THANK YOU FOR READING!

I hope you've enjoyed **The House of Long Shadows**. If you'd like to know about my future work the moment it's released, join my mailing list at the link below!

Please consider leaving a review for this book. Your reviews are invaluable to me; they help me to hone my craft and help new readers find my books.

Subscribe to Ambrose Ibsen's newsletter here:
   http://eepurl.com/bovafj

ABOUT THE AUTHOR

Once upon a time, a young Ambrose Ibsen discovered a collection of ghost stories on his father's bookshelf. He was never the same again.

Apart from horror fiction, he enjoys good coffee, brewed strong.

Connect with author Ambrose Ibsen on his official website:

https://ambroseibsen.com/

Made in the USA
Las Vegas, NV
01 September 2024

94652215R00163